T0129379

"The Puzzle"

PAUL DENSMORE

Order this book online at www.trafford.com
or email orders@trafford.com

Most Trafford titles are also available at major online book retailers.

Author of "The Fall of '68"

Printed in the United States of America.

ISBN: 978-1-4907-4255-7 (sc)
ISBN: 978-1-4907-4254-0 (hc)
ISBN: 978-1-4907-4253-3 (e)

Library of Congress Control Number: 2014913100

Trafford rev. 07/22/2014

 www.trafford.com

North America & international
toll-free: 1 888 232 4444 (USA & Canada)
fax: 812 355 4082

This book is in remembrance of two classmates of mine named on the Vietnam Memorial.

Adolf Hamm
March 14, 1948–September 22, 1968
Memorial number 43W / 62

Delmar Wayne Probst
August 23, 1944–March 08, 1968
Memorial number 43E / 58

ACKNOWLEDGMENTS

Three people gave me valuable help and advice with this book. They are Brian Raynor, Zoe R. May, and Diane W. Heckle. Thank you, my wonderful friends.

He Wishes for the Cloths of Heaven
by William Butler Yeats

Had I the heavens' embroidered cloths,
Enwrought with golden and silver light,
The blue and the dim and the dark cloths
Of night and light and the half light,
I would spread the cloths under your feet:
But I, being poor, have only my dreams;
I have spread my dreams under your feet;
Tread softly because you tread on my dreams.

(From)
Gentlemen-Rankers
Rudyard Kipling

To the legion of the lost ones, to the cohort of the damned,
  To my brethren in their sorrow overseas,
If the home we never write to, and the oaths we never keep,
  And all we know most distant and most dear,
Across the snoring barrack-room return to break our sleep,
  Can you blame us if we soak ourselves in beer?
We have done with Hope and Honor, we are lost to Love and Truth,
  We are dropping down the ladder rung by rung,
And the measure of our torment is the measure of our youth.
  God help us, for we knew the worst too young!
And the Curse of Reuben holds us till an alien turf enfolds us
  And we die, and none can tell Them where we died.
    We're poor little lambs who've lost our way,
       Baa! Baa! Baa!
    We're little black sheep who've gone astray,
       Baa--aa--aa!
    Gentlemen-rankers out on the spree,
    Damned from here to Eternity,
    God ha' mercy on such as we,
       Baa! Yah! Bah!

∞

BOOK ONE

∞

Chapter 1

At the Camp Fire

"When a couple breaks up, one person is always hurt worse than the other. It's a rule of love." Wayne's voice, carrying a contrived tone of authority, came out of the dark on the other side of our small campfire; then, he stepped into the flickering yellow firelight and gave me a challenging smile.

I figuratively leaped at the taunt. "A lot you know!" I snapped back. "How many romances have you been through?" I knew the answer to my own question. I had known Wayne nearly all his life, and now a few weeks after our high school graduation, I knew he had never dated anyone seriously.

"How the hell did we get on this subject?" An irritated voice barked from the open driver's side window of a gray 1961 Falcon parked on the grass almost as close to the campfire as Wayne and I. Brian, the third member of our parody of the three musketeers, was sitting in his car trying to find a clear radio station among the late-night static. "Yacking about romantic crap is for girls," he said, trying to change the subject.

"Don't get sore!" replied Wayne as he retreated into the shadows. "You were the one who got us talking when you said the words 'last date'."

Moments before, Brian had told us the day his last date with his girlfriend, Beth Ann, would be before they each went off to different schools in September. From that comment, our conversation had wandered to the point where Wayne made his gloomy assessment.

Wayne was jealous of Brian and me for having girlfriends, but we understood and tolerated it. Brian and I had romantic problems, but Wayne had a problem vastly greater than ours. Wayne would be inducted into the army in two weeks. The draft had taken him and other members of our class.

"Mike," Brian called to me from the car. "What have you and Sue planned before you leave for school?"

"Just one date. A concert at Chautauqua. Saturday, the twenty-eighth." Chautauqua was a large private, cultural institution and religious retreat on a lake about seventy-five miles from where we lived in rural upstate New York, near Rochester. "Then, we won't see each other for a while."

"Oh, poor Mike. He's going to be lonely." Wayne heckled me for not saying "last date" as Brian had.

I shot back a comment I knew Wayne would not make a wisecrack to. "Okay, soldier boy. Have you told your parents Brian and I are going to go with you to the Induction Center?"

Wayne didn't respond immediately but walked around the fire and slouched against the car next to Brian's window. "Listen. That's a silly idea. It's a long trip, and what the hell good does it do?" Wayne's voice was flat and direct.

I ignored the gravity of his voice and responded directly. "You would do the same if it were one of us going."

Our rambling conversation had laid out who was doing what and when for the last two weeks of August, and Wayne didn't have much to look forward to. Occasionally, I've been told that I talk before thinking. "Hey! Let's all go to the fair next Saturday!" I blurted out.

No one spoke for a moment, and even I was reconsidering the proposition as if someone else had. Brian responded with a question. "The girls, too?" he asked. Then I realized that Wayne's not having a steady date complicated the plan.

"Yeah, sure," I said quickly. And to Wayne I said, "And I don't want to hear about you not being able to dig up a date."

"No way am I pestering someone for a date," Wayne said emphatically.

"You won't have to. I'll ask Sue to talk to someone." Again, my mouth ran off before my brain could catch up.

"Bullshit! Cut it out." Wayne's voice was still calm.

"Listen, I want to have a final fling, something special. Girls love the fair. Come on, Wayne!" I said with emphasis.

Brian ducked his head out of the window and pressured Wayne. "Yeah, it sounds like fun. I'm sure Beth will like the idea. You can be sociable with a girl for one night. I've seen you do it before."

"Damn! I thought you guys were my buddies," Wayne said with a fatalistic sigh as he pushed away from the car. "I've got to take a leak," he said as he walked off into the dark.

"Hey!" I called to him, "if Kathy Bemus can make it, is that okay with you?"

"Sure, sure." Wayne's voice came from behind a tree.

We had been to the drive-in that hot August night in 1965, and now we're performing a ritual: the ritual of returning to the wilderness. Our wilderness was a patch of woods at the bottom of a farmers' cornfield in upstate New York. In years past, the three of us, carrying packs of Boy Scout equipment, had pedaled our bicycles to our version of the Sherwood Forest.

The place was known as "Peterson's Woods" since it was part of old man Peterson's farm. Old man Peterson was a veteran of World War I and had an odd, raspy voice that some said came from his being gassed in the war. He never minded us spending time in his woods and waved to us from his tractor as we bicycled—or, now, drove—down the rutted tractor track between fields that led to the woods from the main road. There had been Peterson children; one died in World War II at the Battle of the Bulge. We had found an old dilapidated campsite in the woods that we suspected was originally built by the Peterson kids.

A major attraction in Peterson's Woods was the Goose Creek, which ran through it. It was a moderate-sized stream that twisted and turned through the overhanging maple, beech, and sycamore trees. The flow of the stream made a sharp turn at a point near the edge of the woods, scouring out a deep pool, perfect for swimming. It was next to that dark pool that we parked that night after having been to the drive-in.

"Anyone going for a swim?" Wayne's voice startled me. He had crept silently back to the fire.

"What? Do you think you are an Indian? No, I'm not going in. A storm is coming." Occasionally, we take a night swim if it was warm. As if on cue, an erratic gust of wind swept around us, stirred the fire into a frenzy, and sent sparks high into the dark above us.

To my relief Wayne suggested we leave. "Yeah, you're right. It's August, not July. And I heard the weather report, too. Well, let's get out of here. I am hungry and tired of slapping mosquitoes."

I didn't want to mention leaving, and probably, Brian didn't either. Our visit to the old hideout had been more for Wayne's sake than for Brian or me. Wayne was going away to a more remote and crueler unknown than we were.

A bat zipped through the light of our fire, but no one said anything. The car door squeaked open, and Brian joined us by the dying fire. "You ever find that swim mask you lost here?" he asked me.

"No, I looked every time I came here the rest of that summer, but never found it." Three or four years before, I had lost a swim mask when I had jumped into the water with it on. Having any such equipment was special, and since we all used it, we were all disappointed when I lost it.

Wayne abruptly interrupted our reminiscing. "Okay! As I said. I'm hungry, and don't you have to go to church tomorrow?" Wayne directed this question to me because my mother often twisted my arm to go to church with her.

"No, I'm not going to church, but let's get out of here. The fire's almost out and rain's coming anyway," I responded.

That was it. We climbed into the car, slamming doors and startling any nocturnal wildlife near us. Brian cranked up the engine, and we left. The trees hung over the narrow lane, creating a tunnel. Our headlights lit up as we bounced along. Just as we broke out of the woods, a long, jagged bolt of lightning silently flashed and turned the night to a white flashbulb-bright day, revealing the tall corn on both sides of the car. An instant later, a clap of thunder rolled over us; and I made the usual comment, "Damn! That was close!"

Brian goosed the Falcon, and the bouncing got worse. "We've got to get out of this cornfield before it rains, and we get stuck in mud," he said in a tense voice. The headlights repeatedly bobbed up to the sky and back down as we followed a road meant only for tractors. Finally with a last thump and jolt, we launched out onto the smooth pavement of the state highway.

Half a mile down the road, fat raindrops began to splatter against the windshield and then quickly turned into a deluge. The rain came too fast for the windshield wipers to keep up, so Brian slowed to a crawl. "Damn! Now I know how headlights work on a submarine," Brian said in a reasonably calm voice.

"Submarine!" I echoed with a laugh in response to the pun.

The lightning gave sharp blasts of static over the radio; and since the song playing was asking us to believe we were on the eve of destruction, Wayne, who was in the front with Brian, reached out and shut the radio off. That left us to listen to the slap, slap of the wipers and the rain beat on the car roof.

Once the squall let up, it took only a minute to get to the turnoff to Opening Hill Road, the narrow county road where Wayne lived. Wayne lived on a modest sized farm that had been in his father's family for generations. Modest sized farms had long since become uneconomic, and his father had sold his herd of dairy cows six years before and now worked in a factory near Rochester. The farm had a tired, slightly dilapidated look about it. The unpainted barn was at least seventy-five years old and sagged in places. Wayne's parents drove an old, rusty car, and several abandoned vehicles hid in high grass and brush thickets around the farm.

This is not to say Wayne came from a poor family. Many of our classmate's families had less. Fortunately, that meant nothing to us kids. Sure, Wayne had to wear his clothes until they were obviously too small for him; but he always had a warm jacket and boots to keep his feet dry and certainly was never hungry.

Wayne's parents still made some money off the farm. They planted corn and baled and sold the hay off the fields. Wayne did a great deal of the work around the farm, driving the equipment and making repairs. I helped Wayne occasionally—mainly so his chores would be done sooner and we could horse around. Wayne's mother often invited me to dinner with the family when I was working or playing there. I always accepted because his mother was a great cook and the whole family was warm, relaxed and entertaining.

The rain had stopped by the time Brian's Falcon pulled into Wayne's drive, the tires crunching over the gravel as we stopped. The house was dark, but two lights were still lit along the long porch that ran the length of the side of the house. "See? They left the lights on for you!" Brian said as Wayne got out of the front seat.

"Thanks for driving," Wayne said to Brian.

"I'll call you about Saturday, and don't chicken out," I said to Wayne as I got out of the back of the car and jumped up next to Brian to ride shotgun.

"You guys make a big deal out of everything!" Wayne said over his shoulder as he walked through the deep shadows up to the house.

Brian was eager to dump me off and get home, so he pushed the Falcon hard as we left Wayne's. A quarter of a mile further down Opening Hill Road, a stop sign came up out of the dark. Brian, seeing no headlights coming, slowed a little and shifted down into second gear; and we hung a bumpy rock scattering right turn onto another narrow road. Spooner Road. Half a mile down that washboard road, we hit the same state highway we had turned off to go to Wayne's but a mile further along. Brian gave this stop sign more respect, slowing nearly to a stop, and shifted down to first to make a left turn. Just a hundred yards from that intersection, he pulled off the highway in front of my house.

We exchanged comments quickly as I hopped out of the car. I thanked Brian for driving and then continued. "I'll drive us all to the fair, and I'll let you know how things work out with Kathy."

"Yeah, fine," Brian responded with a sigh. It was 1:45 a.m. "Sue and Beth will talk. It will work out. The fair is a good idea."

"Okay. See you," I said, and the door squeaked as I shut it.

Now I was alone. I walked a few paces up the gently sloping flagstone walk that led to our house and stopped to listen to the night. Gradually, the sound of Brian's car faded and was replaced by the rustle of the wind in the great old maple trees that stood around our house. In the near silence, my mind picked one incident out of the entire evening to dwell on. It was Wayne's comment that one person is always hurt worse than the other when a couple breaks up. I had it bad for Susan—very bad—and so I was vulnerable. What Wayne didn't say—and may not have known—is that neither person ever knows for certain how deeply in love with them the other person is. Love can turn into a game of evaluating words, tone of voice, the slightest action, all to take the temperature of how one loves another. Ultimately, love is a gamble played for emotions; and I had the feeling I was about to go deeply in debt.

Neither Susan nor I had ever said the "L" word to each other in the eleven months that we had been dating. Still, we had dated no one else and had an affectionate relationship. So why did I worry?

Susan and I were going in opposite directions. She was going to the State University of New York at Albany in eastern New York, and I was going to a small school Marietta College, 500 miles away on the Ohio River. I wanted our relationship to survive the separation, but Susan was giving no such indication.

The thunderstorm had moved away, leaving chilly air behind; even the slight breeze made me shiver. Summer was trickling away, and I was leaving for school in fourteen days.

CHAPTER 2

Calling Susan

There were no private phone calls in our house. The phone was on a low bookcase at the end of the front foyer. The end of the foyer opened on the left to the kitchen and on the right to the living room. When I wanted to make a call, one or both of my parents were likely to be in one of those rooms. So when I called Susan on Sunday evening to set up a date for Wayne, I spoke in a moderately low voice but never aroused curiosity by whispering.

While dialing her number, I focused on sending a telepathic message to Susan that she should answer the phone. I didn't want to have to talk to her parents or sister. My psychic powers worked, and she answered. Her voice disclosed a genuine pleasure at hearing my voice. We exchanged greetings, and then I asked her about the annual family reunion she had been to on Saturday.

"Oh, it was wonderful. My cousin Irene, she graduated from Cornell in June, announced her engagement. Her ring is just divine, and we made a fuss over her. They are planning a December wedding." After giving me a few more details about the newly engaged couple, Susan asked me about my evening at the drive-in. She wasn't amused when I told her the three of us sneaked around the cars, trying to find someone we knew in a compromising situation.

I paced in a small circle as I talked, first wrapping the phone cord one way around myself and then turning and unwrapping the cord. I wanted the phone call to be short, so I got to the important business. "Say, I was thinking about Wayne leaving, and I thought it would be fun if we did something special. What would you think of a triple date to the fair next Saturday?"

"Oh, that sounds like fun!" she responded instantly with enthusiasm; then, just as quickly, she asked the critical question. "So who is Wayne taking?"

With some relief yet still anxious, I continued, "Well, I was hoping Kathy Connelly would like to join us. But Wayne's too shy to ask her." My voice tightened. "So would you mind calling her and suggesting it?"

Susan had anticipated my request, and she responded immediately. "I'll ask Kathy, but if she is willing to go, then Wayne has to call her and discuss the details. It's only polite. Will he do that?"

I looked up at the ceiling in a gesture of thanksgiving and said, "Sure, sure. I'll make him call. Thanks, thanks a lot! You know Wayne, you know. He's shy."

"Yes, Wayne's a wonderful guy, honestly. But he's too old to be depending on you to get him a date."

After only a slight pause from that admonishment, Susan burst out with an excited exclamation about her plans for the next day. "Tomorrow, Mom and I are going shopping in Rochester for the rest of my school list. We will probably have lunch at Bonham's. All the stores are having sales. I saw a wonderful outfit a week ago, and now, it will be on sale. Oh, I hope it's still there!"

When she ran out of breath, I injected a comment. "That sounds great" was all I could say; and that came out in a flat, unenthusiastic tone.

"I've started packing my trunk," she continued, "Everything will fit, as well as whatever I get tomorrow. How about you? Have you started to pack?"

"No, no. Not even," I said quietly.

"Come on, aren't you excited?" she asked urgently.

"Excited?" I responded with an interrogative tone. "Excited about all the studying? Excited about you being 600 miles away from me?" I paused for dramatic effect. "No, I'm not excited."

"Well, you should be" was her weak reply. "You enjoy learning and discovering new ideas. You have lots of friends now, and you will make lots of new ones."

"And so will you!" I emphatically interjected.

We played this verbal charade all summer; and each time we did, the divide between us became clearer. I wanted to continue dating, and she felt that whatever romance we had the past year was now just a polite friendship.

"What time are you thinking of leaving for the fair?" she asked, retreating to the previous subject.

I answered her question, and then asked a question in return. "Are you up for a game of tennis Wednesday?" We had been playing an occasional twilight game of tennis at the high school court during the summer. My invitation seemed awkward after our exchange about going off to school, and she didn't miss the chance to punish me.

"No, not this week. I'll be organizing whatever I get from the sales and checking how things fit in the trunk. You should get organized, too."

Invisible to her, I contorted my face in response to the turndown; but it was imperative that I not sound disappointed. "Okay, I'll see what Brian and Beth are up to," I said in an upbeat manner. It wasn't the tennis that was important, but the anatomical explorations that we did after, after it got dark. She enjoyed that time together as much as I did, but maybe all that had changed.

Susan came back with "Well then, I'll call Kathy right now. And you'll call me back tomorrow night, right?"

"Right, and thanks again for helping Wayne out," I said.

Before I could add a final good-bye, Susan cut back in with a serious tone to her voice.

"Mike, I'm glad you thought about the fair. It's going to be a swell time, just like all our dates. Good-bye!" I heard her receiver click down followed by a dial tone.

I gently hung up the phone, walked into the kitchen, rummaged through a cabinet to get a cookie, and then stood looking out the front kitchen window while eating the cookie.

I had just begun to dwell on the phone call when my mother came into the kitchen behind me and began putting away pots and pans. "I think it's very nice that you and Brian are going with Wayne to the Induction Center. Is Vivienne giving him a going away party of any kind?" Vivienne was Wayne's mother.

Crumbs dropped from my cookie as I turned to answer her. "Oh, no, Wayne wouldn't put up with it if she tried. I suppose there will be a family get-together before he leaves, probably a Sunday dinner." Since I would have to tell my mother anyway, I went ahead and told her about the triple date to the fair the coming Saturday.

"That sounds like fun. Your father and I may go Sunday. I think that's the last day." She paused after closing a cabinet door and faced me. "So you have a full social calendar before you leave. I hope there is room on it to join me at church. Remember, there are only two more Sundays before you leave."

"Sure!" I responded with an artificial enthusiasm. "I'll go the last Sunday. That way, people won't be confused over which Sunday is my last."

"No," my mother said softly but conclusively. "If you go with me at all, please go with me next Sunday. You and Susan will be seeing each other the last Saturday you both are home. You will be less willing to go to church the next day than if you go next week after the fair." She left a moment for the logic to register with me; then, she hit me with an arrow-straight question. "Will you join me at church next Sunday?"

"Yes, I'll go." I answered without hesitation.

My mother stepped up to me and gave me a quick kiss on the cheek. "This is a hard time in your life and a hard time for your father and me too." My mother was wonderful and smart, too. She had gotten an accounting degree (maybe a two-year degree but a degree nonetheless) during the war even while doing defense work. Now, she did part-time accounting for local businesses and had turned my brother's bedroom into an office. My older brother, Ben, had joined the air force two years before and was in Europe.

"Oh, Michael, what evenings are you working this week?" my mother asked as she started to leave the kitchen.

"Everyone's working normal hours, I guess. No one has asked to switch. So it's the usual Monday, Tuesday, Thursday, and Friday." My mother and I agreed on when I would have the family's second car during the week, and then, she returned to the living room with my father.

During this summer and the last, I had a job pumping gas at a Gulf station five miles from home. I usually worked the second shift hours from 3:00 p.m. to closing time at 11:00 p.m.

I wanted to be alone; so I went quietly through the dining room, out the side door, into the garage, out the back door, and then into the backyard. I had to think, to block out emotion, and to come to a conclusion with myself about Susan. I sat in a squeaky lawn chair and looked over the old pasture that began at the edge of the lawn behind our house. The sun had set behind the wood line at the far side of the pasture, giving a pink glow to the bottoms of the clouds on the horizon.

Susan fascinated me. She was genuinely unique, not deliberately different. She was tall and slender—maybe the tallest girl in our class. Her hair was auburn with long seams of blonde, and she wore it shoulder-length. Susan's facial features were sharply defined with thin lips. She had robin's-egg-blue eyes, and her neutral facial expression was a slight smile. It was hard for her to frown.

Occasionally, Susan seemed slightly removed as if she had to be called back from some other place, a place I wanted to know about; however, she was a controlled person and was never rash or impetuous. Socially, she and I both mixed well with our classmates; and we both moved easily between all the subtle circles of friends at school.

Susan's passion was literature, and literature was also our common interest. English was her best subject, and she read voluminously— far more than just the assigned books. I enjoyed novels, too, but not necessarily the same ones she enjoyed; and I certainly didn't read as many. We often talked about the characters in the books and plays assigned to us since we had the same English teacher, but we were in different classes. We amused each other by trying to match Shakespearean quotes to people and situations. It was easy to understand why Susan fascinated me.

With the creak of canvas on aluminum, I got up from the lawn chair and walked to the edge of the lawn, where high grass and a rusty barbed wire fence marked the beginning of the overgrown pasture. It was almost dark; the wind was calm and, except for the crickets, soothingly quite. The evening had trickled away, and I still didn't know what to do about Susan. I needed a simple fantasy-like solution such as saving her from a dragon, but I wasn't stupid. No one can make another person fall in love with him or her. Love was, or love wasn't. Forgetting her, as she seemed to want to forget me, would be a smart move; but I was more stubborn than smart.

Chapter 3

Wayne's Farm

Not having a date with Susan to look forward to made Wednesday a slow, slow day. I briefly considered calling my boss at the gas station to see if he needed extra help. Instead—and at my mother's urging—I reviewed a checklist on preparing for school that Marietta had sent me. Mother had bought me a new, black travel trunk with brass hardware at the corners. I sorted out the clothes I would take and began to pack the trunk.

Susan had called me on Monday evening to say that everything was cool and that Kathy was happy to go with us to the fair; then, I had phoned Wayne and bluntly told him he had to call Kathy.

By one o'clock on Wednesday afternoon, I was bored stiff. I didn't want to call Wayne and bug him to see if he had called Kathy, but I knew it would irritate Susan if he didn't. So I decided to pop over and see Wayne, giving myself something to do and a chance to talk to him about the fair. Going over to Wayne's without calling first was taking a chance since he might not be home. Wayne spent a lot of time working odd hours on other farms, but I thought, *What the hell.*

I had to walk a mile over to Wayne's since my mother was off with the car, seeing one of her business clients. My bike was still in the garage, but somehow, I felt too old to ride it. The walk wouldn't be bad; it was over the same narrow country road Brian and I had rattled along Saturday night. I had walked or ridden the route dozens and dozens of times. I knew who lived in each house along the way, noticed which trees had lost a limb in a storm, and knew which sections of the road the winter winds swept worst.

Shortly after starting down Spooner Road, I regretted not taking my bike. It was hot, even in the occasional pool of shade from the maple trees, whose limbs hung out over the road. If I had ridden my bike, a breeze would have blown over me; and the trip would have been quicker. Occasionally, my footsteps along the gravel at the side of the road flushed a fat brown grasshopper that flew away with a buzz. Only one car passed me in the first half-mile of my walk. I saw the car coming toward me and the rooster tail of dust behind it. When the car rattled past, I shut my eyes and held my breath until the worst of the dust settled. It hadn't rained since Saturday, so the ruts in the road were dry.

Wayne and I each had a brother almost four years older than we were. Our brothers were good company growing up but, naturally, didn't want us little kids joining in their big guys' fun. This created a bond between Wayne and me. In elementary school, Wayne and I ran as a pack, always tried to be on the same team during playground games, helped each other out with pranks, and occasionally sat together in front of the principal's office awaiting discipline. Our friendship survived our becoming adolescents when hormones kicked in and when we discovered girls.

We were tested in school; then we were classified, separated, and told to take different classes. School played God and decided our future. The situation was transparent to Wayne and me; we saw less of each other but were the same buddies when together.

Just before the intersection, where Brian had made his speedway turn the past Saturday night, I left the road and slowly and carefully ducked between two strands of a barbed wire fence and cut across a pasture. The shortcut through the bovine sanctuary would shave a few hundred yards off my walk and was worth the required careful stepping I had to do while walking over the closely trimmed grass. In the distance, I heard a smooth-running tractor strain as it started to pull something. It had to be the Patterson's Farm-All tractor since their other tractor—a two-cylinder John Deere—made a different, deep putt, putt sound.

After making another delicate and successful (that is, my shirt was still whole) traverse of the barbed wire fence, I started across one of the Pattersons' hayfields. The hay had been taken off as was normal in June, but it had been a good summer, and the grass had gotten nearly knee-high again. Wayne was taking a second cutting and had already cut, let dry, and baled the hay. Bales now dotted the field, not as many as in June but enough to make the work worthwhile.

The field sloped gently upward and, just after leaving the fence, I saw the tractor I had heard come over the crest a hundred yards in front of me. Wayne was driving, and the tractor pulled a flatbed wagon that had a few bales of hay stacked on it. Wayne stopped the tractor beside a hay bale, got down, pitched the bale on the wagon, got back on the tractor, and started up again. I hustled to what would be the next bale to be picked up and stood beside it. As he approached, he acknowledged me by a quick flash of his right hand from the steering wheel. "About time you got here!" Wayne yelled with a grin as he drove past me.

Wayne stopped the wagon beside the bale, and I heaved it up onto the wagon; then Wayne pulled the tractor's throttle to idle, set the break, and got off. Wayne wore a faded blue T-shirt with a large, white number ten on the back. I wore a gray, flecked T-shirt that looked like a sweatshirt with short sleeves. We both wore jeans, and Wayne had on a baseball cap while I was bareheaded. "Hi! You want to drive or load?" he asked.

If we had just started working, the answer would have been easy; but Wayne had been at work for a while. "I'll load," I said.

"Okay, use these," Wayne responded and took off his old, worn, oil-stained, canvas work gloves and gave them to me. The gloves were welcome since the twine around the bales chewed up your hands in a hurry.

The bales lay in reasonably neat rows up and down the large field. As Wayne drove and I loaded, we progressed down the row; and at the end, Wayne swung the tractor and wagon around in line with the next row. Wayne stopped at the end of that row, and we switched off. I drove the tractor in first gear and at a low throttle so Wayne had time to walk to the next bale. Keeping a steady, slow pace saved wear on the brakes and clutch. Wayne and his father had taught me how to drive their tractors and a hell of a lot about mechanics as well.

We switched tasks again, and the more bales I heaved onto the wagon, the more the field resembled a barren desert. We took a break once, and after stacking and reorganizing the bales, we sat down in a small patch of shade cast by the wagon.

"I called Kathy," Wayne said after he took a gulp of water from a dented and scuffed old thermos. He passed the Thermos to me and continued. "She's fun to hang out with. She doesn't take our joking around seriously and doesn't expect a fancy time. Did you know she's going to Rochester Business School in a few weeks?"

"No, I didn't know that. Good for her. That school has a wonderful reputation."

"She's going to study accounting so she can do more than just take dictation. If she can earn enough part-time while at RBS, she might go on to a four-year school."

We finished at about four o'clock, and Wayne drove the tractor along an old cow path back to the barn. He pulled into the bottom of the barn through what had been the cattle entrance. It was dark and cool in the barn, and the musty ammonia odor of the cattle still lingered even though they had been gone for years. Empty stanchions and abandoned feed and water troughs remained. "I'll unload tomorrow," Wayne said. He would stack the bales where the cattle had been.

There was a hose beside the porch, at Wayne's house; and we rinsed our hands and arms and shook the hayseeds out of our hair before going into the kitchen. "Michael! Thanks for helping Wayne! I saw you out in the field," Mrs. Patterson exclaimed as we walked through the screen door; she always seemed to be in the kitchen. "Sit down. I'll get you some iced tea." She made great, sweet lemon iced tea.

Mrs. Patterson served the iced tea and homemade sugar cookies and then sat with us and made the usual inquiry about my mother and father. As I told Mrs. Patterson that my parents were fine, I realized I would need an excuse since she invariably invited me to stay for dinner. I was feeling guilty for not having done enough packing and skipping out of the house for longer than I had planned.

"So Mike have another cookie," Mrs. Patterson said as she moved the plate of cookies from the center of the table closer to me. "Wayne's dad doesn't get home till after five, so dinner will be a while yet."

Just as I began to stutter, Wayne cut in to help me out. "Mom, Mike's got a lot more fun going on tonight than having dinner with us. Wednesday is his tennis night at the school with Susan."

"Tennis! Lucky her. That sounds like fun," Wayne's mom said with a big grin as she got up from her chair.

"Yeah," Wayne added as he inspected his third cookie. "They play for ten minutes, at most."

"We'll catch you another time," Mrs. Patterson said as she patted me on the shoulder while walking behind me.

"I don't see her every Wednesday," I protested, "but I do have to get home." I then turned and directed my comment to Mrs. Patterson. "I do love staying for dinner though. You're the best cook, except for my mom."

"You're sweet, Michael. It's nice seeing you," she said over her shoulder as she stood at the stove.

Wayne snickered and in a low voice and mimicked his mother. "You're sweet, Michael."

I had gotten out of dinner but could not convince Wayne to let me walk back home. Since the Farm-All was in the barn hitched to the wagon, Wayne fired up the old, green John Deere. I climbed on behind him, braced my feet on the drawbar, and held onto the back of his wide steel seat.

A tractor cannot be shifted while rolling, so the clutch must be slipped and the beast encouraged into motion from stop while in a higher gear. Wayne did this expertly, and we went bouncing down the road with each of the two cylinders making its own clearly discernible whizzing putt, putt.

"How the hell do you know we play tennis on Wednesdays?" I yelled in Wayne's ear as we bounced along.

"The same way you and I both know where Brian and Beth park before he drops her off from a date," Wayne yelled back without turning his head. I didn't respond; then he added, "And we know where you and Sue go after leaving the court!"

"To church! We go to church."

"Oh, yeah. Church. Right, to church!"

Five o'clock in the afternoon was an odd time to be taking a shower, but I itched from the hayseeds and smelled from sweat. Before I got out of the shower, I gradually adjusted the water to be cooler and cooler until it was nearly cold water splashing over my face and running down my chest and legs. The sensation was not as good as a dip in the creek, but it was satisfying.

The entire afternoon had been satisfying. The hay bales were in the barn safe from the weather. Our labor had turned ordinary grass into winter feed for someone's cattle and provided income for the Patterson family.

"We may as well eat early since your father's away," my mother said to me later as I prowled the kitchen. My father was a civil engineer for the state highway department. He worked at large projects during the summer construction season, usually close to home; but this summer, his project was a bridge 200 miles away in the Adirondack Mountains. He stayed at the job site during the week and came home on weekends. "I hate to think of what those men are eating and the condition of the kitchen. They'll all be sick." My mother speculated. The state had taken over an old motel near the bridge site to house the engineers and workers. My father enjoyed it, so my mother was suspicious.

My mother enjoyed having dinner with me. Four days a week, I was working swing shift at the gas station; my brother was in Europe; and now, my father was happily lost in the woods. So she ate alone often.

"So how many bales did you and Wayne get in?" she asked to get the conversation going. We had corned beef and cabbage—a favorite of mine—for dinner, and I stuffed myself.

"Maybe a hundred. Good for a second cutting," I replied.

We continued talking, and naturally, she asked about my progress in packing for school. She had looked in my bedroom and knew I hadn't done much. "I want you to figure out what you're going to take and what we need to buy this weekend. There are good sales on now that won't last." She cautioned me. Sales certainly motivated women. The phone interrupted us before I could reply.

Nearly all calls were for my mother, so no one else in the house ever bothered to answer the phone. She left the table, and I continued eating and looking out the large dining room window. I saw a red winged blackbird zip between bushes out in the old pasture.

"Oh, Susan, what a pleasant surprise." I heard my mother say in a congenial voice. My mouth froze in mid-chew, and I listened. There was no other Susan than my Susan that my mother would greet in that tone. They exchanged pleasantries while I cleared my palate but did not take another bite. "Yes, he's here. I'll call him," my mother said. I was already by her side to take the phone.

Susan and I exchanged greetings, and then, she continued saying "Kathy called a few minutes ago. Wayne called her yesterday. She is excited about the fair. Wayne sure must have turned on the charm."

"Good, yes. He told me he had called her. I did some work with him this afternoon." Since my mother was in the dining room, I stretched the phone cord to its limit and faced into the living room.

Susan was in a sparkling mood, and she spoke in a fast and excited voice. We talked about the fair, which rides we wanted to take, and if anyone from our school would be showing animals; then she surprised me. "If you're not busy, would you like to come over and see the new outfits I got for school?"

I failed to contain myself and blurted out my reply. "Oh, sure! Now, you mean now?"

"Yes!" she said in her smooth, seductive voice, "I mean now."

Fortunately, I had a car to make the mile-long trip into Conklinville. Just before entering Conklinville, the state highway came down off a hill, giving me a view out over the village. As I slowed the car, I caught a quick glimpse of white church steeples poking up through the furrowed carpet of green treetops. Conklinville had a Congregational church, a Baptist church, a Methodist church, and a small Catholic parish church making the village easily recognizable to Thornton Wilder. Susan and I enjoyed Wilder's play *Our Town* and made comparisons of Conklinville with Grover's Corners, the town in the play.

Even a young person like me, had seen major changes in our village. People, such as Wayne's father, now commuted into Rochester for work. Many families had two cars and did their shopping at the supermarkets, letting the two tiny grocery stores in the village to go out of business. The Grange Hall was now the township's library. Both feed mills were gone; one was replaced by a new post office. We still had two gas stations (one at each end of the village); a café, where the kids hung out; and two tractor and farm implements dealers. The biggest employer in the village was Conklinville Central School, home of the Cougars. The school included elementary, junior high, and high school.

Conklinville residents kept their homes painted and repaired, their yards trimmed and uncluttered. Many grand old houses still looked as good as when they were built 75 or 100 or more years before. There were white Greek revival homes with imposing Doric columns in front, square Federal architecture homes with a copula in the center of the roof, and many elaborate Victorian homes— one of which Susan lived in.

Susan's red brick Victorian home was on the main street of the village. Elaborate filigree wood decorations highlighted the railings and posts of her home's wide porch.

I arrived at Susan's wondering what she would be wearing. How a girl dresses greatly impacts the success of a date. Susan bounced down the wide stone front steps of her home to greet me. She was wearing khaki Bermuda shorts, and an old light blue button-down collar dress-shirt of her father's. The shirt was great, but I would have preferred a skirt.

"Hi!" she exclaimed with a bright smile as she took my hand. "Come in and see what I've got! I'm so lucky they were still on sale." I understood her excitement since her mother sewed very well, and consequently, much of Susan's high school wardrobe was handmade. New store fashions were a special treat to her.

"Most of what I got is for fall and winter, so I can't wear it now," Susan explained as we went through the old wooden door with an oval glass window and white lace curtain. The door opened into a foyer with a grand staircase to the second floor directly in front. We went down a wood paneled hall to the side of the stairs and into the dining room. A clutter of department store shopping bags, garment boxes, and tissue paper covered the dining room table.

"This is my favorite," Susan said with great pride. She picked up a white silk long sleeve, lace-trimmed blouse with one hand and held it to her chest. With the other hand, she held a red, green, and black tartan pleated skirt to her waist. "I am a bonnie Scottish lassie," she said with a grin, "and this is my cutty sark."

"But you are not a witch," I said in a plaintive voice, "and your Granny didn't make it." We were testing each other since we both liked Robert Burns's poem "Tam O'Shanter."

"Well, it's better than being Lady Macbeth," she replied as she turned and put the garments back in their boxes. "It's just like Christmas, but I feel so guilty," she added.

As Susan went on to show me other clothes, I moved close to her as she stepped around the table and gently brushed her arm and hand when it wasn't obviously deliberate. I heard a few ragged piano chords coming from the side drawing room (Susan's sister, no doubt,) but I still didn't know if her parents were home; then I heard the clatter of dishes in the kitchen, and a moment later, Susan's mother came into the dining room.

"Hi, Mike," she said in a friendly tone. What do you think of the lady's wardrobe?" I responded affirmatively and then she urged Susan and me to help ourselves to whatever snacks we could find in the kitchen. "Excuse me, kids. I have to see how your sister's practice is going," Mrs. Holmes said as she left the dining room.

Both of Susan's parents were teachers but in another school district. Her mother taught elementary classes, and her father was a high school math teacher. Susan's sister, Sandra, was two years younger than Susan.

Susan's parents had completely remodeled the kitchen, keeping many of the original 1890s fixtures while still fitting in all modern appliances. One example was the original old icebox now used as a cabinet from which Susan fetched a box of Oreo cookies. "Do your parents know who the original owner of your house was?" I asked Susan as she poured herself a glass of milk and opened a bottle of soda for me.

"Yes, it was a lawyer named Cranston. He was a big shot in local politics and was state representative for a long time," she said, "let's go out on the back porch."

I pushed open the screen door to the side porch with my elbow as I carried my soda and the box of cookies. We walked on around the porch, which surrounded the entire house, to the back and sat down on an old wicker settee. The back porch needed painting, and two of the columns to the roof had dry rot even though they were not original. This contrasted markedly with the front of the house, where everything viewable from the street was renovated. A cement mixer and piles of sand and gravel with shovels stuck in them decorated the back lawn.

"Dad and my uncle are working on the foundation and cellar floor," Susan said as she put her milk on a folding tray table in front of us. "Actually, jacks hold up part of the house right now."

"They do good work," I answered.

"Well, they certainly are experienced."

Her parents had bought the house in a dilapidated state when Susan was a baby and had been renovating it themselves since then.

I leaned closer to her and took her hand as she went on talking about the house. "Can you imagine how many people have lived here? And this seat came with the house. It's not as old as the house, but I bet dozens of different people have sat on this couch and looked out over the yard and garden. They would have had a vegetable garden. There were happy times and sad times." She continued after a short pause. "You know, this house was built before the Spanish American War, and the people in it went through two world wars and the depression."

When Susan talked in this way, I usually just let her continue; but tonight, I leaned over and quickly kissed her cheek. "That was then. This is now," I said.

"Careful!" she exclaimed, pulling away slightly. "My mother might see."

"Yeah," I said with a suspicious tone, "where is your father?"

"Oh, he's bowling and won't be home till about ten o'clock."

This news made me feel better, and a moment passed in silence. "I wonder how many people have kissed out on this porch on a summer evening," Susan speculated, still looking out over the lawn.

"And how many have made nooky?" I responded.

"What! Nooky! Oh, you are terrible," she said with a big smile and laughter in her voice; then, she gave me a playful punch in the arm and leaned a little closer.

"Seriously, our house is like a large depository, a library, or archive of emotions. All the happy events celebrated, and tears shed at sad times." Susan just looked ahead into the darkening shadows of the backyard and drifted away.

"Well, now is one of the good times," I said happily, hoping she would return.

"Do you think it will ever be possible to play back the motions, like on some recorder?" She didn't pause for an answer. "Strong emotions must make some change, like radiation leaves on an X-ray."

I became absorbed in her thoughts. "Sort of like the stars. We see them not as they are now but as they were thousands of years ago because light takes time to travel to us." In unison, we both looked up at an early evening star on the horizon.

"It's impossible to get ahead of light," she said in a factual tone; then we both began to speculate on solutions to a problem just as we might have in our senior physics class.

Susan's voice became flat and devoid of emotion. "I could research documents and newspapers and maybe contact family members that lived here, but it wouldn't give the full emotional impact. People were born in this house and died in this house. I want to relive the events and feel all the emotions."

"Like a time machine," I conjectured.

"Time machines are impossible, silly to think of," Susan responded with a touch of ridicule in her voice, "and I'm not talking of spiritual hocus-pocus or palm readers. I feel strongly that emotional events must leave an impression in some unknown medium."

"Just as Hamlet said to Horatio, 'there are more things in this world than we can dream of.'" I said, giving a battered quote.

"Right! Right!" she answered without looking at me.

"And since I've mentioned a Shakespearean character, what is this I've found?" I pulled a thin paperback edition of *A Midsummer Night's Dream* from between the cushions and showed it to her.

Seeing the volume returned her to reality. "Oh, I reread that every summer. I just love the story."

Before I could respond, we heard the kitchen screen door creak open and then slam shut. Both of us looked to our left to see who would come around the corner of the house. It was Susan's mother, and she poked her head around the corner and said, "Susan, I'm taking Sharon to her piano lesson and doing some shopping while she is there. We'll be back at the usual time." Then she disappeared.

"Fine! See you later!" Susan shouted in the direction where her mother had been. I leaned forward and put the copy of *A Midsummer Night's Dream* on the tray table and took another Oreo cookie. While making these movements, I made an inconspicuous glance at my watch. It was seven forty-five, which left me about an hour and a quarter to work with.

"Well, this isn't an Athenian forest, but it is summer. And there may be fairies in your backyard. Let's go find them," I said as I stood and walked over to the wooden steps that led down to the backyard.

"Puck, we're looking for Puck," Susan informed me as she got up and followed me.

We crossed the yard and walked around the far side of the vegetable garden. The rows of tall sweet corn hid us from the house. Flanking the garden were two rows of blue spruce evergreen trees—all about ten feet tall—planted as windbreak. There was enough room between the rows of the conically shaped trees to walk in. Queen Ann's lace, golden rod, and buttercups grew in the nearly dark avenue between the trees.

"This is it!" I exclaimed as we held hands and walked along. "This is a perfect hideout for the obnoxious little imps."

"It is but I don't think you are serious about finding them," Susan commented with a touch of contrived sarcasm as she plucked a frilly white Queen Ann's lace and casually inspected it.

"Sure, I am," I said as I flopped down onto the grass and flowers, my head coming to rest almost under the bow of a blue spruce.

"But I have to get down close to look under the trees. They're tiny, you know."

Susan sat down beside me but remained sitting up. I reached up around her back with my left arm and pulled her around and down to me. She relaxed against me, and I heard her hum as we shared an anxious kiss. I stroked my hands up and down her back gently pressing with my thumbs.

After a moment, she lifted away slightly from me and said, "You're the imp." Her hair fell down around my face like a veil. I was awash in intoxicating fragrances. Susan wore a light jasmine perfume, but her hair carried the scent of lilac; and then there was the powerful scent of the blue spruce tree just beside me. The cool grass and wild flowers added to the riot of fragrances.

The moment teetered on the edge between reality and dream. Susan kissed my nose and then my lips. I twisted and kissed her earlobe and then her lips again. This went on until she sighed, rolled back, and returned to a sitting position.

I sat up, leaned over to her, and kissed the side of her neck. She turned and kissed my cheek. In response, I moved closer and kissed her chin and continued to kiss down her neck and chest to the point where buttons stopped my progress. She fell back on the grass, and I anxiously leaned over her and continued kissing down her chest as far as possible. I wished that I had had four hands as I explored her hips and down her thigh. All the while, Susan twitched and twisted while making a contented hum.

I continued to press the boundaries by undoing one button of her shirt followed shortly by a second button, which exposed the top of her white lace bra. My lips brushed over a small embroidered flower at the center of her bra. My attempt at a third button prompted a firm resistance from Susan's hand. I complied immediately and, instead, began lightly drawing circles with a finger over her chest, culminating by hooking my finger under her loose bra and stroking as deeply as possible. Susan's movements became sharper, and she was unable to keep her legs still. Finally, in a strained voice Susan asked, "What time is it? We've got to watch the time."

I relaxed, moved back, and strained at my watch to make out that time. The luminescent green dots and lines of my watch showed 8:20 p.m. "It's 8:20. They'll be back at about 9:10, I assume."

"Yes, usually," Susan replied as she sat up, and I remained reclining on one elbow. A few evening birds were chirping goodnight tunes to each other. More stars had come out, but it wasn't completely dark.

"Do you remember the trick Puck played on the sleeping humans in the play?" she asked.

I had studied *A Midsummer Night's Dream* in my junior year English class and didn't care for it as much as *Macbeth*, but I gave her an answer. "He turned someone into a donkey, didn't he?"

"Yes, but the important tricks were where he sprinkled juice from a wildflower on the eyes of the sleeping people. And when they awoke, they fell in love with the first person they saw."

"Oh, right, and that caused all the trouble."

Susan's voice became animated and jovial. "Lie back," she said, and she gave me a push back into my bed of grass. I willingly settled back and said, "Be gentle with me."

"Gentle!" Susan snickered and poked me in the ribs. "Now shut your eyes and go to sleep." She stroked my cheek and kissed my forehead. I closed my eyes. "Keep them closed now. You're asleep."

"Sure, sure," I said but couldn't keep from grinning. I heard her pluck a flower near my head; then she tried to sound serious, but her voice had a tinge of laughter.

"What thou see when thou dost awake do for your truelove take."

Then something soft gently caressed one of my closed eyes. I winced but didn't open my eyes, and then, the same sensation crossed my other eye. Before I could say anything, Susan gave me a quick kiss on the lips and said, "Now awake, my sweet Lysander."

I opened my eyes to see Susan's face close to mine. "Did it work?" she asked softly.

"Oh, yes. Yes, it did," I said and immediately flung my arms up around her and pulled and rolled her across me and into the grass and came above her and kissed her.

After a moment, I pushed up away from her, bracing myself on my arms. "Now it's your turn. Which flower did he use?"

Her lips began to form a word, but then, she froze and her smile disappeared. "Oh, it won't work on me. I am a fairy."

I did not immediately understand her resistance and continued to search the grass next to us for any kind of flower until I made out the white petals of a small daisy and plucked it.

"This will do," I said, but as I turned back to her, she was sitting up. "Come on, now. Cooperate," I urged her.

"But it won't work," she said with her head turned away from me.

"Nuts!" I exclaimed, continuing the game, "the character that fell for the donkey was a fairy."

"We've got to get back," she responded urgently and stood up.

I remained sitting in the grass; and like a fool, I protested, "What's the deal here?"

Susan stepped away from me, shook her hair, adjusted her shirt, and redid the buttons. "Come on, let's go. My sister will be a complete nuisance if she sees me this way." Then she began to walk back to the house.

I sat in the nearly complete darkness and let her walk away. Crickets worked their raspy symphony around me, and I noticed the sky had filled with stars. I was learning the limits of persistence.

Susan was not on the back porch as I approached the house, so I just continued walking down the drive beside the house. I was nearly to the steps to the kitchen when Susan came out of the kitchen door, combing her hair. "Mike!" she called out to me, "wait, Mike!" It was obvious I was going to walk on to the car.

Susan hurried down the steps, and I stopped and faced her. She came up close to me and looked at me. "I'm sorry, Mike. That was a silly game," she said calmly while looking directly into my eyes.

"Yes, a silly game. Do you still want to continue the game Saturday?"

"I very much want to see you Saturday, and it won't be a game." Her voice carried a chill of indignation, which stirred up my confusion again.

"Okay, four o'clock, as we agreed."

"Four o'clock," she repeated. She then put her hand on my left arm, leaned into me, and gave me a quick kiss on the lips.

Chapter 4

The Fair

Thunderstorms had passed through on Friday, and the fair's parking lot—a large field next to the grounds—was still soggy when we arrived late on Saturday afternoon. Low spots in the field had turned into mires of mud ready to snare any fool trying to drive through them. The girls became more excited and now worried about getting their shoes muddy.

"The boys should walk ahead of us, so we know where the mud is," suggested Kathy.

"Don't follow close then because we don't care if we walked in mud," I responded and Brian and Wayne agreed.

We had all packed into my parent's small four-door Corvair, which made a cozy, slow, and low ride to the fair. Three of us sat in front, and three sat in the back. Susan and I would be together, but the other two couples switched off being separated. During the ride to the fair, the girls put down a steady chitchat about clothes and who was doing what since graduation. We boys mostly sat in silence until the subject came up that a couple in our class had gotten married in a rush just after graduation.

"Mike, didn't we sneak up on them the first night the drive-in opened in May?" Wayne asked me.

"Yeah, they were in his old man's '57 Plymouth. The car was shaking so bad I thought the engine was still running but on two cylinders."

The girls squealed, and one of them told us we were "full of it." Brian then added detail. "The best part was those two, gorgeous, white legs poking up in a giant vie from the backseat."

"Stop it! Stop it!" the girls squealed, and Beth slapped her date on the shoulder. It had been a fun ride to the fair, and the evening hadn't even begun.

Later after we all piled out of the car and started walking toward the fair, Susan stopped, leaned against the car, and fumbled with one of her shoes. "Mike, let them go ahead," she said to me. After a moment, we began walking but well back from the group. "I've been miserable since Wednesday. That *Midsummer Night's Dream* stunt was just an impulse. I meant no harm. Do you understand?"

"I'm sure it wasn't intentional," I said while looking ahead at the blinking lights and clusters of tents and buildings. "But what confuses me is why you care if I think it was intentional."

Susan made no immediate response to my confusing statement, so I closed the conversation by saying "I understand you meant no harm, but that's all I understand. Let's talk later." I couldn't articulate an answer while stepping around mud puddles in a rutted hay field. Repeatedly, she demonstrated she was sensitive to my feelings and enjoyed being with me; yet she could not express love for me even through a Shakespearean trick. It was simple, though, if I would only accept it. She cared for me; I loved her. I preferred complete rejection to being cared for.

After we paid and went through the turnstiles, the group huddled up to decide what to do first. Someone suggested rides first, and then Kathy said, "We should check the livestock judging schedule. Fred Dunn is showing his Angus."

"Shame on him!" Wayne chipped in, trying for a joke.

"Food!" I exclaimed, "food!"

"Oh, you're always hungry." Susan chided me while giving a tug on my arm.

"Food!" Wayne shouted, seconding my suggestion.

"Food!" mimicked Brian to make it unanimous among the boys.

So off we went, pushing our way through the chaotic streams of people. After a few steps, we began to separate; so I yelled to the group, "Let's get what we want to eat and meet in the beer tent, near the band." I got acknowledgments or waves of agreement from everyone, so we went our own way.

The beer tent was the riotous center of the fair. Dozens of picnic tables were full of happy people drinking and eating. People pushed carefully through the crowds with arms held high, carrying paper plates made soggy by the baked beans, coleslaw, and butter-drenched corn on the cob. An amateur country and western band played on a small stage at one end of the tent. Clusters of couples danced in front of the band to the massively over amplified music. No one talked in the beer tent; everyone yelled.

Eventually, we were all gathered at one end of a picnic table; but by the time Wayne and Kathy arrived, Brian and Beth had finished eating and were ready to leave. Before they left, everyone agreed we would do the fair separately and meet back at the beer tent near the band at 10:30 p.m.

After we ate, Susan and I followed our noses upwind to the livestock barns and show arenas. Sheep and goats were first. "Show sheep remind me of a big fluffy pillow with legs and head poking out," I commented as we walked down the center aisle of the long barn.

"I can see that," Susan agreed, "especially when they are so clean, but the newly shorn ones look like they're starving."

"No, they look like a wired dog."

"Their faces are so cute, and I love to hear them bleat," Susan said, "and the young ones have springs in their legs."

Livestock was a prominent part of the fair with six barns of displays. Every farm animal was displayed with care. Stables and cages were clean with fresh bedding; every animal had feed, and most were eating. Often, the owners were there busy keeping the animals calm and comfortable. We did not meet anyone we knew.

"Owners must get attached to their animals. Did Wayne ever have a favorite?" Susan asked as we stopped to say hello to a goat.

"Way back in elementary school, his grandfather had an old draft horse named Ned. Old Ned was a family pet, for sure. I loved to feed him carrots. Ned died one January during a hard freeze. The ground was too hard to dig, so they left him out in the field with a tarp over him. Of course, it snowed; and for a couple weeks, I could see this great white lump in the field from the school bus window. Finally, they got a backhoe to dig a hole, and Ned was gone the next day."

"That's sad. Poor Ned," Susan said while reaching in a pen and scratching the ear of our friendly goat.

"Old Ned had a good life, as horse lives go. They could have just hauled him off to the glue factory. Wayne's grandfather had the backhoe operator push a large boulder over the grave so it would never be plowed."

Susan didn't comment but scratched the other ear the goat presented to her. So I added, "And this goat would love to go home with you and keep the lawn clipped."

"Animals have souls," Susan said factually. She paused to let me object to her observation; and when I didn't, she continued, "Animals sustain us. Advanced cultures revere animals and treat them as having spirits."

I reached down and scratched the goat's unattended ear. "Ned's spirit is with me, and this fellow will remember us," I commented.

"And I'll remember the three of us."

"I don't have to be just a memory," I said in return but received no response.

We skipped the smellier animals like the pigs and cattle but went through the chicken barn and spent a lot of time watching rabbits wiggle their ears and noses; then, we went off to the midway to play games and enjoy the rides.

I didn't like the barkers who pushed their near impossible arcade games and implied you were a wimp if you didn't try the game. "I'm going to skip the games. I think they're a rip-off," I said to Susan as we stood watching guys trying to knock over 5-pound lead milk bottles with lightened baseballs.

"Oh, they are a big waste. But I enjoy figuring out what the catch is with them." So we walked from game to game, speculating on what made them difficult to beat. We were enjoying each other.

Finally, we put frugality and logic aside and had fun. We burst balloons with darts, and I tried and failed to ring the bell swinging a huge hammer that had no weight to it. I won a little something for Susan at the shooting gallery, and then we went on rides.

Wayne and Kathy were on the merry-go-round when we got on. "We're going to go around 100 times!" Kathy yelled to us. Later, they told us they had done 106 rounds.

The Ferris wheel was next. It was the tallest ride at the fair. As we shuffled along in the line to get on, I took notice of the clanking, grinding, fuel-spilling motor and drive system. The slow pace suddenly quickened as we got to the front of the line. The short, chubby operator wore a stained white T-shirt and had the stub of a dead cigar held by his yellow teeth. He waved us forward as he held the safety bar up and steadied our seat. We jumped in; the safety bar locked into place, and we were swept up into the night sky like being in a fast open-air elevator. Neither of us spoke as we leaned forward to see the fair suddenly laid out in front and below us. The sounds of the fair faded as we reached the top. A black carpet opened all around us. Streets showed up as twinkling red and white strings of lights. We quickly sank back down into the noise and light of the fair, sweeping past the crowd waiting their turn to ride.

"This is great!" Susan shouted as she leaned against my shoulder, and we held hands.

"It is," I agreed, "it makes me want to fly. I envy pilots."

We went around about four times before the wheel slowed and stopped to let people off and on. The ride started again but stopped suddenly, leaving us at the top.

"Let's go on it again later," Susan said, anticipating the end of our ride.

"Sure," I agreed, "as many times as you want."

The big wheel lurched to a start again but stopped immediately, setting our seat into a gentle swinging motion. Below us, the Ferris wheel's motor sounded different like it was spinning freely. I made a brilliant observation and said, "Sounds like trouble."

Moments later, we heard the operator shout "Hang on! This will be fixed in no time!"

Susan and I congratulated each other at having the good luck to be stopped at the top; then, we didn't speak but looked out at the view. After a time, I spoke up. "This will spoil the moment, but at least, we are alone. What I was getting at out in the parking lot is that I need to know how I fit into your future."

Susan turned to me, no doubt mildly surprised at my comment. "I don't know my future," she said, sounding insulted.

"No, you don't," I countered, "but a smart person, such as you, has thought a great deal about their future. How do you *want* me to fit in your future?" I asked with a distinct emphasis on the word "want."

She did not respond but continued to look out into the dark. Lights, decorating the ride, shone on Susan's face; she wasn't smiling. Wind rocked our seat and played with Susan's hair, and she brushed the hair back into place.

"Are you warm enough?" I finally asked.

"Yes," she responded.

"That's lucky since I don't have anything to offer you if you were cold."

Thankfully, the Ferris wheel jerked to a start, saving us from an awkward moment. We didn't talk seriously again until I dropped her off.

The beer tent was still loud and crowded at 10:30 p.m. After we were back together, we found a table way in the back where we could sit and talk. We exchanged stories about the evening, and it turned out that Brian and Beth had been stuck on the Ferris wheel also. Kathy showed everyone pictures of her and Wayne taken in the photo booth. Beth and Susan immediately wanted photographs. Someone insisted Wayne and Kathy come along so we could get a group photo if we could all fit in the booth. So we trooped off back across the arcade through thinning crowds to the photo booth.

Sue and I went in the booth first, and as we posed cheek to cheek, it occurred to me that this would be the last photo of us together. Brian and Beth did their pose, and then, the great commotion began as we maneuvered to get our faces into one frame. There was plenty of the squeezing going on—some necessary and some deliberate. We got the giggles so bad that one of the pictures had only an arm in it. Eventually, each of us had a picture of all of us; and the trip was complete.

It was midnight when we drove through our village. No one spoke, and the silence set a mood of regret that the evening was over. We passed the Methodist church—my church—and seeing it reminded me I had promised my mother I would go to church with her in the morning. It was difficult to envision myself in the dark; shadow cast building in just a few hours.

The first stop was my house, where we dropped off Brian and Beth. Brian had picked up Beth and then came to my house, where he left the Falcon. Next, we dropped Wayne and Kathy at Wayne's home. Wayne had suggested this and said he would take Kathy home in his father's car. This way, everyone got to say goodnight to their date in private.

My parents' Corvair was no rocket ship and had been straining all evening with a full carload. Now, pulling away from Wayne's, the engine seemed relieved and was much more willing to push us down the dark country roads to the village and to Sue's home. The radio was easier to hear without multiple conversations in the car, so Sue and I just listened and did not talk. The Beach Boys' "California Girls" played, followed by the Righteous Brothers' "You've Lost That Loving Feeling." We had passed under the first street lamp of the village when that song ended.

"I didn't answer the question you asked on the Ferris wheel," Sue said abruptly as though making a confession. "You're absolutely right. We both deserve to know what the other feels about the future." She spoke rapidly and sounded relieved to be talking about the subject. "The problem is that even though you think I do, I don't have everything planned out. There is no instruction manual for becoming an adult." She paused as we went through the empty intersection at the center of the village. It was obvious she was making a sincere effort to say the correct words. "I'm excited about school. To me, the future is school. School is going to be an adventure." Susan's voice brightened up. "School's going to be a huge buffet of ideas, an intellectual buffet."

I glanced over at her as we approached her house when a quick flash from a streetlight showed that she was smiling. It was then, as I stopped the car, that I knew I had lost her. I was not in the vision she saw, the vision that had brought a smile to her face.

"Okay," I said as I parked the car at the curb, shut the motor off, and pulled the parking brake. "Let's work out the details." My voice seemed loud without the sound of the motor or the radio. I turned to her, and continued in a softer tone. "May I visit you at Albany?"

"Oh, it's just too far. It's not practical. What is it, 700 miles from where you will be?"

She had glanced at me as I spoke but then turned and looked at her house. All the porch lights were on, and I could see the hall light through the oval glass in the front door.

"May I write?" I asked in a light, suggestive tone.

"We're both going to be busy, and what good would it do?" she answered. Her voice had become fatalistic, and now, she was looking at her hands.

"May I phone you? It would be nice to talk to you."

"It's awfully hard to coordinate calls. My cousin says the dorms only have one phone for an entire floor of girls." Susan's voice strained.

"Okay, good. I understand," I said and I leaned over and lightly kissed her cheek and then immediately got out of the car, walked around to her side, and opened the door for her. She stepped out, and as I gently closed the door behind her, I notice both our shadows cast on the sidewalk by a street lamp. We walked side by side halfway up the walk; but then I stopped, and she took two steps further before realizing I wasn't beside her. Susan turned, and I could just make out a puzzled look on her face.

"Next Saturday?" I asked softly but with a questioning tone

"Yes," she answered weakly, "of course."

"Okay, four o'clock again?"

"Yes, four o'clock," she responded in a broken whisper. She did not move closer to me.

"I'll see you then. Goodnight."

I turned and walked back to the car, stepping lightly and with my head turned slightly back toward her. She didn't move for a moment, and then, I heard the scuffing of her shoes as she went up the steps.

Chapter 5

Church

Gray-haired Reverend Cope stood in the elaborately paneled pulpit, adjusting his frock as he waited for the congregation to settle into their seats after singing the "Gloria Patri." When the Reverend had everyone's attention, he began to speak in a stern voice (the sermon was serious business). Immediately, my mind wandered off thinking about Judy Clapham, who sat primly with her mother and younger brother just ahead of me and in my left peripheral vision. Judy's raven hair complimented the pastel blue and white lace-trimmed dress she wore. I knew Judy slightly since we had once been on the student council together. She would be starting her senior year in high school. Judy was a pleasant and intelligent girl even if she was a little chilly. No one would notice if I went up to her after the service while everyone chatted on the sidewalk in front of the church. I would wish her luck in her senior year, and she would inquire about the school I was going to and wish me luck, too. Maybe I'd call her at Thanksgiving. I had to remind myself that all things were possible now.

"The answers are in here!" shouted Reverend Cope as he waved a Bible. I had kept my eyes riveted on the Reverend so my mother wouldn't suspect where my mind was. Even so, I had no idea of what he had said before waving the Bible. I didn't belong in church. Church was for those touched by whatever it is that makes them devout. My mother had been touched, but my father and I had been passed over (at least, so far). I was unworthy, just as Reverend Cope was saying.

The Reverend was at the guilt part of the standard sermon. My father had told me (without my mother present) that a standard sermon consisted of three parts: convince the congregation they are guilty sinners, warn them of the inevitable consequences, and then offer them an exclusive way out by repentance and tithing to the church but only that church. My father claimed the structure of the sermon explains why the offering always followed the sermon. My father was right, but I envied my mother's devotion. So now, I went to church more for her than for myself. Someday, I would stop going or be struck by whatever it is—fear, gratitude, elation—that makes a person devout.

My eyes began to flutter while Reverend Cope worked on the repentance part of the sermon, and I had to shift in the pew repeatedly to stay awake. I noticed that a few gray heads in the congregation had already dropped forward. Later, I snapped to attention when the congregation laughed in response to the Reverend's required joke, and at that point, I'm sure my mother knew I was out of it. The upbeat salvation part of the sermon began, and I lasted reasonably well to the end. I liked sunshine more than doom and gloom.

I relaxed as Reverend Cope led the congregation into silent prayer. I felt comfortable during the quiet moments when we conversed with the Father, the Son, and the Holy Ghost. I believed but didn't necessarily accept other's explanation of whom or what these spirits were. For me, God, the Son, and the Holy Ghost were an emotion that did not need personification or explanation.

The small sounds, the rustle of a sleeve, a cough, a small child's whispered complaint hushed by their mother did not distract me as I bowed my head and began giving my thanks; it was only polite to give thanks first. A sense of profound guilt came over me as I realized my blessings were so great that I could never express adequate gratitude. I gave thanks for my family; the peace, security, and the plenty I lived in; and the great friends I had.

Silent prayer did not last long enough, and I had to rush into my pleas. I shot across a prayer for health and happiness for my family and named each of them, including my brother; then I begged that Wayne has an easy time in training, and that whatever he ended doing in the army, that he be safe and come home to a happy life. I squeezed in a wish of success for Brian and Beth Ann and asked specifically that their love survive their separation; then Reverend Cope broke my concentration when he asked the congregation to pray—as we had been taught to pray—the Lord's Prayer. I followed along. "Our father who art in heaven, hallowed be thy name." But my words became garbled because I knew my silent prayer was incomplete. I could not ignore Susan even if she cut me up inside. So I looked up at the sun coming through the stained glass window behind the pulpit and wished her success and happiness and then bowed my head again and finished the Lord's Prayer. "For thine is the kingdom and the power and the glory forever. Amen."

During the benediction, I realized I had not yet said a prayer for myself. Reverend Cope completed the benediction, bidding us to go in peace; and then the organ began the postlude, and people began shuffling and moving out of their pews. I moved along with everyone else. I needed a prayer, what with my going off to school, and my head still full of Susan. But the prayers had to be said correctly, and in church. If not, why go to church? Weren't prayers said while kneeling more likely to be answered than prayers just blurted out? The monks that beat themselves while praying must have all their prayers answered. It was too late for me since I was sarcastic like my father, not pious like my mother.

As we filed out of the church, Reverend Cope shook my hand and wished me well in school. Parishioners gathered in groups on the sidewalk to enjoy the sun and to exchange news and good wishes. I didn't speak to Judy.

CHAPTER 6

The Induction Center

The Wednesday morning trip to the Induction Center started poorly. Brian agreed to drive the two of us, and we were to follow Wayne and his mother on the 80-mile trip to Buffalo. Taking two cars gave Brian and his mother time to talk in private. Wayne wasn't wild about our coming along and had told us emphatically that if we weren't at his house at 8:00 a.m., they would leave without us. Brian pulled into my driveway, beeping his horn at 8:05 a.m. I had just pulled on my pants and was holding a clean shirt in one hand and gathering my sneakers up with the other when I heard him arrive.

We drove down the road in front of Wayne's just in time to see his parents' car disappear over a hill in front of us. Brian and I gave out simultaneous shouts, and Brian gave the Falcon a boost. As we caught up to Wayne, Brian beeped his horn, and we exchanged waves with him and his mom.

"We're going to be starved before lunch," Brian grumbled.

"No doubt about that," I agreed as I leaned forward and tied my shoes.

Our trip didn't go through the village or past Susan's house, so I relaxed and listened to the radio play Sonny and Cher's song "I Got

You Babe" for the millionth time. We were traveling north, and the morning sun was just below the trees on our right and cast long shadows across the road. It was going to be a sunny day, even if it wasn't a happy day.

"Did you hear Adam Hamilton has been drafted?" Brian asked me.

"Oh, no. I hadn't heard that. Well, that's another one. Anybody else?"

"Well, there's Dave and Larry going into the navy together, but they're enlisting."

"Crazy," I said, "the navy is four years like the air force."

There were seventy-five students in our graduating class, and as we drove along, Brian and I totaled up nine guys that we knew had enlisted or had been drafted. "Not good odds for the healthy guys in our class not going on to school," I concluded after we made the tally.

"No," Brian agreed, "more of them should have been fatties like Frederickson."

"Or too tall like Otto," I said.

Otto was over 6'6" tall, and led our school to the basketball championship three years in a row.

Driving along, we passed cornfield after cornfield; and the corn was at full growth, all tasseled out at the top. If I looked close as we whizzed past, I could see fat ears of corn on the stalks at the end of the rows; and the silk on the ears was brown. In a couple weeks, the awkward-looking corn picking machines would cut wide avenues through the corn, leaving some blocks of corn to stand until the frost had turned the cornstalks brittle and brown. Usually, the cornfields weren't completely bare until into November. I wouldn't see any picking this year.

The car hummed along, and curves swayed me left and right. Now the sun came through my side window, warming me; and I realized I'd have to get a conversation going, or I'd be asleep.

"I've gotten all my clothes and other school crap organized and some of it packed. How about you?" I asked Brian.

"Almost, my mother has nagged me. I don't think I'll be done 'til I walk out the door." Brian responded. Brian had been accepted at Kent State in Ohio near Cleveland. "Have you thought any more about what you might major in?" he asked me.

"Well my core electives are a chemistry class and a math class. Everything else is required classes. But who knows? I enjoy English."

Brian was a brain, in the Honor Society, and all that, and was planning to be a business or economics major. I only had a vague idea of what I wanted to study. I had done well in my science classes, so I told everyone I was trying to be an engineer.

"Big difference between Chemistry and English," Brian said as he shifted up through the gears. We had stopped at the four-way intersection of a small hamlet named Cherry Hill.

"Sure is," I agreed and didn't say anything more.

It was time for me to stop talking and start thinking. When I was traveling and had nothing to do but watch the new scenery, I would use the time to think about myself. I hoped the change in environment, seeing new places and people, would give me a new perspective of myself and help me find myself; then when I returned home, I would be eager and confident to go on into the future.

"Oh, I guess we're stopping," Brian said, and my introspection ended before it began.

Ahead of us, Wayne, who was driving, waved from his window and had his right blinker on. Both cars pulled off into the potholed parking lot of Mildred's Café in the village of Acton. I had been in Mildred's before since it was about the distance from home that people needed to stop and use a restroom. Years ago, the café had been a small general store and two-pump gas station. Now, the building had shiny stainless steel siding, a long row of windows, and a blinking red neon sign spelling out "Mildred's Home Cooking." Mildred couldn't sell beer because Acton was a dry township, and this kept Mildred's a friendly place to eat.

"Neat old pickup," I said to Brian as we parked.

A tired-looking late '30s Chevy pickup with scratched and faded red paint sat in the parking lot. Except for the paint, the truck was in good shape: there were no deep dents, and all the pieces were there. The only other vehicle in the lot was a telephone utility repair truck.

"Yeah, I bet the original owner's inside. Some old fart like Old Man Peterson. He should paint it and put a V-8 in it."

We went into Mildred's and found that all four booths along the front window were open. The telephone repair crew sat on stools at the counter, smoking, drinking coffee, and chatting up a young waitress Mildred hired for the morning rush. At the end of the counter was an old man in bib denim overalls, smoking a pipe and reading a newspaper with a cup of coffee in front of him. He was clean-shaven, and his clothes were neatly pressed.

"The pickup driver," Brian whispered to me as we slid across the red vinyl seat of the booth.

The quick doughnuts and coffee perked us all up. Mrs. Patterson insisted on paying, so Brian and I each left $.50 for the tip. Most importantly, Mrs. Patterson gave Brian a hand-drawn map to the Induction Center. We would likely be separated in traffic as we got into the suburbs of Buffalo.

Back on the road, I didn't want to start thinking about myself again, so I talked more about school. Beth Ann had always talked of teaching and had been in the Future Teachers club in high school. "Does Beth Ann want to teach elementary or high school?"

"She wants to be a high school science teacher. She thinks more girls, or rather women, should get into science, and she wants to be an example."

"Great, great!" I said with sincere enthusiasm. Beth Ann was going to a New York state university near Buffalo. Brian would only have a three-hour drive from Kent to visit her.

"And I guess Susan wants to study literature?" Brian asked.

"Yeah, right. She's even talked about a PhD and being a university professor."

"She's smart enough," Brian responded.

Now, I regretted talking about school and let the conversation drop. It seemed everyone had their shit together for school, except me. I just watched the green country go by for a time. Every village we went through could have been our village. There were Methodist churches that had a vague resemblance to a fort but with stained-glass windows. There were bright white clapboard Congregational churches with tall steeples and Baptist churches (also white). The villages usually had a gas station at the four corners, a small frame Post Office, and a down-and-out-looking grocery store. There were farm implement dealers with tractors and combines lined up by the road. The schools we passed were nearly identical with ours—two-story brick buildings with clearly distinguishable additions added over the years. I thought of all the guys from these villages drafted like Wayne. There were an awful lot of lives getting crapped up.

Gradually, the villages merged; and we were in the suburbs of Buffalo. Brian and I became separated from Wayne at a traffic light, but Wayne pulled to the side of the boulevard and waited for us. I was checking Mrs. Patterson's map as we went along.

"We should be getting closer," I commented to Brian.

We went through an intersection and, what—at first—appeared to be a park, began on our right. A high chain-link fence with three strands of barbed wire at the top ran along the street, so I knew it wasn't a park. Next, I noticed rows of long, white wooden two-story barracks with exterior stairs on the ends of the buildings. They were identical with the buildings I'd seen many times in old newsreels or movies about World War II.

"They're turning in." Brian said.

A large, white sign with black lettering, reading "Camp Baker U.S. Military Reservation," stood beside the driveway to a large nearly empty parking lot. We pulled in and parked beside Wayne. There were a few cars parked at one end of the lot by a sign reading "Staff Parking Only." Three drab olive school buses with "U.S. Military" and "Official Use Only" stenciled in white on their sides sat parked near the entrance gate. A large sign at the gate read "Inductees Read This:" but the rest was too small to read from a distance.

"A serious-looking place," Brian said to me as we got out of the car, walked to the back, and stretched, all the while looking around.

Wayne walked up to us and said, "We're early. My mother suggested that, if there is enough time, we have lunch before I sign in. I'm going to check with those guys at the gate."

Wayne, carrying a large manila mailing envelope, walked over to the entrance where three guys in crisp pressed khaki uniforms stood. Mrs. Patterson was still sitting in the car, and I noticed her blowing her nose into a white handkerchief.

"Check out the footprints," I said to Brian as I motioned to an area of the parking lot behind the ugly buses. Sets of white footprints were painted on the asphalt in four neat rows of about 20 sets to a row.

"I suppose that saves a lot of instruction to people not used to taking instruction," Brian commented.

From a distance, we could see Wayne taking papers out of his envelope and talking to the soldiers. Brian and I walked over to the fence and took a closer look at the buildings in the compound. Administrative buildings were clustered just beyond the entrance gate. They were plain brick two-story buildings with identification numbers painted on their sides. Wide, paved driveways ran among the buildings rather than normal sidewalks. Each building had sets of white footprints painted on the asphalt near its entrance, with one exception. There was no landscaping or decoration to the grounds. The exception was the walkway to one building lined with rocks painted white.

"This place makes a cemetery look like an amusement park." Brian observed as we left the fence and returned to the car.

"Sterile," I said and then made a suggestion. "How about if we say goodbye to Wayne after lunch, at the restaurant, and head home from there?"

"Fine," Brian said, "I don't want to come back here."

When Wayne returned, his face held a serious expression, and his voice was businesslike. "I've got lots of time. They say everyone puts it off until the last possible minute. I'll ask Mom what she wants to do." He walked over and talked to his mother through her car window; then he came back to us. "There's a Howard Johnson's further down the street. Let's go have lunch."

It was impossible to miss the orange tiled roof and white cupola with a weather vane that distinguished all Howard Johnson's. I had brought five bucks for lunch, so I felt I could afford a nice place to eat. McDonald's was great for the price, but going to Howard Johnson's made it a special occasion. A pleasant and attractive hostess took us to our booth. Potted plants and framed photographs decorated the dining room.

We looked over our menus in silence and only spoke when the waitress (also attractive and wearing a light blue uniform with white lace trimmed apron) came to take our orders. After she left, I considered making a comment about this being Wayne's last good meal for a while. Fortunately, I said something else.

"Well, Wayne. When you get an address, we'll write and tell you all the news." My comment sounded lame.

Wayne gave me a forced smile. "Sure, sure. It may take a week or so since there is a lot of processing before I get to basic training." Then his smile evaporated, and he turned his head and looked out the window. I didn't say anything more and just sat there fingering my silverware and sipping at my ice water.

Finally, our food came; and we brightened up and exchanged comments about them. "Why can't Mildred cook like this?" I said while holding up my big cheeseburger with a juicy, fresh-cut tomato; thick-sliced onion; and crispy, fresh lettuce. Melted cheese had dripped onto my fingers.

Brian answered quickly, "Because her clientele wouldn't pay the price."

Wayne hadn't spoken for a while, so I asked him a direct question. "So are you going to ask for particular branch of the army or just let them decide?"

"I'm going to ask for the artillery. If I get in, I'll be going way out to Oklahoma for training," he said, "my father was what he called a 'Cannon Cocker.' He says you ride in trucks that pull the guns and carry the shells, so it beats marching."

"Makes sense," I responded, "all I know about the army is what I see in newsreels and movies. Some of the guns are track-mounted now. I've seen that. Large helicopters carry around smaller guns. Moving around by helicopter might be fun."

Looking at his food, (not at me) Wayne simply said, "Yeah, fun."

After we had finished eating, Brian worked on Wayne to get a little more information.

"When do you think you'll get your first leave?"

"Those guys at the gate said I'd definitely get a Christmas leave since I'll still be in training. They said maybe I'd get a week."

I piped up immediately, saying "Well, time flies. It will be Christmas before you know it." Again I regretted my unimaginative comment.

Mrs. Patterson finally joined the conversation to help me out. "It's true!" She said emphatically as she leaned over the table and looked at each of the three of us in succession. "All of you will be very busy this fall, and that does make the time pass faster. Always remember to look out into the future and see the happy times ahead. You will get tired and discouraged if you only look at the hard work in front of you." She paused and looked at Brian and me. "I'm already planning what to serve at our New Year's Eve party, and you and all your friends are invited."

We were taking the last gurgling pulls on our soda straws when Wayne spoke up. "Why don't you guys head home from here? There's no point in your going back to the Induction Center."

Brian and I did a poor job at hiding our surprise and relief. We both began to answer at the same time; then we each stopped speaking to let the other talk. Brian finally continued. "Yeah, we were thinking the same thing."

Out in the parking lot, Wayne politely got the car door for his mother and then came to the front of the Falcon, where Brian and I stood. His mood changed after the solemn lunch.

"Okay, you reprobates, I'm glad you came. What the hell! Misery loves company."

He stuck out his hand to Brian first, and as they shook hands, Brian guided him off to the other side of the Falcon. I idly walked a few parking spaces away and watched the traffic on the Boulevard. A silver split window Corvette went past shifting from second to third and giving a rap to the exhaust note. Mercifully, this distracted me for a moment. When I did turn back, Brian and Wayne were walking toward me.

"You guys plotting something without me?" I joked as I stepped up to them.

"You bet, and it's going to be a lot of fun," Wayne said as he put his hand on my shoulder, and we began to walk back to where I had been watching traffic. "Did you see that Corvette?" he asked, "I bet you have one of those someday, and when you do, I'll whip your ass with my Mustang."

"You're on!" I exclaimed, "and we'll do it right out there." And I pointed to the Boulevard.

"Anyway, good luck in school. You will hit a home run no matter what you do. Don't pay any attention to how Brian is doing. Do your own thing."

"Yeah, well, I am going to sleep better now that I know you're protecting me from those Commies and their evil plot to pollute our precious bodily fluids."

"Damn, right! I'll hunt down those deviated prevert Commies."

"Wouldn't you be surprised if you get a commander named Ripper!" We both exploded in laughter and then shadowboxed with each other and slapped each other on the back.

We had taken a few paces back toward Brian when Wayne stopped, and I turned to face him. "Mike, about girls . . ." He paused a moment. "Don't sweat it. Beth Ann says she and other girls think you have what they call sensitivity, and that must be some kind of magic with them. Besides, women change their minds like the weather and then change them back again. Anyway, everything will work out one way or another."

"Yeah, sure. No big deal," I said in return.

The three of us did a final round of handshaking, and it was then that I noticed Mrs. Patterson in the car blowing her nose into a blue handkerchief. We loaded up, and Brian and I headed home; and Wayne headed off to the army.

Going home, I felt a person was missing from our car even though Wayne hadn't ridden to the Induction Center with Brian and me. There was a cold, empty space that neither Brian nor I wanted to talk about, so we didn't speak at all for the first half hour of our trip home.

We were listening to one of the powerful Buffalo rock stations when the announcer said he was going to play an oldie; then Elvis's deep mellow voice came on singing, "Didja ever get, didja ever get one of them days?" Elvis was one of the few passions of mine that I was willing to admit to. And so I started knee slapping to the song.

"That was on 'G.I. Blues' wasn't it!" I remarked.

"I don't know. If you say so. You know Elvis?" Brian responded.

"I just thought of something," I said in a cheery voice, "Wayne will probably be sent to Germany. He might be able to hook up with my brother and have a few beers. I know German girls are great-looking. Wayne may come back married. Wouldn't that be a hoot?"

"Well, if you believe the movie, Elvis had a good time over there," Brian answered but with less enthusiasm than me.

Thinking of Wayne in Germany made me feel much better, and I ran a vision through my mind of Wayne in a khaki uniform, sitting at a table under a tree in a sunny German beer garden. A blond, blue-eyed, full-busted Viking princess sat close to Wayne and was running her hand up the inside of his leg. Wayne ignored her and sipped his beer from a great beer stein, which left him with a white beer mustache. The girl pressed herself to Wayne and kissed the foam mustache until it was gone.

Brian interrupted my daydreaming. "Kathy may have something to say about Wayne's coming back married. According to Beth Ann, they saw each other Monday and Tuesday."

"Good. Maybe she will write to him. I understand letters mean a lot."

After driving about a quarter of a mile, Brian continued. "Girls are fickle," he said factually, "you can never tell what they will do. They say one thing and mean another."

"Not all girls are fickle. Some mean exactly what they say," I responded bluntly.

"Are you sure?"

"Yeah, I'm sure," I said and left the conversation at that.

Another Beatles song was playing on the radio. This time, it was "You Can't Hide Your Love Away." The Beatles were touring in the States, so many of their songs were on the air. My happy thoughts of Wayne evaporated. Clearly, everyone knew Susan was dumping me. Sensitivity. What the hell was sensitivity?

"Do you need to stop at Mildred's?" Brian asked as he slowed the Falcon coming into Acton.

"No, I'm good, but stop if you want."

"Well, let's get on home then," Brian said, and we went on past the diner. A few of what looked like junior high school boys were riding bikes in circles in Mildred's parking lot while giggling girls the same age clustered on the sidewalk.

Passing Mildred's reminded me we were getting close to home, and I hadn't given any more thought to my problems. I considered saying a silent prayer, but instead, I resolved to make college a new beginning and leave everything else behind. I would make a success of school. It wasn't necessary to know what I would major in; whatever I studied, I'd get a degree; then I said a quick, silent prayer. "Dear Lord, help me succeed at school. Help me get through it." The prayer probably didn't count since I wasn't in church.

The resolution completed my journey, so I let my mind go back to following the music on the radio. It was four o'clock, and the news cut into the music; so I reached down and punched a button on the radio to change the station. Immediately, Brian's hand came down from the steering wheel; and he pushed the previous button to get back to the news.

"Sorry," he said, "I want to hear about the space shot. It's Gemini V, and Conrad and Cooper may stay up for a record long flight."

"Fine, sure," I said sincerely.

Brian loved the rocket shots and talked as though he knew the astronauts personally. Eventually, the radio announcer got to the space story. The mission's rendezvous experiment had problems, but a long duration flight record looked like it could still be made. A report about Vietnam followed the Gemini V story. The announcer excitedly described what he called "the first planned set piece battle of the war." The marines had been kicking the Vietcong's ass in someplace called the Batangan Peninsula, which was south of another odd-sounding place called Chu Lai. The Jug Heads had whipped them good, knocking off 600 V.C. while suffering only 45 killed in action. The announcer didn't name any of the 45 GIs; only numbers were important. Numbers didn't have homes and families.

I had a home, and when Brian dropped me off, I walked in the door and smelled dinner cooking.

CHAPTER 7

Last Date

Late Friday morning, I was sitting at our dining room table copying names and addresses from my mother's address book into a new one that my mother told me I must take to school. Many days before, my mother had said to me, "Copy your aunts' and uncles' addresses. You'll want to write to them, and don't forget your brother's military address."

"All right, all right, I'll do it!" I had agreed after a brief and foolish protest. I had hoped that would be the last I would hear of the subject. But, just days from leaving home for school, I still hadn't learned that my mother never forgot details. "Have you filled out your address book as I asked you?" she asked me that morning as I bowed my head over a bowl of Cheerios.

So I sat there wishing I could honestly say I had to leave early for work; then my mother's infallible memory hit me with another punch. "Have you made a reservation for dinner tomorrow night? I assume you're taking Susan to dinner as you did in July," she asked me from the kitchen.

"Oh, damn!" I exclaimed slapping down my pencil and leaning back in my chair.

"Don't swear!" My mother scolded back at me. "Just take care of it. I hope school teaches you not to procrastinate." My mother was still an optimist even after being married to my father for years and raising two sons.

It took two hours to drive to Chautauqua. This made it more convenient to start early and have dinner on the institution grounds. Obviously, we both had assumed we would do this again but hadn't confirmed it with each other. I had to make sure we were thinking the same, so I got up to call Susan. My mother gave me privacy by going upstairs to do some unnecessary task as I dialed Susan's phone number.

Crap! I thought to myself as I heard Susan's sister answer the phone. Despite what I was thinking, I greeted her politely; and as I held up my crossed fingers, I asked for Susan. The brat didn't disappoint my initial reaction on hearing her voice.

"Oh, she's busy. She's looking at information she's gotten in the mail from sororities at Albany. Albany is a big university, you know, not just a small college. They have lots of sororities and fraternities and all kinds of social activities. Susan is so smart. I bet she even gets to know graduate students."

My voice strained. "Would you please just ask her to talk to me about dinner tomorrow night?"

"Well, I'll see if she can speak to you."

I heard distant voices and then a shout and a clearly recognizable exclamation from Susan. "You said what!" Then came an unconvincing scream of "That hurt!" from the brat.

"Hi, Mike! She's terrible! Please use her as a punching bag when you pick me up tomorrow."

"I will. I'll do just that."

"Yes, we will need to do something about dinner before the concert."

We agreed the La Vie En Rose would work a second time. The La Vie En Rose was more a café than a restaurant and served a limited but good menu of European dishes.

"How did the trip to the Induction Center go?" Susan asked.

"Well enough. It wasn't a happy trip. Camp Baker is a bleak place. Have you ever seen it?"

"Yes, we've driven past it when driving to Canada, but I never paid any attention to it. Until the draft got so big, it was just used by the National Guard. Kathy told me this morning that Wayne's at Fort Dix, New Jersey, now."

"I think he assumed that. Everyone we know that went into the army ended up there. Say, when did Kathy decide Wayne was an okay kind of guy?"

"At the same time he decided she was an okay kind of girl."

Wisely, for once, I let the subject drop. "So what are you reading?"

"Oh, something light. Arthur Hailey's *Hotel*. I was lucky the library had a copy since it's so popular."

"Well, light reading is good, too. Give the classics a break and read something contemporary."

"Yes, yes, but this is so trite I'm worried I'm wasting my time."

Earlier in the summer, Susan had read Virginia Woolf's *Mrs. Dalloway* because she thought it might help with her freshman English class in the fall.

"Well, *The Reivers* wasn't exactly Faulkner's gloomiest work, and I think it should be the first book of his that a person reads. Tell that to your English professor." Susan realized I said this lightheartedly. She and I had verbally jousted before on what makes a book literature rather than just popular reading material.

"*The Reivers* is a wonderful book, but if it had been Faulkner's only book, it wouldn't have won him the Nobel."

We went on talking about authors, ideas, style, and the purpose of books until I realized more than half an hour had past. Susan was going on about library censorship when I cut in saying "I'm sorry, but I just saw the time. I've got to get ready for work." We wrapped up our conversation, and finally I said, "Okay. I'll see you tomorrow at four. Bye."

"I'm glad you called, Mike. It's so good to talk like this. Summer is so boring. I hope it's an easy day at work for you. Bye."

I hung up the phone, raced up to my room, and dug through the center drawer of my desk until I found a receipt to the La Vie En Rose I had saved from our July date. The receipt had a phone number, and I went downstairs and phoned the restaurant (long-distance) and made the reservation.

Later, during the few minutes I had alone while driving the Corvair to work, I thought of Susan and our phone call. Our conversation had been so relaxed and enjoyable that it was hard to believe that a week before, Susan had told me she didn't want to have any contact with me for months to come. A cold rage built up in me quickly replaced by simple disbelief, confusion, consternation, whatever you call it when a person is punished without explanation.

Wayne had left on Wednesday, and now, Friday was my last day at work for the summer. I pulled into the station and drove around back and parked among the stacks of bald tires and rusting worn-out car parts. Ed Crookshank owned and operated the gas station. Everyone knew Ed as "Crankshaft"; I had even heard him addressed as Mr. Crankshaft.

Crankshaft was middle-aged, balding, and as round as a bowling ball. He wore the same clothes all week with Monday being the day we looked forward to when he started a new set. Sick cars talked to Crankshaft and told him what their problems were. He was so good that rival mechanics stopped at the station carrying beer or a bottle of booze as a gift and had embarrassing conversations with him about a problem they couldn't fix. Crankshaft never cheated a customer, and consequently, the station was always swamped with repair work.

Crankshaft tutored us young guys in the art of profanity. He delivered profanity with the gusto of a good Shakespearean actor, his booming voice echoing from under a jacked up car while he lay underneath on a mechanics creeper. No woman dared bring a car in for repair since Crankshaft couldn't say a civil sentence without at least a "hell" or "damn." He claimed he learned the art of profanity while a marine infantryman in the South Pacific during World War II and he had the tattoos and scars to back up the claim.

Crankshaft also delivered anatomy and sex education lessons to us green high school kids. We considered these lessons as a bonus to our pay. He would roar with laughter when he saw our blank, disbelieving faces as he described impossibly contorted body positions; however, he gave his most valuable lecture in full seriousness. The lesson concerned how to make a girl as happy with sex as we men. He claimed patience was the key and gave exacting detail on how to find all of the girl's hot spots. Prof. Crankshaft condemned what he called hit-and-run sex. If the girl wasn't happy, he warned, she wouldn't invite you back.

At five o'clock each Friday, Crankshaft handed out pay envelopes as he stood behind the cash register. He demanded that each of us go through a ritual he called reporting for pay.

When it was my turn and when I stepped in front of him at the cash register, he yelled out "Who the hell are you?" as though he didn't know me.

"Mike Collins," I barked as loud as I could.

"What the hell do you want?" Crankshaft hollered back.

"My pay!"

After grumbling that, I and all my coworkers were worthless and didn't deserve a penny; he handed me my envelope. That ended the ritual, and Crankshaft immediately became his old self, laughing and asking how my parents were and if my brother had a German child yet. This odd behavior frightened new employees and startled any customers that heard the shouting. I enjoyed the game.

This Friday, he asked me about Susan. "You still date that bookish Hanson girl?"

I told him I did.

"She's a hard case," he said as he picked up a flyswatter from the countertop, turned, and swatted a fly sitting on an oilcan on the shelf behind him. "But it's just a shell. I know because she is just like her mother, and I went to high school with her mother. I could have cracked that shell," he said while idly swinging the flyswatter and looking around for another fly. "But there were plenty of easier touches. We're still friends, believe it or not."

I stood with a blank look trying to comprehend what he was saying.

"Wipe that stupid look off your face," Crankshaft said as he pulled out his wallet and gave me a twenty-dollar bill.

"What?" was all I said as I took the money.

"This is your last day for the summer. When you're working, the till is always straight with the gallons pumped. You don't goof off much, and you know a box wrench from an open-end wrench, the hot-wire from the ground wire. Have some fun with the money."

"Damn! Thanks!" I said as I turned and stepped out of the office.

Behind me, I heard Crankshaft grumble, "College kids!"

The extra twenty bucks made the hot and muggy evening easier to get through. Friday evening, the start of the weekend, brought extra traffic to the station; and I was happy to switch off all the lights and pumps at eleven o'clock. A refreshing night breeze blew through my open window as I drove home, and my mind wandered back to what Crankshaft had said about his high school philandering. All of that had gone down more than twenty years before, and time had wiped away all record of his youth, except what was in his mind.

Saturday evening was to be the end of a precious set of memories for Susan and me. This made me wonder what, in future years, would remind us of our high school romance. I had given Susan a few gifts but nothing exceptional. There were a few pictures, certainly our high school yearbook, but I thought there should be another more personal token or remembrance of our affection for each other, even as obviously lopsided that affection was.

All the usual gifts seemed trite and commercial. I considered writing a poem, but knowing her appreciation of the art, I ditched that idea quickly. I thought of one thing and then another but couldn't agree with myself; however as I drove through the night, a fuzzy, unfocused idea grew in my mind. I decided the gift would be a quirky gift that might perplex her or might annoy her or might be immediately trashed by her.

Saturday morning, I worked out the details of the gift and began making it. My arts and crafts skills rivaled my ballet abilities, so the project was tenuous at best. First, I rummaged through the heaps of old toys in the back of my closet and pulled out an old picture puzzle in its box. The box was crushed and leaking parts, but it didn't matter if the puzzle was complete or not. I carefully selected four parts that interlocked in a column though it didn't matter what part of the puzzle the parts came from; then I pushed crap out of the way, opened a small corner of my desk, put the pieces down, and got out my pocketknife. I used the blade of my knife to peel the photo layer off, each piece leaving four blank pieces. I found a black ink pen and, leaning intently over each piece, I printed a letter on each piece. The letters were L, O, V, and E. It wasn't calligraphy, but all the letters were legible and of the same size; it would do the job. Now the problem was how to wrap four small puzzle pieces.

No solution came to mind, so I took my usual option and procrastinated. I continued with the chores of what was my last weekend at home for nearly three months.

I mowed the lawn, as I had dozens of times in the past years. The lawn would need one—maybe two—more mowing in the fall, and my father could do that. What leaves didn't blow away, I would take care of in Thanksgiving. I would be missed but not because I left chores undone.

At two o'clock, I had to start cleaning myself up if I were to be on time to pick up Susan at four o'clock. After taking a shower, I was in my room wondering what to wear when I again saw the puzzle pieces on my desk. I considered looking around the house for a jewelry box left over from a gift to my mother, but then, I realized such a box would scare the hell out of Susan if it were the size of a ring box. I was about to give up on the whole damn, fool idea when I thought of the perfect solution for presenting the puzzle.

When I was small, my aunt had given my brother and I a special gift—gold-foil-wrapped chocolate coins—in our Christmas stockings. The coins came in a small pouch made of scarlet velvet, lined with satin- and gold-braided drawstring. I had saved a number of the pouches, and one would be perfect to put the puzzle pieces into. While still in my underwear, I spent the next ten minutes searching my room for that special, unforgettable place where I had stashed the keepsake pouches. Just as desperation was setting in, I found them in the back of my sock drawer. I put the puzzle pieces in a pouch, put on my clothes, and took the pouch to the car, leaving it there so I wouldn't forget to take it. I didn't trust my memory any more than my mother did.

I parked the car in Susan's drive at 3:50 p.m., and as I pulled the brass knob of the antique doorbell, I hoped Susan would be ready and greet me at the door. I didn't want to speak to either of her parents or the brat. But I had no luck, and her mother greeted me.

Mrs. Holden and I exchanged greetings; and I began to worry that, for no reason at all, I would blurt out "Crankshaft."

"Come in, sit down. Susan is almost ready," Mrs. Holden said as she motioned to me and stepped into what, in the past, was called the parlor. I eyed the black and white photographs of stern-faced ancestors hung on the walls in oval frames as I gently sat down on a flimsy-looking old chair with legs, which looked like an animal's claw gripping a ball. She sat on a mini couch that I heard was called a love seat, but looked too uncomfortable for love to me.

"Did your mother tell you that Susan's father and I saw your parents at Chautauqua the first weekend of the season this year? We were all at the opera and met at intermission. It was a wonderful performance of 'Die Fledermaus.' The husbands are willing to go because the performances are in English, and your mother and I love the costumes." She laughed and continued praising Chautauqua, and I never did get to tell her that my mother had told me about the meeting.

I heard heavy thumping on the stairs behind me. "Here I am!" shouted Susan as she popped into the parlor. She wore navy blue slacks that, instead of cuffs, had stirrup bands around her feet, which held the slacks tight and close to her ankles. Her white long-sleeved blouse had ruffles down the front and a narrow collar. Her fresh jasmine perfume immediately filled the room as we greeted each other.

Susan and her mother discussed the weather and finally agreed that Susan would be fine taking just a sweater. We had almost made it out the door when Mrs. Holden commented on the occasion. "You two have had a wonderful summer and best of luck to you, Mike, at school. You'll meet lots of new friends and enjoy the challenge. You'll do just fine"

"Thank you" was all I said. Collaboration between mother and daughter didn't surprise me; it just disappointed me.

We drove south out of the village, the opposite direction from my journey last Wednesday. Billowing towers of white cumulus clouds dominated this sky, but there was no threat of rain. The clouds kept the air cool, and fortunately, my mother had insisted I take a sweater. The nearly two-hour trip was entirely through open country and small hamlets like Conklinville.

Chautauqua Institution was on the shore of Chautauqua Lake, a narrow 28-mile-long lake. Chautauqua Lake was shaped similar to the Finger Lakes but was a hundred miles west of those lakes. The lake was renowned for sport fishing, especially for the spunky muskellunge. Hardwood forests of maple and oak carpeted the shores right to the water's edge, making the lake an ideal resort destination.

"I'm looking forward to a great show tonight. This is the second year in a row Ferrante and Teicher have come to Chautauqua," Susan commented as we drove out of the village past our empty and lonely-looking high school. Ferrante and Teicher were the classical piano duo that we were going to see perform.

My musical knowledge ended at the eighth note of the scales, so I made only a weak reply. Susan went on to talk about how Mary Pardee, a girl in our class, had auditioned for and had been accepted in the choir of the Sunday morning worship service at Chautauqua. Mary had made the long trip to Chautauqua and back every Sunday morning throughout this summer. The Institution had been founded in the early 1870s as a summer revival camp and school for training Sunday school teachers. Now, Chautauqua was refreshingly ecumenical and reasonably secular though it retained its fundamental spiritual character.

After talking about Mary, we went on to talk about teachers we had had through school. That topic evolved into exchanging bits of information about classmates. We laughed a lot and occasionally challenged the plausibility of a story. The hot topic was the contagion of pregnancy that two of our classmates had contracted. One girl had left school the previous January. The father in that case was from the class ahead of us and was going to a southern university. They had gotten married and set up housekeeping near his campus. The other couple was in our class, and the news hadn't broken until after graduation. Neither Susan nor I knew what the couple's plans were.

Our nostalgic conversation went on through the entire trip, interrupted only by brief pauses to listen to a good song on the radio. We heard Sonny and Cher at least three times during the trip.

Chautauqua Institution had a mystique that was enhanced by the black wrought iron fences and pleasantly patterned red brick walls that surround the approximately 400 acres. Nonresidents had to pay to enter the Institution during the July and August season.

I parked in one of the large parking lots on the other side of the state highway that ran past the Institution. Visitors could not drive or park on the grounds during the season. I fished my sweater out of the backseat, checked to be sure that the pouch of puzzle pieces was in my pocket, and we joined the trickle of people crossing the highway at a traffic light at the main gate. The crowd was dressed casually, and some carried picnic blankets to either sit on or to cover their legs with during the concert. Popular concerts, lectures, and the Sunday morning worship services were held in the covered, open-air amphitheater, which was complete with a marvelous organ and a stage large enough for a symphony orchestra. Long fixed wooden pews provided multilevel seating for about four thousand. These flat wooden pews became harder the longer a concert went unless you had a blanket to sit on.

The will-call window was in the administration building at the front gate. After getting our tickets, I rejoined Susan; and we began the quarter-mile walk down a sloping brick street tightly lined with narrow three- and sometimes four-story houses. Nearly all the houses had a door and front porch at each story of the building. A common Chautauqua pastime was sitting in a wicker chair and watching people on the street.

Walking into Chautauqua gave you a mild shock since it was that different from the rural countryside just outside its gates. The change always prompted comments from Susan and me.

"I now make a pledge to myself," Susan said emphatically, "I will come to Chautauqua for at least a weeklong stay and as soon as possible."

"It is different, pleasantly different," I said, "everyone walks and the streets are only wide enough for one car anyway. I wonder why the houses are so narrow and close together."

"It's because Chautauqua began as a planned community but planned only for tents on platforms or, at most, small summer cottages. The Institution became popular faster than I bet they expected, and people replaced the tents with boarding houses and small hotels. I've heard there are about 8000 people here in the summer." Susan was truly enchanted by Chautauqua.

"Well, this place looks like an amusement park. Maybe like Disneyland without the rides and commercialism," I responded

Chautauqua intimidated me mildly. The people summering at Chautauqua were predominantly the well-to-do from Buffalo,

Cleveland, Pittsburgh, and even New York City—old industrial money from the turn of the century and before. We locals didn't have the money to pursue the arts, philosophy, and religion within a gated community.

A plaza, roughly the dimension of a football field, was notched out of the sloping terrain halfway down to the lakeshore. Wide sidewalks bisected the expanse of grass and trees, and there was a large fountain in the middle. This was Bestor Plaza, named for a prominent former president of the Institution and was the center of the community. A two-story brick administration building with wide stone steps leading up to a colonnade occupied the width of one end of the plaza. At the other end was an impressive two-story brick library worthy of a small city. An impeccably maintained wood-framed hotel from the turn-of-the-century dominated one side of the plaza. Along the other side was a commercial building with a post office, a café, shops on the upper level, and a large bookstore in the basement level. The park-like plaza was ringed with grand old maple, beech, sycamore, and oak trees. The trees shaded the grass, the sidewalks, and the people who were walking in all directions.

A short walk from the plaza was the Hollyhock Hotel. The La Vie En Rose restaurant rambled through multiple rooms of the first floor of the hotel. The Hollyhock was actually two homes along a steep lane that had somehow been joined. A hostess guided Susan and me through a short, narrow hall of the restaurant; down three steps; through a windowless dining room, where we sat during our July date; and into another dining room. Fortunately this time, we were seated next to a window where we could look out at a small rose garden, the sidewalk, and the lane in front of the hotel.

"So here we are again. We must like French cooking," I said as I helped Susan with her chair and then sat down myself. "So what do you know about France?"

"What I know, most of all, is I want to go there," Susan replied as she peeked from behind her menu.

"But I thought you were coming here to immerse yourself in the arts."

"Not at all in the same category," she answered.

Since we knew the menu, we ordered quickly. The food was okay but probably as authentic French as what I could make in my mother's kitchen; however, every dish had a thick butter sauce, which must have qualified it as French.

The conversation died after we ordered, and we didn't have the menus to hide behind. Eventually, we both blurted out something at the same time, our words mixing in a confusion neither of us understood. I insisted she speak first.

"Oh, I was just going to say the flowers are nice." She motioned to the white porcelain bud vase at the end of our table holding a single yellow rose.

"Right, right. Each table has one," I said in return; then I leaned across the table and said in a low voice, "It looks like they collected up the vases from yard sales. Everyone is different." And I looked around at the other tables.

She smiled and said, "It could be. Businesses don't try to be elaborate here since they're only open two months a year."

Neither of us spoke for a long moment, leaving only the background conversation of the one other couple in the dining room with us; then Susan turned quickly from looking out the window.

"Oh, what were you going to say before?" she asked.

I grimaced at her and sheepishly said, "I don't remember. It must have been something about France, I guess."

"Well, I know," Susan said as if discovering a solution to the silence. "What's your favorite movie set in France?"

I dropped the fork I was idly playing with. "There was one I saw last week on the late show after getting home from work. It was *It Takes a Thief*, a romance/comedy/mystery set on the Riviera. Now that's a place I'd like to go. It had old, funny-looking French cars, too." I talked some more about the movie and Susan said she liked *Charade* with Audrey Hepburn; she had seen the movie twice the year before. Our dinners came, and after commenting about our food, we ate quickly without talking. I was thinking about what to say to Susan when I gave her the puzzle pieces. I planned to do it just after our dinner plates were taken away, but the more time passed, the dumber the whole idea seemed.

It was time to present the puzzle or forget it came after the waitress cleared our plates, but I tried to stall. "Would you like dessert?" I asked immediately after my empty plate passed under my nose.

"No, I don't think we have time," replied Susan as she looked at her watch and straightened in her chair.

"Okay, but wait a moment." I reached into my pocket and pulled out the velvet pouch. "May I ask a favor of you? Would you take this as a remembrance of this summer?" I said as I placed the crimson pouch directly in front of her on the white tablecloth. She looked surprised and didn't immediately reach for the pouch. "It's a trivial gift, not what you would expect."

Susan looked up at me and gave me a weak smile but didn't speak as she reached for the pouch. She pressed her hand on the pouch as she picked it up in an effort to feel what was inside. Her expression grew confused as she pulled open the gold cords and looked into the pouch. She put a finger in the pouch but still didn't get a clue what was inside, so she turned the pouch over and shook out the pieces. Perplexed, she frowned as she looked at the four cardboard puzzle pieces, some with the letter side up and others with a blank side up.

"I know," I said as I reached across to the puzzle pieces. "It's an odd gift, but it may mean something someday." I turned over the upside down pieces so all the letters showed. Her face cleared as she recognized the four letters, and she took the index finger of her right hand and moved the pieces in order to spell "love." But none of the pieces fit, and she looked up at me.

"No, they don't fit," I said as I reached across the table with both hands and picked up the pieces, not wanting her to work the puzzle more, and put the pieces back in the pouch. "Maybe someday, when we look at life differently, they will fit." And I laid the pouch down again. "Would you at least take it now? You can do whatever you want with it later."

"Oh, of course, it's lovely! Yes. Yes, I'll take it," she exclaimed as she picked up the pouch and put it in her purse. I listened closely, and her voice sounded sincere.

"Well, we had better get going," I said as I slid back my chair and stood up. For me, the most important event of the evening was over.

I started a conversation as soon as we left the restaurant and began walking to the amphitheater. "I think we will be in time to get good seats, not blocked by a post," I said just to be talking. The amphitheater had a semicircle of structural posts among the seats that blocked the view. The amphitheater was open seating, making early arrival more important.

"Right. We're early enough, and I've seen the sidewalk more crowded than this before a concert and still gotten good seats."

We walked back up to the plaza and turned left to join the flow of people moving toward the amphitheater. Most streets in the Institution were in a grid pattern. Consequently, a street was either going up and down the slope to the lakeshore or running horizontally with the shore.

"The gardens are lovely," Susan said as we walked along; she sounded like she was trying to make conversation. We were passing church congregation houses, and each had a small flower garden between the sidewalk and the porch, and a discreet sign naming the denomination. We walked past the Baptist House and the Church of Christ House and others. Some of the houses had the original frame building in front but extended in the back into modern dormitory like buildings. Church retreats were held in these buildings all year.

An usher gave us a program as we went through one of the gates of the amphitheater. The entrance ticket to the Institution grounds included admission to all of the Institution's venues, including the opera house, the stage theater, the amphitheater, and any of the smaller attractions.

From the top tier of the amphitheater, Susan and I began the ritual of finding the best possible seating. We looked down and scanned a section, conferred with each other, and then moved on around and scanned another section where we found room on a pew that provided a reasonable view. We quickly walked down the sloping aisle and shuffled our way across the long bench and to the open spot. Many people were still scouting for seats right up to and past show time.

After a rousing introduction, out came two old guys dressed in identical loud red tuxedos with black satin lapels, oversized black bow ties, and ruffled white shirts. They looked almost like twins with matching haircuts and identical, heavy black-rimmed glasses. I thought they were a pair of sissy boys until during the program when one of them spoke to the audience of his wife and children. Their grand pianos faced each other and nested together on the stage. A tall curtain made of multicolored and reflective streamers ran the width of the stage behind them. Spotlights played on the cover of streamers, giving a sparkling wave affect.

After bowing to the audience, they took their seats—or benches—and pounded out a rousing rendition of "Rhapsody in Blue." The audience loved it and clapped and cheered their approval. Ferrante and Teicher were great, even to someone like me who didn't know stick about music. The entire program went on like that, and my palms were sore from clapping. They were true showmen; and at one point, each of them stood, reached forward into their open pianos, and plucked the strings giving a unique sound while still playing the keys with the other hand.

My favorite tune of the concert was "Autumn Leaves," although the theme from *Exodus* was also good. I preferred "Autumn Leaves" because it was near autumn, and it was a sadly melodic tune that left a feeling of futility and finality. "I'll miss you most of all, my darling, when autumn leaves begin to fall."

Ferrante and Teicher called it a night after the second encore. The houselights came up, and we joined the crowd in the slow shuffle up and out of the amphitheater and along the narrow streets and sidewalks. Neither of us attempted to speak as we moved along, but when the crowd had thinned and we were side-by-side, Susan blurted out, "Oh, they were great! It's a pity the season's over."

"Well, there's next season," I answered. She didn't respond, leaving only the muffled and broken conversation of the other walkers around us; so I quickly continued. "This place must be a ghost town in the winter. Have you ever been over here then?"

"No, but it's an incorporated village, and there are permanent residences. The Post office, library, and a few stores stay open all winter."

"And I suppose there are the church meetings and whatever permanent staff the Institution has," I added.

We continued having a pleasant conversation about how unique Chautauqua was until we reached the car; then we began the drive home with the headlights pushing back the dark a short distance in front of us, giving the impression of driving through a long, twisting tunnel. I turned on the radio at a low volume; Susan folded up her sweater, put it up to her window and, using it as a pillow, fell asleep. I watched for deer on the side of the road and we made it safely back to Conklinville.

Susan didn't respond when I stopped the car in her driveway, so I waited a moment. The front porch light was on, and I saw a shadow at the parlor window; and the white lace curtain moved.

"Okay. End of the line," I said reasonably softly as I touched her shoulder.

She snapped awake and sat up but just looked ahead saying, "Oh my, oh my."

"Are you okay?" I asked.

"Yes, yes," she responded but still looked directly forward.

"They're waiting for you. We had better not take long."

"Yes, okay," she responded as she turned to me and reached out and touched my hand.

I got out of the car, walked around, and opened her door. She got out, stood in front of me and, putting her hands on my shoulders, leaned into me and gave me a quick kiss; then she fell against me, putting her head against my chest. I put my arms around her and kissed her hair and enjoyed the fragrance of her perfume.

In a voice muffled by my sweater, she said, "I couldn't have asked for a better time. You're wonderful. It's just so difficult." She pushed back and looked up at me; and I kissed her, hugged her, and patted her on the back. There was no passion in our kiss, just sorrow.

She stepped back from me but then leaned forward and gave me another quick kiss, moved away again, and walked quickly to the side porch steps. She looked back and said, "Goodnight." And she went up the steps.

As I backed the car out of her drive, Peter and Gordon were playing on the radio, singing about falling to pieces and almost crying. If our romance had been a play, the last act was a disaster.

∞

BOOK TWO

∞

CHAPTER 1

Thanksgiving

A cold rain soaked the Marietta campus on Wednesday afternoon, the day before Thanksgiving. I ignored the drizzle and ran from the freshman men's dorm to a car waiting at the curb. I was riding home in a red and black 1963 Pontiac Tempest Le Mans with a 326-cubic-inch engine. A junior from Rochester named Allen Harding had posted the ride on a bulletin board. The lucky guy was driving me and two others home.

As I approached the car, the passenger side door opened; and a guy I didn't know got out, letting me into the backseat. I was carrying an armful of books and a small duffel bag of laundry. When I went to get into the backseat, I realized that the fourth guy was already sitting in the back on the drivers' side.

"How about if I dump my books in the trunk?" I asked Allen.

Allen turned toward me from the driver's seat and said in a raised voice, "No, put the bag up under the rear window and the books on the floor. Hurry up! It's late."

When I arranged the ride, Allen had urged me to cut my two o'clock class. I refused, so now we were leaving well after 3:00 p.m.

The car was as fast as I expected, and Allen demonstrated it when starting away from each traffic light as we made our way out of town. I introduced myself to the other two guys, and it turned out that they and Allen were all Alpha Alpha Omega fraternity brothers. Tom, riding up front with Allen, was a junior and lived at the fraternity house with Allen. Ed, sitting in the backseat with me, was a sophomore living in an upper-class dorm. Tom was from Rochester also, so he would do the whole ride. Ed lived near Cleveland and so was only going halfway.

It took only a few minutes to get out of Marietta—what there was of it—and into the steep hills and valleys of Southern Ohio. Allen had the Tempest's lights on and ran the windshield wipers when the rain got heavy. We took state Route 21 which ran the 300 miles from Marietta north to Cleveland. Radio reception was terrible for the first few hours of the drive.

Alpha Alpha Omega was categorized as the fraternity of party-going future executives, who are mildly interested in athletics. During my first three months at school, I learned the categorization of the six fraternities and, to a lesser extent, the six sororities on campus. It was possible to write a short—in some cases one-word—but accurate description of each fraternity. Freshman needed to fit themselves quickly into one of the Greek slots since, of the eighteen hundred students on campus, all but two or three hundred were Greek. Marietta College was a small school faraway from everywhere, so the Greeks were the only social life.

I went to one rush party during October rush week but not at Alpha Alpha Omega. The butt-sniffing interview process was disgusting, so I decided to remain independent. I would forgo the automatic social support for my own circle of sincere friends. Money was another big issue; I didn't have enough.

Gradually, the car warmed up; and except for my cold feet, I was comfortable. I was wearing a wool navy peacoat I'd found in a secondhand store. Unfortunately, military surplus clothes were becoming popular; but I liked it most because it was warm on trips like this.

The Tempest had a unique driveshaft, so there was hardly any floor tunnel, which gave room on the floor for my books. I was still short on sleep from midterm exams the week before, so I fell asleep shortly after we left the city limits. My black pessimism about the workload in college came true. My head was just above the tide of reading, lab reports, and papers due when midterms washed over me in November. Now, I was hoping Thanksgiving would give me a chance to surface and catch a breath of air.

A voice I didn't recognize was calling loudly to me. "Hey, wake up! It's time to eat."

"Right, okay," I stammered after sitting up and realizing we had pulled into a McDonald's. The doors of the car opened, and cold air flooded in, giving us incentive to tumble out and rush into the temple of food.

When I walked into the warmth and smelled the hamburgers and french fries, my stomach knotted up as though I was starving. My watch read 5:30 p.m., showing we had been on the road for only two hours of the eight-hour drive. While in line to order, I asked where we were. Without looking at me, Allen responded saying we were in Cambridge; then, I realized I had asked a dumb question since I didn't know any towns between Marietta and Cleveland.

We stopped at a new McDonald's that had a few tables in what looked like a large enclosed patio. One of Allen's rules of the road was no eating or drinking in the car, so we sat at a table stuffing and gulping our food. Everyone was eager to get back on the road.

I finished my two cheeseburgers and two large packets of fries, so I asked Allen about the Tempest. "The magazines say your car handles great because the transmission is in the back with an independent suspension. What do you think? Does it feel good to you?"

"The transmission's where?" he asked.

"In the back as part of the rear axle. That's why there's no big hump up front."

"Yeah, it's fine," he said with no enthusiasm.

Tom asked Allen why he'd gotten a Pontiac. "It was for high school graduation. One of my father's clients is a Pontiac dealer. So my old man got a good deal," answered Allen.

That exchange prompted Ed to ask Allen what his father did. It turned out that both Allen and Tom's fathers were lawyers in Rochester. Ed volunteered that his father was a partner in what he called "a significant accounting firm in Cleveland." The conversation hadn't included me, so I said nothing.

The three fraternity brothers continued talking after we hit the road again. Allen and Tom were already planning on graduate school; both of them intended on going to the same law schools their fathers had graduated from. Ed wasn't enthusiastic about accounting but planned on going to graduate school, if for no other reason than to avoid the draft.

Radio reception improved as we traveled north out of the hills. We had been forced to listen to the twang of country music but now received a good rock station from Cleveland worth listening to. Snow began to mix with the rain, but the weather report from Cleveland promised a clearing, which encouraged us.

Two more hours of driving got us through Akron and onto the beltway of superhighways surrounding Cleveland. Ed lived in Shaker Heights, the small suburb-city of Cleveland that was just inside the Beltway. Allen had driven Ed home before; so he had navigated onto Shaker Boulevard, a grand divided avenue with a wide park-like median, before asking for directions. "Which oval was it?" Allen asked over his shoulder to Ed.

"Belvoir Oval," Ed replied, "it's about a quarter of a mile ahead."

We turned off Shaker Boulevard and came to an intersection, where Allen turned right on a street marked as West Belvoir Oval. The street began a gentle left curve, and I imagined how the east and west halves formed the elongated Belvoir Oval. Impressive large homes, all set back the same distance, lined both sides of the street. Many had semicircular drives that curved up to the formal entrances at the center of a large home. It was obvious these were custom, architect-designed homes. The planning included landscaping, as each manicured bush complemented the design.

"Yell when we get close," Allen said to Ed.

"It's coming up. The next house on the right after this one."

Ed's house did not have a curving drive up to the front door. It was a two-story home of earth-toned brick with large bay windows and forest green shutters. The exterior accent lights showed up on the brick at just the right places. We pulled into a concrete driveway lined by small lights and drove in past the side of the house to a large turn-around area in front of a three-car detached garage. It was then that I realized I hadn't seen any garages along the street. I looked closer and realized that the architects placed the garages out of sight.

Allen turned the car around and stopped heading back out the driveway. Multiple floodlights snapped on as Allen got out of the

Tempest to let Ed out of the backseat. Ed pulled the laundry bag out with him, said a hasty goodbye to us, and went up onto the patio, where I saw his parents at the back door.

Not hesitating at all, Allen pulled out and turned down the street in the same direction we had been going. Immediately, the constantly left curving street came to a three-way intersection with East Belvoir Oval. We were at the other entrance to Belvoir Oval. Allen turned left onto a large boulevard and soon passed a wide drive flanked by lighted fieldstone columns. A large brass plaque announcing "Canterbury Country Club" adorned one column.

"Nice neighborhood," said Tom as we drove back toward the interstate.

"Yeah, Ed thinks so. But no better than ours," Allen answered.

"True, but the country club's closer."

I hadn't realized until then that Allen and Tom lived near each other. Fortunately, Allen was dropping me off at an all-night restaurant at his exit from the New York State toll road. My father would pick me up there.

After we were back on the interstate, I stretched out over the backseat and used my laundry bag as a pillow. There would be nothing to see for the next four hours. We took Interstate 90 from Ohio through a short stretch of Pennsylvania and then into New York, where the route became the New York state toll road called the Thruway. After crossing into New York, we made a stop for gas, a snack, and a restroom break. I phoned my parents from the gas station and told them where we were and when I expected to be at the Rochester exit. Tom took over driving from there, and the Tempest ate up the miles while doing an effortless 70 or better on the now dry pavement.

We exited the Thruway at 11:50 p.m. and paid the toll, and Allen and Tom dropped me off at a 24-hour coffee shop. My father judged my arrival well and pulled into the restaurant parking lot just after I finished a chocolate milkshake.

Thursday morning, I repeatedly came close to waking up but drifted back to sleep. Finally, I woke startled and confused, not knowing where I was. I groaned at my foolishness and considered trying to go back to sleep but realized it was impossible. I heard faint kitchen sounds from downstairs and remembered hearing the same sounds from other Thanksgiving mornings, as my mother was up early baking pies.

This Thanksgiving would be different from those previous holidays. For the first time in my memory, there would be no guests leaving, just my parents and I to celebrate. All my grandparents had passed away in the last four years; then my brother was off to the service, and there were only aunts and uncles to exchange visits with. This year, everyone but my parents had minor health problems; so we were staying home. I relaxed; there would be less commotion over the long weekend.

My mother took a break from baking and had a cup of coffee with me as I ate my second bowl of cornflakes at the dining room table. She sat down across from me without speaking and added cream and sugar to her coffee from a china set that had decorated our table for decades. I continued munching my flakes as she stirred her coffee, and her spoon clicked against the cup. After taking a sip and putting the cup down, she spoke, "I have some news about Christmas vacation." She stopped with that, as if to let my curiosity build, and took another sip of coffee.

I didn't mind the tease and spoke up, "Oh, what's the news?"

"Mrs. Putnam, other mothers and I, are putting on a New Year's Eve party at the Putnams' home for Wayne. He'll be home for Christmas, you know."

I suppressed my surprise and finished my cornflakes. I remembered Wayne's mother mentioning a party when we dropped Wayne off at the Induction Center but never thought it would happen. I played with my spoon and didn't look at my mother.

"Does Wayne know?"

My mother responded with a slightly superior tone, "Yes, he knows. Marion had him send her a list of names to invite."

"Well," I said, "that should be fun. Honest it sounds like a good time."

"I hope so. Marion was disappointed she couldn't do something for him when he left. Oh, and the parents won't be hanging around. We will have our own party, but we'll come and get anyone that needs a ride home. We don't want any accidents."

In my mind, I pictured Wayne's tenth birthday party. Only, instead of fourth graders, we were adults. I quickly responded to my mother. "Right, yes. And there might be bad weather, which would make it worse."

"I know you people have been on your own, but we still feel responsible. The party will make Marion and all of us mothers feel good, so you might look on it as a Christmas gift to us."

"Well, it's a gift to all of us, too, and we appreciate it. Wayne will too, even if he doesn't admit it."

My mother continued to sip her coffee, and we talked about the quality of the food in the campus dining halls; then she checked her watch, which prompted me to check mine. It was 10:45 a.m. Time was crucial that morning because the pinnacle event of the day would not be dinner but rather a phone call from my brother scheduled for about noon. The phone call thrilled my parents since they still thought of the telegram as intercontinental communications.

My mother went back to finish baking, and I sat at the table looking through the back window, out over the stunted but still green lawn and out over the field now brown from frost. At the edge of the woods, the cold wind whipped the bare tree branches, giving the impression that the trees were clawing at the gray sky.

I broke out of my trance and helped my mother clean up the kitchen. She put the small bird in the oven, preheated from the pies, at 11:00 a.m. for a planned one o'clock feast. Gradually, the fragrance in the kitchen changed from pies baking to turkey roasting.

My brother's call came through at 12:15 p.m., and the ring of the phone set off an explosion of scurrying to take the call. My father and I stood in the hall by the front door as my mother answered the phone and chatted with my brother. She asked motherly questions such as how he kept warm while working outside on the flight line, seeing some cultural sites while in Europe, and where his friends came from. She was beginning to sniffle after she handed the phone to my father. My father spoke to my brother just long enough to tell him not to bust his knuckles and that he should ask for electronics training since there would be more money in that when he got out of the service. When I took the phone, I could not ask my brother the questions I wanted to such as if German women were as buxom and willing as I imagined them to be. Instead, we talked about the planes he worked on, his duty hours, and what kinds of mechanical problems cropped up on supersonic fighter jets. He spoke with enthusiasm and confidence. We could have talked much longer, but I knew it was costing a lot to make the call; so I said goodbye and gave the phone back to my father for him to say goodbye. He was very short—just wishing my brother a happy holiday—and then gave the phone to my mother. She was all choked up but said our final farewell.

I spent the last hour before dinner in my room, unpacking dirty laundry and shuffling the books and notebooks I had brought home. I figured out just what I had to study over the weekend. My conversation with my brother had tweaked my envy of him. He had achieved a respected position in the real world. I was at the bottom of the heap at an ivory tower of academia, populated with wealthy and conceited classmates.

Mother and I took half an hour to set the table for three. Guests or not, it was a holiday; and she used her mother's china and my father's mother's silver. My mother retrained me on how to properly position each type of fork and spoon.

Mother had made an effort to cook smaller portions, but she served all the typical dishes; and so bowls, terrines, and platters crowded the table. Dinner conversation was sparse compared to other holidays when a dozen people seemed to talk at the same time. My father discussed the previous summer's bridge work and described the next summer's projects that he was working on at the design office in Buffalo over the winter. My mother told me the gossip from the village, including who in my class had gotten married or drafted. She also mentioned that she planned to work a few weeks the next summer in the accounting office at Chautauqua Institution. She planned to stay at the Institution during the week. This put my father and me on notice that we would have to care for ourselves during the summer.

We agreed to have pie and coffee later, so dinner was over. My father stood and stretched and said, "Weren't we both lucky to miss the blackout!" He was referring to the massive blackout that had darkened most of the northeast earlier in the month. "We were far enough west, and our power company had its act together."

The new American Football League complicated Thanksgiving Day football. Now there were two football games that afternoon, and the AFL game was particularly important because the Buffalo Bills were playing the San Diego Chargers. As strange as those team names were, my father and I had to follow the local team. That game was on the radio, and the traditional Detroit Lions game—the Lions were playing the Baltimore Colts—was on TV. We watched the Lions' game while having a radio tuned to the Buffalo game but at low volume. When there was a pause in the TV game, I turned up the volume on the radio. Both games were exciting, with the Bills and Colts coming back in the last quarter to tie their game.

I lay sprawled on the couch after the games when the phone rang. As usual, neither my father nor I made any effort to answer the phone; and I assumed it was an aunt calling to wish us a happy holiday.

"Oh, yes. He's here," I heard my mother say, and my eyes opened wide; and I tensed to listen.

"Michael, It's for you!" She called out. I snap rolled off the couch and started for the phone. My mother didn't say who the call was from until I neared the phone. "It's Brian," she said, handing me the phone. I disguised my disappointment.

"Hey, hi, what's up?" I said with an upbeat tone.

"Just checking to see if you came home. You're so far away I thought you might just hang out at school. Did you watch the game?" We discussed the football games and were both happy that Buffalo had clinched the division title.

"I'm glad Unitas woke up in the second half, but I wish he'd won the game." I commented, talking about the Baltimore-Detroit game.

"Unitas is good, but I still think Starr is the best," Brian countered and then continued. "How about swinging the rackets tomorrow if it's not pouring down rain?"

"Sure. When?"

"Any time after one. I've got some shopping to do in Rochester in the morning."

"Oh, your mom's taking you out to get new underwear at the sales."

"At least I wear underwear," Brian responded.

"Okay. I'll see you at the courts about one."

"Okay," Brian said, and the conversation was over.

I hung up the phone and immediately felt guilty. I needed to spend both Friday and Saturday studying, and here I had just blown away a good part of Friday, playing tennis.

Brian and I both enjoyed tennis; and in an unusual but pleasant twist, we both wanted only fun from the game, not competition. We didn't keep score when we played but, instead, made keeping a volley going as long as possible our goal. We were both nearly identically inept players with Brian being slightly better than me. We played on the courts at the school, and only snow on the courts or driving rain kept us from playing. In the winter, we wore pants and as light a jacket as possible. In the summer, we and other friends had often played at night by the faint light from streetlights near the courts. One night, the Justice of the Peace told us to knock off our night game because our shouting and laughing were disturbing neighbors near the school.

Thanksgiving evening television programs were all tearjerker holiday specials, so I spent some time in my room reading a couple chapters of the book assigned for American Literature. Later, I came down and had a slice of apple pie and a wedge of cheddar cheese while sitting alone in the dining room. The holiday issue of the morning paper was on the table, so I looked through it. I passed over the front page quickly since the headlines were still about the 100 or more GIs killed during the previous week in another weird-sounding place in Vietnam, the Ia Dang Valley. At least the papers had stopped writing about the war-protesting Quaker, who burned himself up at the Pentagon a few weeks before. Another great holiday headline was the deadly natural gas explosion at a square dance held at the armory in a small Iowa town. So I read the Christmas ads instead of the news and let myself dream childish dreams about what I wanted for Christmas.

I felt awkward shaking hands when greeting my friends. We were adults, but acting like one still seemed odd. So Brian and I exchanged weak handshakes when we met at the tennis courts by Friday afternoon.

"What the hell are we doing playing tennis in November, almost December?" I asked Brian.

"We've played in worse. We're in control, not the weather," he said as he pulled a navy knit stocking cap down over his ears. It was forty degrees with gusting winds and occasional snow flurries drifting past.

Brian asked me about school. "So has Marietta turned out to be what you expected?"

I paused longer than I should have and then answered weakly, "Yeah, pretty much."

Brian picked up on my hesitation. "Oh, well. You're still getting settled."

"How about Kent?" I asked in return.

"Great, great. Hectic but great. The dorm's a madhouse. I bet there are 500 freshman men in my dorm alone. The town is alive, even during the week."

We talked a little more and then began volleying to each other. After a time, Brian shouted over the net, "Have you heard from Wayne?"

"I wrote him as soon as I got his address, and he answered in early October. He was still in basic training at Fort Dix. It was a real short letter. Said he wouldn't be home for Thanksgiving because he would be going all the way to Oklahoma for more training before the holiday. He did say he would be home for Christmas."

After a few more shouts between us, we concluded we had both gotten essentially the same short letter back from Wayne. Neither Brian nor I had answered Wayne, and I felt guilty.

We played for almost half an hour without a break; then, after a wide returned by Brian and a wild swing and miss by me, I retrieved the ball and walked up to the net instead of continuing play.

Brian came up to the net breathing hard. "That was fun. You get a chance to play at school?"

"You kidding?"

"Right. My roommate and I played one Sunday afternoon, but that's been it. How did your roommate turn out?"

"I don't know. I never see him. So, come to think of it, he has turned out fine."

"Well, does he leave the place a mess?"

"No, because he literally isn't there. He's only slept in the room a few times. He's a legacy. His father went to Marietta, and he is going to pledge the same fraternity as his father. He spends all his time at the fraternity house, sleeping and eating there."

"He's a freshman like you, right?"

"Yeah, but it's all unofficial. I guess they have empty rooms at the house or bunk beds. I don't know. The guy has loads of money and keeps a car at the fraternity house even though freshmen are not allowed to have cars."

"Well, that gives you peace and quiet."

"Whoever heard of a quiet dorm?" Before Brian responded, I continued, changing the subject. "Say, have you heard about the New Year's Eve party at Wayne's?"

"Oh, yeah! I heard I'm going, which I would anyway. So your mother told you?"

"Yeah, but it's okay. I'm glad Wayne's mother went through with it."

"Beth and I are looking forward to it. We wouldn't all get together unless this was going on."

"Who else is going?" After I asked Brian, I realized he might think I was inquiring about Susan.

"I haven't heard. The parents are probably rounding up the usual suspects over Thanksgiving."

"Well, let's get on with my demonstration of how to play Grand Slam tennis. You're improving, but I'll get to Wimbledon before you."

"Bullshit!" replied Brian as we both retreated to our respective baselines. "I'm taking time off from school in January and going down under for the Australian Open."

The cold wind blew stronger with erratic gusts driving last summer's leaves into swirling circles and tightly packed drifts at the corners of the court. We only managed to play another fifteen minutes before Brian yelled over to me. "That's it, I'm too damn cold!"

We walked over to our cars, and Brian suggested we get into the Falcon and warm up. I got in, and after a few minutes of running the engine, the heat came up.

"Did you get to drive home for the weekend?" I asked as I held my hands to the heater vents on the dash.

"No, but I drove up to Buffalo for Beth's homecoming weekend." Brian also leaned forward with his hands over a vent.

"Hey, swell. That must have been great."

"It was. Yeah, it was." Brian was thoughtful enough not to elaborate or ask about Susan and changed the subject. "When will you be home for Christmas?"

"The Wednesday before," I responded. (Christmas was on Saturday.)

We talked about Christmas vacation and decided we would have to go up to Rochester with Wayne. Going up to Rochester was code between us and other friends for going barhopping at spots popular with the University of Rochester students. We had done some carousing the previous spring and summer as we turned eighteen, the legal drinking age in New York.

"So are you seeing Beth tomorrow?" I asked Brian.

"Yeah, she's with relatives all day today."

"Say 'hi' for me."

"Sure, I'll do that."

We said goodbye to each other and wished each other well in school; then I began the drive home, taking the same odd combination of side streets through the village as I had taken coming to the courts. The detour from the main street avoided driving past Susan's house. I didn't want to risk her seeing me drive past. To my relief, Brian hadn't mentioned Susan. That left only my mother, who might blunder on to the subject; and since she hadn't mentioned it yet, I suspected she knew Susan and me were through. I wasn't seeing any other friends this trip home. This gave people more time to forget I had dated Susan.

I spent Saturday studying and eating Thanksgiving leftovers. I studied enough to avoid disaster when I got back to school but should have done more. Saturday evening, my mother made pizza; and we watched Jackie Gleason and Gunsmoke. Except for my brother not being there, the evening was the same as many Saturday evenings in the past.

The news of the day was a protest march at the White House. Reports claimed that twenty thousand protesters marched around telling LBJ to stop the war. I felt guilty for not having written Wayne more, and I wondered what kind of Thanksgiving he was having.

At 8:30 a.m. on Sunday, I was back at the restaurant near the Thruway exit, waiting for Allen and Tom to pick me up. My mother had joined my father to drive me the half-hour north. There was an artificial, lighthearted atmosphere in the car as we drove to my drop-off point; my parents were trying to help the best they could. I insisted they not wait, and I sat sipping coffee in the restaurant until my ride arrived.

Driving back in daylight was a damn sight better than driving in the dark as all but an hour or so of the trip home had been. White clouds dotted the sky that morning, and there was more sunshine than I had seen all weekend. I sat in the back watching miles of bare trees and brown fallow farm fields roll past as Allen and Tom chatted in the front seat.

The front seat conversation was about the girls they had met at the country club over the holiday. When the laughing and jokes stopped, Allen cautioned Tom saying "Remember, the only way Jackie and Marion could hear about this is if one of us runs our mouth off. Understand me?"

Tom turned toward Allen and responded in an irritated voice, "Yeah, I understand. And I hope you can keep quiet."

From the backseat, I could see Allen reset his grip on the steering wheel and clinched it tighter. "I can keep quiet. Just watch yourself," he shot back.

Allen and Tom were right to ignore my presence since their friends would never believe me if I suggested Allen and Tom had cheated on their girlfriends. Anyway, knowing some of the sororities on campus, there was a distinct possibility Allen and Tom's girlfriends were having a similar conversation on their way back to campus.

I relaxed as the distance from home grew. Most likely, Susan was doing 65 mph in the opposite direction—east—towards Albany. Unfortunately, I would never be able to go home and pal around with my high school friends without worrying about seeing her. Wayne's party was going to be an example of that. I had a few weeks to figure out what to do about the party, but the whole thing pissed me off.

We got into the Cleveland area around noon and stopped at a McDonald's again for lunch. Allen called Ed after lunch and told him we would be picking him up shortly. After picking up Ed, we began driving directly south to Marietta. Gray clouds had built-up, and when we passed Akron, a light cold rain had started.

I used the time at home reasonably well, which caught me up on reading assignments; however, now began the crunch before final exams in January. It would have been nice had the semester ended at Christmas, but that would be too modern a calendar for the 130-year-old institution; old was good at Marietta.

I would have to do a damn sight better on final exams than I had done on midterms. My grade point average equated to a C- with Chemistry and Math, supposedly my core subjects, even worse. My Economics and American Literature grades had saved me from scholastic probation.

I needed to make changes socially as well as academically, which meant mixing more. Susan wasn't the last girl in the world, but no girl was going to prostrate herself in front of me and beg me to ravish her.

As we neared the school, the others talked of their girlfriends and the holiday parties the fraternities and sororities had planned. My spirits mirrored the steady rain coming down. Allen dropped me off first, and I got soaked getting out of the car and ran into the dorm with my books and laundry bag.

Chapter 2

Christmas

Beyond the obvious near bald haircut, Wayne looked thinner and taller as he got out of his parents' car and came up the walk to my house on Thursday morning before Christmas. I opened the door and greeted him with a booming "Hey, look at you! The army's got you in shape" as I pumped his arm and slapped him on the shoulder.

"You're looking good, too! School food must be edible."

A cold wind prompted us to step back into the foyer and to close the door. My mother came rushing from the kitchen and gave Wayne a big hug.

"Wayne! You've grown an inch!" My mother shouted.

"No, they just teach us to stand tall."

"Well, come in and sit down," she insisted, "I've made doughnuts from scratch for the holidays, and I'll make coffee."

"We can't stay long," Wayne cautioned as he took off his jacket and dropped it over the back of a chair, and we sat down at the dining room table. "Mike has to help me play Santa Claus. I have no idea what to get for Christmas gifts."

Wayne had called me the previous evening and asked me to join him on a shopping trip to Rochester. Christmas was on Saturday, leaving only two days to shop. During the phone call, I suggested that, after shopping, we knock back a celebratory welcome home beer at a pizza joint called Mike and Sam's. I told Wayne I would try to get Brian to come with us.

During the few minutes we sat at the table drinking coffee and eating doughnuts, my mother brought up the subject of the New Year's Eve party. "Wayne, are you looking forward to New Year's Eve? You kids will have the run of your house, no adults."

Her remark irritated me. "Mom, we're not kids. Please!"

"Oh, I'm looking forward to it. It'll be swell to see everyone again," Wayne replied. He then told us how he had left Fort Sill, Oklahoma, on Tuesday and, after taking buses and planes, had gotten home on Wednesday afternoon.

"So how long do you have?" I asked.

"I've got to be back Monday the third, but I'm leaving Saturday, New Year's day. Just in case there is bad weather or broken down buses. The army is serious about getting us back from leave. I don't want the MPs looking for me or have my pay docked as punishment for being late," he spoke authoritatively as though he were an old veteran.

After chatting more, and Wayne promising my mother to come again during the holidays, Wayne and I walked out to his car.

"Head over to Brian's," I said as I slid into the front seat of the cream-colored 1962 Ford Fairlane 500. "He's got shopping to do and wants to come along."

"Great!" answered Wayne as he turned in his seat, looked over his shoulder, and backed the car down my parents' drive.

Brian's mother welcomed Wayne just as my mother had, only this time, we ate homemade apple strudel. I received a share of the attention when Brian's mother asked me about school, and I described Marietta. We were on the road again shortly after eleven o'clock, and we took the same road out of the village as we had taken in August going to the Induction Center.

"We missed the fall. It was green the last time we drove this way," I said as we drove north, "anyone hear how the Panthers did in football this year?" (Our high school mascot was the panther.)

"They went 7 and 3," Brian answered but then changed the subject. "Say, Wayne, what's this party business? Are you becoming hospitable as well as romantic?"

"You guys know very well what the story is. Your mothers are involved, too, and I bet neither of you said no to your mother."

"Hey, Beth and I are looking forward to it. I was just razzing you," Brian replied.

"It'll be a good time," I added, "but we can't sound too happy about it to our mothers."

As we passed through Acton, I noticed the Christmas decorations at Mildred's diner. Mildred decorated the same this year as the year before and the year before that for as far back as I could remember. The same larger-than-life plywood Santa Claus stood by the entrance, waving to the passing traffic; only this year, Mildred had repainted Santa's red suit, black belt, and white trim, making the jolly gentleman look shiny and new.

Brian spoke up, saying "Hey, get this. My mother gave me some news about George Felton. 'Seems he has gone off to Canada to dodge the draft."

"What the hell! He's at Syracuse. Didn't he have a deferment?"

"He didn't go back this fall. My mother says he's been working at his father's Cadillac dealership in Rochester. He was fair game for the draft board."

Jeff was in the class ahead of us in high school. Neither of the three of us had been close friends with him, but he was a well-known and unique member of his class—unique because his family had money. Jeff's ancestors pioneered this part of western New York and were entrepreneurs or professionals. Now, Jeff's father owned two car and truck dealerships, with one started by Jeff's grandfather.

"I'm not surprised he didn't make it at Syracuse. He never cracked a book in high school. He was always too busy driving girls around in hot cars from his father's used car lot," I commented.

"You know, that's right," Wayne said sounding puzzled, "so how did he get accepted at Syracuse?"

Brian had the answer. "His old man's a Syracuse alumnus, which makes Jeff a legacy. Money talks."

"What the hell was he thinking?" I asked rhetorically. "He should have taken basket weaving just to stay in school."

"I think he was doing just that, but even then, you've got to go to class," Brian answered.

"I know what he was thinking," Wayne said dryly, "he was thinking his father could pull strings and get him in the National

Guard or maybe get a doctor to give Jeff some bogus medical condition. I wonder what went wrong." Wayne's voice trailed off.

"His father sold lemons to too many members of the draft board!" I said with a laugh.

"But it does break the rule," Wayne insisted.

"What rule is that?" I asked.

"The rule that, if you are somebody, rules don't apply to you."

"Going to Canada craps up his life. The FBI will be after him forever."

"But his old man has enough money. Maybe Jeff will start a dealership in Canada and forget about the U.S.," Brian speculated

The news irritated me. "He may have big money, but he has no honor. Honor is the reward for your actions. Honor can't be bought." I paused and then continued, "I feel sorry for him. Now when he shaves, he will look in the mirror and see . . ." I fumbled for words.

"He'll see a chicken shit," Wayne cut in emphatically. "There's no polite way to put it. We are talking life-and-death here. This war is separating the good from the bad."

The DJ on the radio cut into our conversation. "Here is the hottest couple on the air!"

Wayne's right hand immediately punched randomly at the radio buttons to change the station. "I'm sick of those two," Wayne growled as the first few bars of 'I got you Babe' were cut off and replaced by a used car pitchman.

"Where are we going to do this shopping anyway?" I asked, "and what's the big deal about picking something out?"

"The big deal is I don't know what to get Kathy," Wayne replied, "you guys are the big Romeos, so you should know. And I thought we should start downtown at the department stores."

"Well, I'm getting Beth some perfume and an album. *Rubber Soul,*" Brian replied.

"Okay, that's good for you, but I need something extraordinary. You see Beth all the time. I'm going to be gone for a hell of a long time."

"Get her a ring. That'll knock her socks off," I said jokingly.

"No, we talked all that out last night. I went over to her place after settling in with my parents. There is no sense in getting all that stirred up when I'll be leaving the country after I'm done at Ft. Sill. She was willing, but I won't have any of it. I don't want her to be committed."

No one spoke, except the used car salesman on the radio finishing his pitch. "So come on down for a free hotdog. We're open till midnight and will leave the lights on for you."

I silently cursed myself for suggesting a ring. Wayne's comment about being gone gave me the willies.

Wayne got the conversation going again. "The important thing now is that I find a special gift."

"Okay, no problem. Like you say, Brian and I are specialists, and department stores are a good place to start."

"And after shopping, we get a pizza at Mike and Sam's," Brian added conclusively.

"Absolutely!" Wayne confirmed.

I understood Wayne's predicament because a year before, I was searching for a special gift for Susan. I didn't have that problem this year though I wished I had. For me, Santa Claus was dead; his obituary was written the previous August.

The forty-minute trip into Rochester ended at a municipal parking lot. The lot was new—the city having replaced old buildings with a parking lot—hoping to attract shoppers, who were beginning to shop in the suburbs. It was a warm day for December—in the high forties—so the walk to the center of the city at Main and Clinton streets was comfortable. The sidewalks became crowded, and we elbowed our way slowly along dodging women burdened with multiple department store shopping bags swinging from each hand. Brian paused as we were about to enter Sibley's Department Store and dropped a few coins in the Salvation Army kettle. In return, he received a blessing from the bell ringer, an old lady wearing a red and black bonnet and cape. Wayne and I quickly fished into our pockets and contributed and received the same blessing.

After pushing through the revolving door, we stepped into the cosmetics department, where clerks in white lab smocks were performing what appeared to be serious life-saving procedures on anxious looking women sitting on bar stools.

"Holy mackerel," commented Wayne. "It smells like a thousand girls going to the prom in here."

We moved off to the side and found a spot out of the rushing flow of traffic so we could discuss how we were going to attack the shopping problem.

Brian began the strategy session. "I'm going to get some perfume here and then go up to the floor, where they have records, and get an album. How about if you guys do your thing, and we meet back here in an hour?"

We agreed to that plan, and Brian walked away and began sniffing around the counters.

"I don't want to get her perfume," declared Wayne. "Why would I want Kathy to smell great when I'm on the other side of the world?"

"Good point!" I responded with a laugh even though Wayne's comment worried me since I believed in self-fulfilling prophecies. "Okay, so let's go on up to the jewelry department." I tapped my finger on a wood display case.

We squirmed our way through the crowd to the escalators and went up to the mezzanine. The crowd was thinner, and I let Wayne move well ahead of me so as not to pressure him as we drifted among the dazzling glass display cases. He paused a couple times but seemed intimidated when a saleslady tried to help him, and he quickly moved on. After fifteen minutes of this, he walked up to me.

"This sucks. Everything here is the same old stuff, nothing really special, and it costs a fortune. I don't know what to do," his voice trailed off in exasperation.

"Well, let's look at it logically. We've eliminated perfume and jewelry, so that leaves entertainment things like records and books. Clothes are obviously out of the question. Let's go up a few floors and see what we find."

"No," Wayne said flatly, "all that's the same crap, and there is no sentiment in a book."

A flash of anger came over me at his stubborn response. My anger quickly changed to sympathy though, sympathy for someone in love beyond hope. I had an idea, and I spoke up in a calm voice.

"Hey, it just hit me. My mother likes to go to this antique shop on St. Paul Street, down by the river. So I've been in there, and I've seen some unique old jewelry and other trinkets women love. You know, old stuff, stuff that makes them think they are characters in an English novel. I bet we could find something unique down there."

Wayne gave me a blank look, and I wondered if he understood what I had said; then he responded, "Anything is better than this place."

We went back down to our rendezvous point, and within minutes, Brian showed up carrying two string handled shopping bags. The three of us agreed to meet again at the same spot in an hour although Brian was anxious about our pizza lunch and told us to hurry.

A shadow of guilt crossed my mind as Wayne and I walked the two blocks west on Main St. to the intersection with St. Paul Street. I'd only told Wayne part of my story about the antique shop. I knew the place from my mother, just as I had said; however what I didn't tell Wayne was that, a year ago, I had solved my own girlfriend shopping problem when I found a Victorian era pendant necklace for Susan at the antique shop.

St. Paul Street paralleled the Genesee River, but multiple-story brick buildings from the previous century on the river side of the street blocked any water view. It was a seedy part of town now, and no holiday shoppers crowded the sidewalks. A thick wooden sign with "Canterbury Antiques" carved into it, marked the shop. The sign hung out over the sidewalk from a wrought iron bracket.

Wayne entered first, and I hoped the proprietor would not recognize me. The old, crudely made, colonial furniture—probably the most valuable in the store—was at the left. Victorian chairs, tables, and china closets that reminded me of Susan's home were in the center of the store. To the right of the door was the art deco furniture and decorative items; all with simple lines; solid, bright colors; and shining chrome. The wood and glass display cases, where I had found jewelry a year before, were still in the center of the store; and Wayne went directly to them. The bearded, middle-aged proprietor dressed in a white shirt, black bow tie, and wide black suspenders—all identical to when I last saw him—went to help Wayne. I drifted off to look at the old radios. The radios in giant wooden cabinets were like the one my grandparents had.

Wayne and the proprietor spoke for a moment, and the next time I glanced across the store, I saw Wayne inspecting an item; but I was too far away to see what it was. No more than five minutes later, Wayne came up beside me so fast that he startled me.

"This is it! Take a look."

He opened his fist to show a pastel blue porcelain oval graced with the ivory white cameo profile of a woman's face. Fine gold lace surrounded the blue oval, and a gold chain completed the jewel.

"It's pretty, but that's not the best part." Wayne gently snapped open the pendant to reveal a tiny antique photograph of a man with mutton chop whiskers.

"The salesman says he has a camera and can take a picture of me and reduce it, so it fits inside. Isn't it great?"

"Oh, yeah," I answered as I touched the locket with my right index finger as it rested in Wayne's hand.

"This is just great. Just great!" Wayne exclaimed again in an excited tone as he turned, and walked back across the store.

It was a unique gift, and I would have chosen it had it been there a year ago. But, then, what a waste it would have been.

Wayne had his picture taken in the back office of the antique store. The picture would be ready to be put in the locket the next day, Christmas Eve. We were now in the true Christmas spirit as we walked back to the center of town to meet Brian.

"I think Kathy will like the locket. I owe you buddy," Wayne said repeatedly, but using different words each time as we walked back uptown.

The shoppers were still thick as Wayne and I walked up to Brian at the perfume fragrant rendezvous point. Wayne's excitement hadn't diminished as he presented the locket to Brian. "Wow, terrific!" Brian said. "Now, let's get lunch. It's two forty-five already."

Mike and Sam's was a neighborhood Italian restaurant and bar near the University of Rochester campus. The place was a favorite with students, and that's why the three of us had taken up the spot as our first watering hole after turning eighteen. The place had, and deserved, the reputation for serving the absolute best pizza in town.

"Wow, look at that! A parking space right in front," Wayne exclaimed as he parked at the curb directly in front of Mike and Sam's. The place was so popular that parking was usually hard to find.

"Amazing!" I agreed, "well, it's a weekday afternoon, and school's out. The place will probably be empty."

Mike and Sam's was in an older brick building that had been a store of some sort in the past. We walked in to find the place nearly empty as we anticipated. Portly Sam was busy behind the bar putting freshly washed beer glasses into neat rows in anticipation of the evening rush. Mike was taller and thinner than Sam, so it was easy to tell who was who. Two old guys sat at the bar, talking to each other at the same time; and two old ladies—probably the barfly's wives—sat at a table, drinking coffee.

"Seems like locals take over when school's out," Wayne said softly as we sat at a table by a large front window that gave a view of the street.

"It even smells different in here," I said, being polite and not saying the place smelled of sour beer.

"That's because the place isn't full of smoke as usual," Brian suggested. None of us smoked.

"You haven't seen smoking until you've been in the army," Wayne said as he looked at the one-sheet, laminated, and slightly sticky menu. The menu wasn't necessary since we always ordered a pizza with half sausage and half cheese (only the size varied) and a pitcher of beer.

"What you want?" asked the round, elderly waitress dressed in black. We speculated she was Mike or Sam's wife since she bossed all her coworkers, including Mike and Sam.

We ordered, and as we listened to the old waitress barking our order in Italian to the chef, Brian made a speculation. "I wonder if she is Mussolini's daughter."

We laughed but said nothing more until the intimidating waitress served the pitcher of beer. I filled everyone's glasses and then made a toast. "Here's to Wayne. Welcome home!"

We clinked glasses and took a swig. As I set my glass down, I asked Wayne a question. "So how is army life? As hard as it's made out to be?"

Wayne brought his glass down, looked at me, lifted the glass again, and took another drink. After setting his class down again, he answered me. "It's no picnic." He paused, studied his beer glass, and continued. "We get up at five thirty, have to be in formation at six, so there is only time to dress and make your bunk. You have to shit, shower, and shave the night before. Then it's PT, physical training. Usually calisthenics and a long run, followed by chow at seven o'clock. By eight o'clock, we're in the trailer of a tractor-trailer rig that we call a "cattle car" because it has no seats, so everyone has to stand and hang on. They take us out to a range way out, where there are no barracks. Rain, shine, or snow we sit on open bleachers and get instructions on all things army, weapons mostly. We fire weapons and all that stuff."

Wayne stopped and took a long drink. "We often have lunch out on the range, served from big green insulated tubs. Actually, the food isn't bad. We're always hungry, so I suppose that helps the food. Everyone misses not having a snack whenever we want one."

I wanted to cut in and change the subject, but he spoke faster. "There's more PT before evening chow, and the evening is always completely taken up with cleaning the mud and dirt from the day, in the barracks, on yourself, on your equipment, on your boots— especially your boots!" Wayne's voice rose, and he waved a finger at us. "If your boots don't shine, your ass is grass, and the drill instructor is the lawnmower. You're doing push-ups with your nose in the dirt. We are constantly tired, dead tired. They push us constantly, never a free minute. Getting us ready for battle, I suppose."

Wayne took another deep drink of beer, emptying his glass. As he refilled the glass, I tried to finish the army talk. "We're proud of you, buddy. Everyone is proud of you, remember that. And training is probably the hardest part, sort of like getting into shape before the first game." I turned in my chair and looked toward the kitchen. "I wonder if the pizza is coming from Italy."

"I could tell you a shitload of stories, oh, a shit load of stories," Wayne said as he leaned back in his chair. "The characters you meet— oh, my God! It's like some crazy movie— no, like an insane asylum with every kind of screwball represented. In basic training down in New Jersey, we had a real honest-to-God hillbilly that I'm sure must never have been more than twenty miles from his home in the holler. He didn't know shit about anything. I don't think he saw much TV. I have no idea how he passed the IQ test. The army is getting desperate. Anyway, he fell to pieces after two weeks. He cried just like in the movies. He cried, honestly cried. We were standing in ranks, and the DI, Drill Instructor, was ripping him a new asshole. And the kid just sat down on the pavement and cried. His squad members got him calmed down enough to get through the rest of the day, but that night after lights-out, the kid started crying again. You've never heard such a pitiful thing in your life as hearing a grown man cry in a dark barracks with forty other men listening. He was still crying when I fell asleep."

Wayne took another drink and quickly continued. "So the next morning, the kid refuses to get out of his bunk. So the DI dumps him out of his rack, fortunately, the bottom bunk. And the kid just curled up on the floor, wearing just his shorts, and refused to move. The platoon went on with the day, and we never saw him again. The DI said he was in jail, but we suspected they just sent him back to the holler."

Brian and I said nothing, just looked down at our beer while Wayne took another drink and started up again. "And the city slickers, they're the worst. They con and steal from everyone, including their own kind."

"Okay, here is your pizza," interrupted Mussolini's daughter as she dropped the 16-inch pizza on the table, saving us from more army stories.

"Oh, hey! We'd like plates, forks, and some extra napkins please," Brian called after her.

"And another pitcher!" Wayne added in a loud voice.

"This place is a lot friendlier at night when the young waitresses are working," Brian commented.

We didn't wait for the plates but leaned in over the table to get the best hand position under our chosen slice. The first bite is the supreme moment of the pizza experience. That's when you're the hungriest and the pizza of the hottest and so the most flavorful. I lifted out my slice, pulling out long strings of hot mozzarella cheese with it. A painful experience had taught me to test the point of the pizza wedge carefully to avoid burning my tongue. The pizza was as good as I remembered: a delightful combination of warm cheese, zesty tomato sauce, spicy pepperoni, and crunchy nut-flavored crust.

"If you had your choice between a girl and a pizza, which would you take?" asked Wayne in a voice muffled by pizza.

"Right now, the pizza," Brian answered.

"Depends on what the girl is willing to do," I responded, causing us all to snicker and snort with our mouths full.

After the initial feeding frenzy, Wayne spoke up. "So you know about army life. How's college life?"

"Embarrassing, compared with what you're doing," Brian answered.

"Bullshit— I didn't mean it that way. I know going off to school is damned hard. Lots of people don't make it."

"You're right. It is hard. I guess all of us are learning how to take care of ourselves, break away from home, where Mama took care of us. I've been okay. The food could be better, and its hell not having a refrigerator to raid, but we squirrel food away in our rooms. There is a hell of a lot more studying. A hell of a lot more."

"What about the babes? Are they as free with their favors as Playboy makes them out?"

"Well, I get up to Buffalo to see Beth whenever I can," Brian then looked over at me. "But from what he didn't say at Thanksgiving, I guess Old Mike here is leading a pretty quiet life."

I was in the middle of a bite of pizza but, finally, was able to defend myself. "Hey, I've made friends. I guess it's taken time, but there are lots of people like me that aren't in the hot social life."

"So any girls?" Wayne pressed me.

"Sure, there're girls," I said emphatically, "none I am wild about, but I've been downtown a few times with a group of people."

I hoped I had not, as Shakespeare said, protested too much. The people I was hanging out with were casual friends that were in my classes. We traded class notes and comments about our professors while having coffee in the student union. Occasionally, we had gone downtown to hang out at a place called Pink's. There were girls in the group, but I wasn't attracted to any one of them. I wasn't burning a candle or holding out hope for Susan, but I couldn't say that to Wayne and Brian; just saying so would convince them I was lying.

Laughter and girls' voices broke out at the door. Wayne looked past Brian and me towards the door and said, "Girls. Four of them."

Brian and I squirmed in our seats but resisted turning around to look. Luckily, they took the booth that, with minor side glances, gave us a view of them.

"High school girls," I said after sneaking a peek.

"Yeah, we're so much older," Brian said with a touch of sarcasm, "and I bet they are 18, or they wouldn't be in here."

Sure enough, they showed their driver's licenses and were served a pitcher of beer.

"I'm going to check them out," Wayne said. He then got up and made a purposely slow stroll past the girls, to the jukebox. At the jukebox, Wayne leaned over the selection display and, after some deliberation, dropped coins in the slot and punched buttons. As he made his way back past the girls, Petula Clark began to sing out, urging us to go downtown.

Wayne sat down at the table, drained his glass, and then refilled it as well as topping off my glass and Brian's. He took another drink, set his glass down, and announced, "Giggling teenyboppers."

Another of Wayne's jukebox selections—this time, Tom Jones asking his pussycat what's new—filled the room with music, and I noticed the girls bobbing their heads to the beat.

"Either of you see the movie?" Wayne asked.

None of us had seen *What's New Pussycat*, but all of us had seen *Thunderball* and were sure we qualified for a license to kill. We went on eating, drinking, and talking for some time; and eventually, the second pitcher of beer was served.

Other groups came in from the fading late afternoon light. Three couples about our age came in as a group, chatting and happy; then a family came in, and the waitress greeted them warmly as though they were frequent customers. Still, the place seemed empty compared to a Friday or Saturday night during the university school year; then you couldn't get a seat and so stood drinking in a crowd by the door.

I was wondering when we should leave when Wayne piped up, "Would you believe I'm getting mail from Mrs. Johnson?"

Mrs. Johnson was our most popular high school history and sociology teacher. She was older but understood and respected her students.

"No kidding," Brian commented.

"That's damn nice of her," I added, "does she give you the school gossip?"

"Yeah, some of that. I'm not a special case. She writes to a number of her old students in the military. A lot of what she writes is a combination history lesson and patriotic pep talk."

"I wonder if she writes to George Felton?" Brian mused as he picked up a now lukewarm slice of pizza and maneuvered it to his mouth.

"I'll ask her. I've got to stop by and thank her while I'm home."

"So what's the history lesson about," I asked.

Wayne had refilled his glass. "Oh, just making the case the Communists and Russia, in particular, are a big threat. She remembers, as a kid, the Bolsheviks knocking off the Czar and family, including the young princesses that were nearer her age."

"I remember her talking about her son having served in Korea. I suppose she doesn't like the Chinese Communists either."

"I'll say. She included them as bad guys, pointing out what a big chunk of the globe Russia and China make."

"What about half of Europe? She must have stewed over that," Brian asked.

"Oh, sure. And the Berlin wall is evidence of how those countries are captives."

"Damn, are you sure you want that kind of happy mail?" Brian asked.

"She mixes it with news of the town and school, how the football team's doing, who is dating who. She intends the political stuff to be a morale booster, like we're guarding the homeland."

"She's a neat old lady," I said, "it reminds me of how upset she was during the Cuban missile crisis. That was the first class I had with her."

"Yeah, they gave you smart kids the good teachers even as sophomores," Wayne teased me.

"Bullshit," I replied.

"Bullshit is right. This guy shouldn't have been in my classes," Brian said smugly.

I turned and gave him a playful shove, making him spill the beer he was about to sip. He pushed me back, and we traded more good-natured insults.

Wayne stared out the window as he spoke about school. "I could have gone to Genesee Community College instead of waiting for the draft."

Brian and I got serious at this comment. "Oh, damned right! Hell yeah!" I told Wayne. "Sure, you could have. You did fine in high school."

"Absolutely!" Brian emphasized.

"Well, it's your fault—both of you—that I didn't." Wayne was still looking out the window. A light rain had started, and the headlights of passing cars cast long wedge-shaped reflections of light on the wet pavement.

Neither Brian nor I said anything as we sat, trying to understand this serious remark.

"Oh, I'm just kidding," Wayne said as he turned back to us and flashed a smile. "But in a way, it's true. If you guys had set me up with Kathy—say, for prom—I bet I would have applied to community college and be hitting the books now like you guys."

Both Brian and I began to blurt our response, but Wayne cut us off and continued. "Yes, yes, I know," he said, raising a hand to figuratively deflect the comments we were about to make. "I remember you bugged me to go to the prom, both junior and senior year." He turned and looked out the window again. "It's strange." He paused, but neither Brian nor I spoke. "I've known Kathy since seventh grade, when we moved up from elementary school. I've sat near her in classes. We've talked and been friendly, but now it's all different, all changed. Like a season has changed. Spring has come." Wayne avoided the forbidden "L" word.

I managed a lame comment. "It's great, really great. Things are going to be swell now."

"But it's strange." Wayne used the word again. "No one can explain why things happen when they do. I mean, you can break your neck over a girl, and she just shoots you down. But then, a wonderful girl you've known for years suddenly smiles, and you're head over heels. It's all a crapshoot." Wayne took another drink and continued. "And now both of us are stuck for two years, and the crapshoot goes on."

"But look at it this way. You're on a run. Just as Mike says, things are going to be okay now. And there's this. You're going to have GI benefits in one year and seven months, and that'll pay for school and help with buying a house, too, if you want."

I cut in quickly to add to Brian's list of good thoughts. "And now, you're done with the draft while it's still hanging over Brian and me. You know some draft boards take guys out of school. No deferment is guaranteed." I paused and added one more point. "Who knows? Maybe the war will still be going on when we graduate, then what?"

"Hey!" Wayne raised his hand. "I don't want you guys to have to get into this mess."

"No, we understand. We're just saying you're getting it over with. In a way, you're lucky."

"That's hard to see," Wayne replied as he pushed back from the table and stood up." I'm going to the latrine—restroom to you civilians—and then I'm going to feed the jukebox again."

"Shit," I said to Brian after Wayne left, "I wish he hadn't said that."

"Hey, it's his life. He's kicking himself, but he shouldn't. A lot of life is just as he says. A crapshoot."

Brian and I took turns going to the restroom as Wayne reviewed the playlists on the jukebox. The Rolling Stones were halfway through complaining about not getting any satisfaction by the time Wayne returned, carrying another pitcher of beer in one hand and three large bags of beer nuts in the other.

"Hey, we're swimming here already, Wayne," Brian protested as Wayne put the pitcher down. "That's too much beer."

"You guys must learn how to drink like a trooper. After all, just as you say, you may end up like me someday." Wayne topped off our glasses, which were nearly full already, and then filled his empty glass. "Now I'm going to teach you Jodie's how-to-sing cadence." He took a long sip of beer. "Now, repeat after me . . . 'I want to be in airborne Ranger . . .'"

"Hey, we don't want to sing in public. You know we can't sing."

"Sing or I'll sing alone. Singing makes you feel better no matter how miserable you are. That's why we sing while marching."

Wayne started again, "'I want to be an airborne Ranger . . .'" And he pointed at us.

Brian and I reluctantly began to speak more than sing. "'I want to be an airborne Ranger.'"

"'I want to live a life of danger,'" sang Wayne, and he pointed at us again.

We smiled and leaned back in our chairs and sang, "'I want to live a life of danger.'"

"'I'm in a big bird in the sky.'"

"'I'm in a big bird in the sky.'"

"'All will jump and some will die.'"

"'All will jump and some will die.'"

"'Off to battle, we will go.'"

"'Off to battle, we will go.'"

"'To live or die, hell, I don't know.'"

"'To live or die, hell, I don't know.'"

"'Jagged shrapnel on the fly.'"

"'Jagged shrapnel on-the-fly.'"

"'Kills my buddy, makes me cry.'"

"'Kills my buddy, makes me cry.'"

"'If I die in a combat zone.'"

"'If I die in a combat zone.'"

"'Box me up and send me home.'"

"'Box me up and send me home.'"

"'Tell my girl I did my best.'"

"'Tell my girl I did my best.'"

"'Bury me in the leaning rest.'"

"'Bury me in the leaning rest.'"

"'Hail, hail oh, infantry.'"

"'Hail, hail oh, infantry.'"

"'Queen of battle, follow me.'"

"'Queen of battle, follow me.'"

"'One, two, three, four . . . Ha!'"

"'One, two, three, four . . . Ha!'"

"Now drink!" Wayne instructed as he raised his glass.

"To us!" I exclaimed.

"To us!" repeated both Brian and Wayne. We clinked glasses and took a long drink. It was true; the song transformed our mood.

"You see, starting from a standing position, you step off with your left foot first. So the cadence should end on your second right stride," Wayne told us. He stopped speaking and looked over at a guy, who had walked up to the end of our table.

The guy, about our age and wearing a University of Rochester sweatshirt, spoke to Wayne. "From the haircuts, I'd say you are the one home on leave."

"Yeah, I guess it shows," Wayne answered as he stroked his left hand over his short bristly hair.

"Well, many of us don't like the war and don't like hearing singing glorifying the war."

"Well, I don't like it either man," Wayne shot back with distinct irritation.

"If you don't like it, don't sing about it."

The guy's condescending voice triggered an immediate response from me, and I stood up quickly, knocking my chair back with a clatter. "Look, we'll turn the volume down, but we will sing what we want when we want!" I then wrapped the knuckles of my right fist on the table. Brian stood, too, and we glared at the guy.

"Fools," he muttered as he turned and went back to his table.

"Asshole," I said as I sat down and took a belt of beer.

"Thanks. I couldn't have said it better." Wayne complimented me.

"He may have been one of those protesters at the White House, Thanksgiving weekend." Wayne suggested.

"I wish I had been," Wayne said as he emptied a bag of beer nuts into the palm of his hand.

The complainer and his group put on their coats and left, but we didn't sing anymore; the confrontation broke the good mood.

"Okay, we've got a problem," Wayne spoke up after finishing his beer nuts and draining his glass. "I can't drive, but how are you guys going to get home from my place without calling your parents?"

"I've got it figured out," I said, "I'll drive from here, drop Brian off at his place, and he will get the Falcon and follow us to your house and take me home."

We agreed but were not anxious to leave. The day was a memorable addition to the many other days the three of us had enjoyed together. But it was late, and we were all expected at our homes; so we put on our coats and headed for the door.

"Merry Christmas to you gentlemen and good luck to you soldier!" shouted Sam from behind the bar as we went out the door into the cold.

"Merry Christmas to you! We'll be back!" Wayne called in return as he gave a big wave of the arm.

"Here, open it up quick. It's cold out here!" Wayne barked in a voice strained by the chill as he gave me the keys to the car. I unlocked and opened the passenger side door, got in, and slid across to the driver's seat. Brian tumbled in after me, followed by Wayne. It would be warmer in the front, so no one wanted to ride in the back. I drove familiar streets out of the city and into the suburbs. Strings of holiday lights decorated homes, and occasionally, a brightly lit Christmas tree showed for an instant through a window as we drove past. The engine warmed, and finally, heat began to blow from the vents on the dashboard. As we got comfortable, a conversation began.

"I'm going to an aunt and uncle's for dinner Wednesday next week, but that's all there is on my thrilling holiday calendar. What are you guys up to?" I asked as I watched the dark, wet road ahead.

"Between Kathy, my mother, and a mess of relatives that want to see me, I'm all tied up. I don't know the details until I'm told where to go and what to do," Wayne answered.

"About the same with me. Beth wants me to join her family at an uncle's house for dinner. When are your finals?" Brian asked me.

"The week of the seventeenth. Three weeks," I answered, letting my voice trailed off. "I suppose you didn't have to bring a single book home for Christmas?" Kent was on the quarter system, so Brian had finals before Christmas vacation.

"Nope, not one," Brian responded with justified smugness. "But think about hopping on a bus and coming up to Kent when you're through finals. Classes will have started, but I'll have time to hang out."

"Okay, I'll keep it in mind and call you," I replied. I then asked Wayne about his training.

"So when are you done with Oklahoma?"

"Sometime in February. I'm nearly finished with artillery basics, and then, they train me on a specific gun before I am assigned to a battery. I'll get another leave if I am shipped overseas, and everyone is."

I had no response for Wayne's last comment. I considered people silly that, out of misguided kindness, object to or make light of another person's accurate but grim assessment of a personal situation. Wayne and Kathy were in a jam; they knew it, and we knew it. The best anyone could do is wishing them good luck, so I did.

"Well, good luck." My comment ended the conversation.

The car was toasty warm now, and out of the corner of my eye, I could see Wayne's head nodding and finally his chin drop to his chest. Brian was already asleep and slumped against my right shoulder.

The radio kept me company. Every other song was a Christmas themed rock song. The Beach Boys sang about a Merry Little St.

Nick and, then, came my favorite: Elvis complaining about his blue, blue Christmas. I agreed; it was a blue Christmas without her, without someone.

After Elvis and I finished lamenting our lonely Christmas, the radio broadcast a short blurb of news. The top story was LBJ's intention to put four hundred thousand GIs into Vietnam.

I went to church with my mother on Christmas Eve; she would have gone alone if I hadn't joined her. My mother and father must have had a titanic struggle about church after they married. My father had won because I never remember his going to church. I had not figured out what he had given up to win, so my mother may still hold his "I owe you."

It was a pity my father didn't go with us on Christmas Eve because it was a moving program of Christmas hymns, music solos, and candlelight. There was no sermon; the words of the hymns said what was necessary.

The service gave me a calm feeling of gratitude and security. I wished everyone was as blessed as me. Also, the program gave me optimism for my future and the future of all those I remembered during the service, especially Wayne.

Gift giving on Christmas morning had become awkward since I was older and my brother was gone. My gifts to my parents were unimaginative. My parents gave me a small six transistor AM/FM radio with a leather case and earphones. The radio used two penlight batteries and would be great to listen to while studying, even in the library. Also, I received a gift certificate, which I knew I should use for clothes, to Sibley's department store.

The aunt and uncle that couldn't make it at Thanksgiving joined us for Christmas dinner. Still, it was a small gathering and so a relaxed affair. My brother had called Christmas Eve morning when he could get a phone line.

As they said, Wayne and Brian were tied up during Christmas week. Neither of them called, and since we already discussed it, I didn't try to set anything up with them. I was not as close to my other high school buddies as I was to Wayne and Brian, so I just let my social life slide for the week. The high point of a dull week was going back to Rochester to get clothes with my Christmas gift certificate.

Other than that, I slept, ate, and studied for finals. I did watch TV in the evenings, which was a pleasant change since I saw very little TV at school.

Chapter 3

New Year's Eve Party

On the last day of the year, a bright sun climbed a few degrees higher into an empty pale blue sky, making the day slightly longer than the day before. But despite the day being longer, the temperature only reached twenty degrees. So that evening was painfully cold, and my every step in the snow sounded with a crunch as I walked from the Corvair up the driveway to Wayne's house. I took a moment and glanced up to see the coal-black sky sprinkled with the sharp white points of a million stars, but I didn't make a wish on any of them.

I carried a wicker pie basket that had a tureen of Swedish meatballs inside. This was my mother's contribution to what I suspected would be a feast. Half a dozen cars sat in the plowed drive, which now included part of the frozen hard lawn. I could see people through the kitchen window as I came up onto the porch and, without knocking, went quickly inside to escape the cold.

"It's about time you got here! The party is almost over," Wayne scolded me even though I was early.

The kitchen was abuzz with girls, all anxious to help lay out the food and to do whatever else was necessary. Kathy acted as hostess and greeted me. "Mike! I'm so glad you're here. Let me take your basket, and you can put your coat in Wayne's bedroom down the hall."

My glasses fogged over as usual when coming in from the cold, so I took them off as I passed through the dining room. I didn't want to bump blindly into Susan before I could avoid her. I hadn't asked Wayne if Susan accepted her invitation, so I prepared myself as though she was there.

Coming back to the dining room from dropping off my coat, I stopped and talked to Wayne's cousin Frank, whom I'd met when he had visited Wayne in past summers. Frank was a year older than Wayne and lived in Buffalo. Other high school classmates joined the party, and everyone mingled and helped themselves to the food and the punch bowl on the dining room table.

"Great decorating!" I said to Kathy at one point, "did Wayne help at least a little?"

"A little," she responded, "but Beth and I did most of it." And we laughed together.

A banner reading "Happy New Year 1966" stretched across one wall of the dining room; and twisted, multicolored crepe paper decorated every room. Stacks of conical party hats sat here and there, and Kathy urged everyone to put one on. Beth brought her Crosley portable stereo record player along with some albums and 45s. Kathy brought her *Rubber Soul* Christmas gift album, as well as other records. Many of the other girls had brought records also, so constant music came from the living room.

I stayed out of the kitchen since everyone arrived through that door, and I didn't want to be standing there when Susan came—if she came. So I stood in the living room, talking to people I hadn't seen since the evening we graduated, way back in the summer. I went into the dining room occasionally to get another of the tiny sandwiches with a toothpick in it and another cup of punch. The punch was terrific with gobs of ice cream floating in it.

Kathy sought me out again by the punch bowl and made a fuss over me. She was wearing her Christmas locket. "Michael," she said formally, "it was so sweet of you to help Wayne with my Christmas present." And then she put her hands on my shoulders, stood on tiptoe, and gave me a kiss on the cheek.

The scent of her perfume triggered a reflex, and my arms came up to embrace her; but I only grasped her outstretched arms. It had been a long time since I had enjoyed such perfume.

"I love the locket," she continued. The polished gold lace borders around the pale blue porcelain oval showed against Cathy's black party dress.

After kissing me, Kathy looked down at the locket and snapped it open. "See, Wayne is close to my heart all the time."

I leaned down and saw a small picture of Wayne; only, the short haircut betrayed his being in the army. "Oh, yeah," I said, "what a handsome guy."

"You are wonderful!" Kathy said emphatically and reached up and gently patted my cheek.

Kathy went back into the kitchen; and I was feeling sorry for myself when, as if on cue, Susan popped in the kitchen door. I felt a draft of cold air all the way into the dining room.

"Oh, Lord! It's cold out there!" Susan exclaimed, and Wayne and all the girls in the kitchen greeted her warmly.

I scooted into the living room to hold up in a corner behind the end table, where the portable stereo sat. I decided to play disk jockey and change the records.

People came and went from the small, dimly lit living room. One couple attempted to slow dance on the rug while another couple was content to cuddle on the couch. I had a conversation with a girl—Loretta—I knew well from high school but was, unfortunately, with a date. Half an hour later, while I fumbled putting an album back into its cover, the inevitable happened.

"There you are! How are you Mike?" Susan called from behind me.

As I turned to face her, I instantly transformed into an Academy Award-winning actor, spontaneously performing an unscripted part.

"Susan! I'm fine, and you look great! That's a stunning dress, and the shoes are a perfect match." I did not approach her or even offer a genteel handshake.

"Oh, you like it?" She responded with a broad smile while moving slightly into profile to model the dress.

"Yes, sure. You look festive."

She looked elegant, as well. Her dark blue velvet dress hugged her hips and gave subtle reflections of light along her curves. A circle of black lace adorned the cuffs of her mid-length sleeves, and she wore a single string of white pearls of uniform size.

"So how has Albany been?" I asked her.

"Fine, fine, everything I'd hoped it would be. And how is Marietta?"

I fed her the typical response, and we went on to talk about classes and how long it took each of us to drive to school. We talked with the same ease as any two, old friends. The conversation went on until I couldn't stand the charade any longer and made a stupid remark. Looking past her into the dining room, I said, "Hey, I see Brian's back. He was on an errand for Beth—food or something—when I got here. Would you mind? I'm going to ask him if he's here to stay." I stepped back from her.

"Not at all. I want to say hello to Loretta." I moved further away when she raised a hand and continued. "But, Mike, just a second. I'm leaving in a few minutes and going to a party near Rochester with some other Albany kids. I won't be here at midnight, so I want to wish you a happy new year!" Her smile radiated sincerity.

I responded appropriately, "Well, that sounds like fun and thanks!" I gave a wide smile. "And Happy New Year to you, too!" Again, I began to move away when her hand reached out; and she firmly grasped my forearm, leaned up, and gave me a kiss on the cheek.

"I mean it, Mike. Happy New Year and good luck." Our eyes locked.

"Yes, absolutely. Good luck to you!" I responded with equal sincerity, and we parted.

I was damn glad that interview was over, and I headed for the punch bowl.

Wayne's cousin Frank was at the punch bowl again, and I realized why after I filled my cup.

"Here, let me help you with that cup," he said as he came up close to me, fumbled into his pocket, and pulled out a flask. "A little Ron Bacardi Superior will liven up the taste," he suggested and splashed enough in my cup to bring it to nearly overflowing. "Next time, don't put in so much punch. I've got plenty of Bacardi."

"Thanks, thanks a lot!" I said with a smile. I sipped from my cup— so I wouldn't spill it on the carpet—grabbed a few more mini sandwiches, and went on into the kitchen.

The kitchen was the conversation center, and eight or nine people were milling about, elbow to elbow. One moment, everyone was in one large discussion about the same subject; and then suddenly, separate conversations started. I knew everyone, and after a moment of listening, I joined in. The first conversation I joined was all about who had married who, who was engaged to who, and who was expecting a baby. There was only one other guy in the group, and he looked like he was asleep standing up; so I moved on. Two guys were standing by the refrigerator, talking about the new Mustang fastback, so I joined them. I was speculating on Ford's chance at winning the French 24 Hour road race at Le Mans when Susan came into the kitchen. Susan began talking to Kathy and Wayne. And soon, Beth and another person joined the group. I watched as inconspicuously as possible, and at one moment, I saw Susan give Wayne a kiss on the cheek; then she made an announcement to the entire group.

"Excuse me, everyone. I've got to leave now so goodnight and Happy New Year. Next time, I promise to stay until midnight." Many people wished her a happy new year as she put on her coat. She turned toward the door and was waving when, for an instant, she looked directly at me; and her smile brightened, and her eyes twinkled brighter. I took a mental photograph of her, a photograph I would store away and periodically pull out to torment myself with.

The fellows I had been talking to were in another conversation, so I walked back through the dining room. Frank smiled and patted his pocket, so I stopped for a refill.

"There you go," Frank said as he topped off my cup from the flask. "You see, I'm doing this for Wayne's sake, so he can honestly tell his mother he didn't provide any booze." We laughed, and I went on back to messing with the records.

The couples in the living room were getting cozy, so I put on "I'll Never Find Another You" by the Seekers. With Susan gone, I felt more relaxed. The pinnacle of my Christmas vacation was now past, and the only big event left was getting back to Ohio. I suspected that, in the future, seeing Susan would get easier; and I might not even see her often since she had out-of-town friends. She probably had already become very good friends with someone.

Later around eleven o'clock, I decided I'd talk to Wayne about his leaving. If I talked to him before midnight, I could make a quick exit immediately after the celebration. Wayne was still in the kitchen with a cup of punch in one hand and a circle of girls, including Kathy, around him. "Say, soldier, may I take you away from your fan club?" I asked and motioned for him to follow me.

"This sounds serious," he replied, "and it had better be serious to take me away from these beauties." He smiled back at the girls only to have them accuse him of spreading manure.

Both Wayne and I got refills from Wayne's cousin as we passed through the dining room. It was obvious Frank was being generous to himself as well, which led Wayne to make a comment. "He's staying here tonight, so he has nothing to worry about."

Wayne and I ducked into the short hall off the living room that led to the bathroom and bedrooms.

"I wanted to say I'm not going to be hanging around after midnight. The lights will go out, and people will have better things to do than talk."

"Well, if you weren't such a stick in the mud, you would have fun too. Why not make a pass on Judy Cameron? She's not with a date."

"No, no, I don't want to stir anything up that doesn't have a future in it. It's tacky to maul a girl just for jollies."

"What if she wants to maul you?" Wayne said with a snicker.

"Let's not get into all that. Are you still planning on leaving tomorrow?"

"Yeah, I've stuffed my duffel bag full. The folks and Kathy are taking me to the Buffalo airport at noon if I'm out of bed." He paused a moment and took a sip of punch. "Leaving is a tremendous pain in the ass. The women cry and all that. It would be a lot easier if I had just left last summer and come back in two years when it's all over."

"Well, who knows? Maybe the politicians will start to listen and wise up. And they won't need you, and they'll let you out early."

"Wishful thinking. I've got to push forward, drive on whatever the consequences."

"True, true. So I just want you to know Brian and I are thinking about you even if we don't write."

"Oh, don't worry. Kathy and the folks in the relatives send me mail, and anyway then, I don't have to answer your mail." We both laughed.

"You said you might be back in February. I doubt I'll be able to make it back to see you."

"That's okay. I understand. I'll probably be back a year after I finished training at Fort Sill."

"I'll catch you again as I leave," I told Wayne as we both moved back toward the living room.

"Sure. And, Mike, don't be so picky about girls. Lightning doesn't always strike on the first kiss."

"Yeah, sure. This coming from you. Now you're an old pro?"

"I am, I am. Thanks to you and Brian."

We walked into the dining room and found Kathy talking to Cousin Frank, the punch bowl dispenser. Wayne joined them, and I went on into the kitchen, which was buzzing with people chatting

I stood for a moment and considered which conversation cluster to join when I heard the rising voice of a girl firmly say, "Either you don't understand, or you don't know the facts."

I recognized the voice as Mary Fenton, another member of our high school class and a mutual friend of Susan, Beth, and Kathy. Mary was attractive with glistening, straight black hair down below her shoulders. She was intelligent—Honor Society and all that— but Mary had a touch of arrogance about her, not like Susan or the other two girls. I suspected booze was bringing out the arrogance and superiority streak tonight.

I moved closer to them and realized Mary was talking to a girl Wayne had introduced to me earlier, his cousin Connie. My glass was empty, so as an excuse, I moved across the kitchen to get ice from the ice bucket on the counter next to the girls. I wasn't able to hear Connie's response to Mary's exclamation, but after pushing up next to them and scooping up a few ice cubes, I heard Mary again.

"I'm very proud of Wayne, too. I've told him I'm proud of him so he would understand it's not personal. The point is the draft takes Wayne and others like him while wealthy kids get deferments. The less fortunate disproportionately sacrifice their lives."

Connie's face froze over, and she said sternly, "Wayne is not going to die." Before Mary could reply, Connie turned and maneuvered her way between people and out of the kitchen.

Mary turned and looked at me. "Well, I did it again. It's a wonder I'm still invited to parties."

"Wayne and I will talk to her. Don't worry. It was mentioning death that did it. No one dies in war. No one you know, anyway. Johnny always comes marching home again."

"I'm so frustrated I could cry. Actually, I do cry. Don't people realize this war is folly? Some wars have at least reasonable justification, but this has none. It's a big con job of the military and industry just like Eisenhower said. We're stepping in where the French were ten years ago, so of course, we look like an old European colonial power."

She was all cranked up, and I didn't want to hear it. "Look, it's New Year's Eve. Let's skip the heavy stuff. Come on, let's find Brian and Beth."

We found Brian and Beth in the living room and began exchanging old stories of high school.

Fifteen minutes before midnight, Kathy, the complete hostess, began preparing her guests for the celebration. She instructed us to get hats, noisemakers, and beverages for the toast. Brian checked the film in his camera and stuffed his pockets with flashbulbs. Someone turned on the lights in the living room and warmed up the TV, tuning it to the CBS channel.

After a moment, the gray fuzzy images on the TV sharpened; and we saw a stiff, formal-looking old guy with slicked back, dark hair and wearing a bow tie. He was swinging a baton in front of a ballroom orchestra that appeared as though it were hatched out of a time machine, direct from 1940.

One of the girls in the group piped up saying "Oh, my parents love this guy. Can't we find another channel?"

Someone else countered with "But that's Guy Lombardo. He's a tradition and does do the best New Year's song."

"Do you get NBC?" Brian asked Wayne. Wayne clicked the channel knobs around just in time to see Johnny Carson speculating on how the Times Square New Year's ball will drop; then the scene changed to a reporter in Times Square.

Brian and Beth were beside me, and Beth put the buzz on Brian to go to New York City. "We've just got to go someday," she said whimsically as she snuggled against his arm.

Far above a giant "Allied Chemical" sign, the ball started to drop while the reporter shot his mouth about 1965 bringing a much hotter war in Vietnam but that the stock market had gone up. For Kathy's sake, I wished the blabbermouth had left out talk of Vietnam.

Our group began counting down the seconds, and when the ball went out, everyone erupted in cheers of "Happy New Year," blew horns, and passed kisses all around. Brian managed to pop off a few flash pictures. I clicked the TV channel back to the ballroom orchestra, and the melodic rendition of "Auld Lang Syne" sent the group into a sentimental mood, for at least as long as the music played.

Playing "Auld Lang Syne" was a conspiracy of fate designed to make me feel like hell. Susan and I both enjoyed Robert Burns's poetry, and a year before, we had read the original Scots version of "Auld Lang Syne," as well as a crude English translation. No one else in the crowd had a clue about the origin of the song. I wanted to talk to someone about the spirit and emotion of the song, but there was no one. Susan truly was from "Old Long Past."

As soon as the revelry had quieted down, I started extricating myself. First, I spoke to Brian and Beth. "Okay," I said to Brian, "let's plan. I'll take a bus up to Kent for a day or two after my finals."

Brian gave me the name and phone number of his dorm, and I wrote it on a napkin so I wouldn't forget. Beth gave me a goodbye kiss on the cheek, and we all wished each other a Happy New Year again and good luck.

Cousin Frank sat slouched in a chair, having enjoyed Ron Bacardi's company. He attempted to get up; but I kept him in his chair, shook his hand, and thanked him for his service during the evening.

Frank responded in a slurred voice saying "You're a damn nice guy, you know that? You're a damn nice guy." And we exchanged hopes of seeing each other again.

The TV was off, and Johnny Mathis crooned about what the chances are. Wayne and Kathy embraced, swinging to the music. I cooled my heels in a corner, waiting for a break between songs before interrupting the romantic scene.

"So I'll see you in about a year?" I said to Wayne as a designated DJ changed records.

"About that. I doubt I'll make next year's New Year's Eve but, hopefully, Valentine's Day. Valentine's Day 1967."

Kathy began tearing up, and I regretted having mentioned the length of time. Wayne and I shook hands, embraced, and slapped each other on the back

"Best of luck, best of luck," I told him.

"Thanks and the same to you. Good luck in school."

I turned to Kathy. "And I'll see you sometime this spring to check on up on this guy."

"I'm looking forward to it," she responded as she came up to me and gave me a kiss on the cheek. Her face was moist with warm tears, tears of love and fear. Wayne was lucky.

I said a quick goodbye to other people and began bundling up at the kitchen door. After buttoning up tight and putting on gloves, I gave everyone a last salute and plunged out into the frigid single-digit air.

I checked the sky again as I trudged back to the Corvair. The stars had rotated around Polaris, and the Big Dipper had settled below the horizon. I suspected cold, clear, calm nights thrilled astronomers. I'd never make it as an astronomer.

With great anxiety, I put the key in the Corvair's ignition and gave a twist. The battery had enough juice to give the engine a good whirl, but the engine refused to start; so I continued to worry. On the next try, a sputter gave me hope; and then the engine shook to life. I relaxed, beat my gloved hands together, and made sure I had the heater control pushed over to max.

New Year's Day was football day. There were parades, too, that my mother watched; but it was a football day. The previous summer, I had helped my father change a burned-out tube in our TV; and we had replaced all the weak tubes at the same time. Now our picture, even if it was black and white, was crisp on the NBC channel where the Rose, Sugar, and Orange bowls were being broadcast. The Rose Bowl game was the best of the three. Underdog UCLA used lots of surprise razzle dazzle plays to beat heavily favored Michigan State.

Besides watching football and eating, I packed and got ready for the trip back to Ohio the next day, Sunday. My situation was not remotely as stressful as Wayne's, but I felt similar emotions about packing up and leaving when it felt like I had just gotten home. All of us were going to have to get used to that emotional yo-yo since we would be doing a lot of coming and going in the years ahead.

I had ridden home with Alan and Tom again. The trip had been similar to Thanksgiving, convincing me I would find another ride, or take the bus for spring break.

The next three weeks would be a grind with a paper due and finals. Freshmen are told that first semester is the worst, and I certainly hoped that was true. But, thanks to Brian, I had a trip to Kent to look forward to.

CHAPTER 4

Semester Break

My bus arrived at the downtown Kent bus station at 5:15 p.m., Thursday afternoon, January 27. The 160-mile trip had taken five hours because of all the stops in little farm villages—villages like my own. At a number of the stops, GIs in uniform got on the bus. Invariably, a group of parents, siblings, and a girlfriend clustered around the guy to give him a cheery sendoff. The smiles always deteriorated into crying and wailing as the G.I. got on the bus.

My hair wasn't long, and my jacket didn't display the name of my school; so I wasn't an obvious draft dodger, but I still kept a low profile during the trip.

From the bus station, I hiked up the Main Street grade up to the campus. Along the way, I passed the obvious student drinking and eating spots. While passing one place, the wonderful fragrance of warm pizza drifted out the door and reminded me I was hungry.

Going through the school's main gate, I found the campus immense compared to mine. Eventually, I arrived at Brian's dorm, Lake Hall, a new but utilitarian-looking building and went up to his room. Brian's room was one of a four-room suite on a short hall that came off an exterior walkway.

I pounded on Brian's door while yelling "Open the door! This is the FBI. We know you're smoking pot in there."

"Whatever you're selling, we don't want it!" I heard Brian's voice as the door opened. After greeting each other, Brian introduced me his roommate, Randy; and the three of us went off to dinner at the freshman dining hall.

"So how large is the freshman class?" I asked Brian as we sat set our trays down at a table amid the chaotic clatter and buzz of conversations around us.

"About two thousand," he answered.

"Big. Big," I said while thinking to myself that his class was larger than my school's entire student body.

Being a large university didn't make the food served any better than on my small campus. The food was the same, bland, cooked-in-enormous-volume, take-it-or-leave-it fare I got at Marietta.

Thursday evening, Brian and Randy had to study for Friday classes; so I spent some time at the student union—also a large layout—drinking a Coke, reading the campus newspaper, and watching girls. The girls came into the union in pairs or in threes, rarely alone.

I was hanging out more at my own campus student union. The casual study group I had mentioned to Brian and Wayne at Christmas was the center of my social life, and in the group was a girl with whom I had an unusual relation. Unusual because we weren't at all romantically attracted to each other, but still, we enjoyed each other. Most of the time. The girl—Natalie was her name—suffered from wild mood swings that were much more extreme than a typical girl's moods. When she was depressed, I consoled her. My kindness would lead to passionate moments,

moments that would end abruptly and later be forgotten by both of us. I was still looking for someone, but I was being cautious; Susan had been a painful lesson.

Friday was cold with low clouds. Brian and Randy were off at classes, so I gave myself a tour of the campus. I felt conspicuous walking around, so to blend in better, I ducked into the bookstore and bought a notebook with a large Kent state logo on it to carry around. I spent the afternoon in the vast periodicals section of the library. I fell asleep for nearly two hours in one of the many comfortable lounge chairs.

The dining hall was just as noisy on Friday evening as the night before. After gulping my dinner in silence, I sat idly, pushing leftovers around my plate with my fork; and then Brian spoke up. "So what do you want to do for the rest of the weekend?"

"Doesn't matter," I replied, "a movie, I suppose, since the basketball team is on the road. I saw the new 007 movie is in town."

Randy piped up, "Yeah, I want to see that, too. But how about tomorrow night? I want to go to the teach-in at seven o'clock tonight."

"Teach-in? Haven't you had enough class time for one day?"

Brian explained, "It's like an informal seminar about the Vietnam War. There is a question-and-answer session with supposed experts and faculty members."

Randy went on to describe how the University of Michigan and the University of California at Berkeley had initiated student awareness lecturing about the war.

"It's not protesting," Randy added, "it's nothing like what went on in Washington in November."

"No, thanks. I'll skip it," I told them, "I'll dig up something else for tonight. Don't worry about me."

So I spent the evening watching a color TV in the dorm lounge. It was a treat since the TV in my dorm lounge was a black-and-white.

On Saturday, unusually warm air pushed up from the south, making the day feel more like April than January. It seemed the entire student body took advantage of this brief burst of spring and went outside to lie on blankets, shoot hoops on the outdoor courts, play tennis, or just sit on a bench in the sun and read.

Good weather gave Brian, Randy, and me an opportunity to perform a religious ritual of sorts: tossing the Frisbee. We went out onto the rolling green lawn of central campus, and in that sanctuary, we renewed our spirits. We ignored the world for a time and concentrated solely on a spinning red plastic disk. With the swing of the arm and a flick of the wrist, we sent the disc arcing up among the bare tree limbs and watched it drift and settle down until one of us snatched it out of the air. After an hour of devotion, we sat on a bench in front of the library to catch our breath, the knees of our jeans damp and grass-stained. The temperature had passed its peak, and it was getting cooler fast.

"So tonight's the '007' movie," Randy said to no one in particular.

"Right, another training film for me," I responded with artificial smugness. "Soon, I'll have my license to kill." Brian and Randy groaned and hissed at me.

Samantha purred like a kitten as I stroked her bare back with my mink gloved hand. She lay face down on the bed, and I sat on the edge and turned toward her. I leaned down and ran my fingers through her strawberry blond hair, and then I kissed her between the shoulders.

She responded saying "This is divine, just divine" as she squirmed deeper into the blankets.

I turned to position myself to kiss lower and lower down her back when a familiar voice spoiled my dream. "I'm going to keep count. This is the second time with the same girl," whispered Brian as he leaned toward me in the dark theater.

James Bond was my only fantasy. Otherwise, I was as rigidly realistic and practical as my parents. I knew the fantasy was silly, but why couldn't I be 007? This was the time of my life to make decisions and set goals. So I'd be a suave spy conquering women all over the world. Why not?

On the screen, James was flirting with Money Penny. It was a great movie, but it was just a movie. I resigned myself to reality and began enjoying the show.

A B-17 snatched James and Domino up out of their life raft, and the great adventure ended. The house lights came up, and we stood and shuffled down our row of seats, kicking empty popcorn boxes on the floor as we went.

"Come on, James," Brian said to me over his shoulder, "you've frightened enough fish for one night."

From the theater lobby, we stepped out onto a much busier street than when we had gone in. The sidewalk was elbow-to-elbow with what seemed like the entire student body of the University.

The scene reminded me of a street festival. Knots of people developed on the sidewalk as people stopped to chat. The blocked sidewalks forced others to walk in the street, which then slowed traffic. Cars crept along so slow in both directions that drivers and passengers held conversations between cars. I had the feeling I was on Bourbon Street in New Orleans during Mardi Gras.

"Where did all the people come from?" I exclaimed

"All the bars are on this street and one other street, all within walking distance of campus. So everyone comes down here," Brian exclaimed over the street noise.

"Damn! Now, *this* is a party town," I said, "Marietta is a graveyard compared to this."

We ducked up an alley to a set of steps leading down to a bar located in a basement named, appropriately, The Cellar Door. The place was a smoky, hot, humid madhouse of noise and confusion. Our waitress told us that, because of fire codes and occupancy laws, we couldn't order until a table opened up. We hung around, watching girls and suffering from a pathetic local rock and roll band until we snagged a table. More minutes passed before we were able to catch a waitress and order. But a commotion hit before we got our beer.

The band mercifully took a break, and just after the music stopped, a stern voice from the back of the room managed to rise above the din and yell, "This is the fire marshal! Everyone take their seat. If you don't have a seat, you must leave."

Yelling, laughter, and cursing erupted; and suddenly, a girl—a good-looking girl—pulled at my shoulders saying loudly "Let me sit. Let me sit on your lap."

And she did. She just plopped onto my lap while, at the same time, a friend of hers dropped onto Brian's. The noise and confusion were so bad that I couldn't talk to her although she made no effort to talk to me.

The crowd thinned rapidly with mostly boys without dates flooding out, up the stairs and into the alley. Only moments later, a person on the band platform yelled out "Okay, they are gone. Sorry for the interruption."

The girl was up and out of my lap just as suddenly as she had appeared. Brian's girl was gone, too, and I yelled over to him, "What was that all about?"

"Hell, I don't know. Fire laws, I guess."

After waiting a while, our beer hadn't been served; and the band took the stage again.

"Let's split!" yelled Randy. Brian and I nodded, and we escaped from the cellar, back up to the fresh air of the alley. Brian and Randy spoke to each other for a moment, and then Brian turned to me. "How about a great hotdog?"

We ended up two blocks away, well beyond the student fun zone, at a classic working man's lunch counter that had a flickering red neon sign in the window saying "Van's Texas Hots." The place was a single narrow room between two other brick buildings and was just big enough for a ten-stool-counter. The simple fixtures behind the counter included a grill, a sink full of dirty dishes, a tired old refrigerator, a few cabinets, and a soda dispenser.

The proprietor, Van, I assumed, wore an apron that obviously he hadn't changed all day along with a gray dishtowel flipped over one shoulder. "How many?" Van asked each of us in a tired, slightly irritated voice.

There was no menu at Van's. You just told him how many dogs you wanted and whether you wanted Coke or Seven-Up. Each of us ordered two dogs and a Coke.

Van dropped six unusually long hot dogs on the grill. After he had rolled the sizzling dogs back and forth with a spatula for a few minutes, he went to a gadget that steamed hotdog buns and took out six buns. He balanced all of the buns on his left arm and hand; then, with deft skill, he snatched up dogs with a set of tongs and loaded the buns. Next, he added the secret chili sauce. Still balancing the dogs, he moved to a large cast iron kettle at the side of the grill, took up a soup ladle, and anointed each dog with a wide line of thick, chunky red sauce. He didn't flinch as rivulets of the sauce dripped on his bare arm; then Van dropped the dogs on plates he had previously set in front of us. Van served our drinks and a bowl of chopped onions, and we began to eat. We smiled at each other and gave muffled grunts of satisfaction. The long bus ride to Kent would have been worth it just for Van's Texas Hots.

CHAPTER 5

Spring Break

The January bus ride to see Brian at Kent left me with serious doubts about taking the bus home for spring break. I did it anyway, traveling on Saturday, April 9, the day before Easter. Connections were impossible on Good Friday if I left after my last class, making Saturday the only alternative. The trip was long and slow just like my other ride, and as before, there were many guys in uniform on the bus.

I had a lot to do during the week at home. I had to work on getting a summer job, and as always, I was behind on my reading as well as having a term paper to research.

Then there was Kathy, whom I had promised to visit while at home. Now I regretted committing to the visit. Wayne was in Vietnam, which made it hard to talk to Kathy. My mother had told me the news during a February phone call, but she had no address for me. Later, in early March when I did get an address, I wrote a short—very short—letter. I hadn't gotten a reply until just the previous week. Wayne's letter (a note, really) just said he was fine and that he was on a big, secure artillery base. He gave a two-sentence description of the country as strange, primitive, smelly, and like living in a National Geographic Magazine story. He told me not to worry about writing him since it would be hard for him to reply. Wayne's letter came in an interesting envelope. He and all the troops, I supposed, didn't need to put a stamp on the envelope but just wrote "free" where the stamp would have gone.

My mother reminded me about Easter that evening when I was in the kitchen helping her make homemade pizza.

"Are you going to church with me tomorrow?" She asked as she spooned tomato sauce (of her own recipe) on the stretched pizza dough.

"Yeah, sure. I went at Christmas," I responded as I cut slices of pepperoni off a long sausage.

"Someday, I hope you will want to go for yourself, not as an obligation to me." I felt like hell, and I took a moment to respond. There was no sense in denying my ambivalence; this was my mother I was talking to.

"It will come someday. Then I will feel the reward and want to go. Until then, I'll just keep trying."

She stopped her work and put a hand on my arm. "Yes, yes," she said, "I'm so proud of you, and I so wish your father would make an effort. A person must be willing to submit and recognize their place. I think your father still wants an engineering explanation, as strange as that seems."

I was growing apart from my parents, which made coming home harder.

Easter morning was ideal with sunshine and the temperature near forty-five degrees when the church service began. Christmas Eve, the last time I'd been in a church, seemed a long time ago. The decorations in the church reflected the change of season. Lilies were everywhere, as well as fragrant hyacinths and other more common but just as precious, spring flowers such as daffodils. A shaft of bright sunlight shining through the stained glass windows enhanced the colors of the flowers, as well as the bright colors of the congregation's spring wardrobes.

My mother and I sat in our usual pew as the organist played a muted prelude. A dozen or so smiling people greeted us as we entered the church. I was alert as the service progressed, having drunk two cups of coffee at breakfast. I had a different reaction to the silent prayer than at Christmas. The silence intimidated me, leaving me wondering how to pray. Prayer would be easier for me if I knew someone was listening. An immediate response to my prayer would be helpful, maybe a mild electric shock to the foot on contact with the divine. I recalled my Christmas prayer for Wayne, so I repeated it. My life was going well. I wasn't on academic probation, so I expressed sincere gratitude for my grades. But beyond that, I was unwilling to make specific requests. I had the feeling that the deity would do what he or she wanted. At best, I only suggested.

It was Tuesday evening before my guilt prompted me to call Kathy. "Hi, this is Mike. Pardon me for taking so long to call," I began the conversation.

"Mike! You didn't forget! How are you?"

We passed the usual pleasantries, and I hoped just a phone call would suffice; but Kathy wanted to get together.

"How about you stop by my house tomorrow at five, and we can go up to Mildred's for a burger and root beer float for dinner. I get home from school about four. Oh, and dutch treat."

"That sounds swell," I responded, "only, one thing. It will not be dutch treat. You're a lady, and I am a gentleman, remember?"

"Okay, okay, you win."

So we were set although I felt odd having even the most casual date with Kathy.

I hadn't visited Mildred's for dinner, and I found the place different in the late afternoon. The patrons, tired from a day's work, talked less and spoke quieter. Mildred wasn't there either; her staff had taken over, and they weren't as jovial as she.

I slid back into our booth across from Kathy after selecting four songs for a quarter on the jukebox. We had talked about Kathy's school and classes during our drive to the diner, so now, I asked her about Wayne.

"So what do you hear from our soldier boy?"

"It might sound strange, but he seems reasonably content though he misses me. Has he written to you?"

"Yes, we've exchanged short letters, but we've agreed not to write much." I then told her Wayne had described Vietnam as a primitive country, a world apart from our modern Western culture. Kathy went on to add other details Wayne had written her.

"He uses the word 'gun', not 'cannon', and he is serving on a gun he calls a 175MM. The gun is mounted on tank tracks, so it can be moved around."

I didn't know much more about army equipment than Kathy, so I just listened. She went on to describe how Wayne lived. "He lives in a cave-like room partially dug into the ground with thick walls of sandbags and a thick roof covered by sandbags, too. Would you believe they have rats? They even name rats, but then they make a game of killing them."

Hearing that made me think Wayne would consider my comparatively clean, bright, and sunny dorm room a hotel room.

She continued, "All the guys from his gun live together, and they do what he calls 'fire missions' when the infantry calls and needs help. This can happen anytime and may go on for hours. He says other guns in his battery join in, and they just miss sleep if it goes on all night. They never have a day off."

While Kathy was speaking, a tired-looking but pleasant-speaking waitress served our hamburgers, fries, and root beer floats. Mildred's hamburgers were works of culinary art. The beef came from local farms and was so fresh that I might have seen the sacrificial beast in the pasture just days before. The buns were from a local bakery, and the cheese was from a nearby dairy. Most importantly, the chef made the burgers individually, and they were generous in size. The production line food from McDonald's was cheap, not inexpensive.

As we ate, Kathy mentioned that Wayne ate his meals at the mess hall he described as a tin-roofed pavilion with crude picnic tables. Wayne's parents sent him packages of snacks and sundry items, toiletries, and other small items that he couldn't get out in a combat zone.

"Wayne misses being able to go to the store, any kind of store," Kathy said as she stirred her root beer float with a long spoon. "He says some of the guys that have been there longer are going stir-crazy and act strange." Her voice grew fainter. "Only, he doesn't say how they act strange."

"Come on, now, we all know Wayne is a rock," I said in a matter-of-fact voice. "Besides, I'm sure your letters keep his spirits up. He is a lucky guy and knows it."

Kathy didn't respond to my encouragement and just continued eating, so I tried to make small talk. "I've seen newsreels where GIs are watching movies. Does he get anything like that?"

"Yes, he talked about movies. In one letter, he described how they show the movies outside against a sheet of plywood painted white. He says the mosquitoes feast on the audience." She stopped speaking and took a long look out the window as if she could see Wayne across the thousands of miles.

We continued our meal while making quiet comments about the few other patrons in the diner and how good the food was; then, as I neared finishing my burger, Kathy dropped a verbal bomb on me.

"Have you seen Susan since you've been home?"

I looked up at her and said, "No." But the questioning tone of my voice and my blank look made it obvious that I wondered why she asked.

Kathy continued, "She was seriously ill in February. She had such a bad cold the doctor feared it might turn into pneumonia. Her mother brought her home, and she missed four days of classes. She called me while she was home and told me all about it. We've kept in touch since."

"Oh, that's too bad," I said with relief in my voice, "so is she okay now?"

"Yes, but she had to take it easy and get lots of sleep when she was back at school, so her grades suffered. She's home on break. I saw her last night."

"Good, good," I said and took a long drag on the straw in my root beer float.

"Now she feels constantly behind. According to her, she had a hard time even before she got sick. I think she's a bit panicked."

"It's the big leagues, alright. You know that. She sounded in good spirits at New Year's Eve, like she was doing okay and fitting in at Albany."

"Oh, she's worried about that, too. She says everyone else in the English program is brilliant and more creative than her."

"Susan will get over it. I'll guarantee you that." My remark was blunt and revealed my bitterness. I should have shown compassion.

"Yes, but it's difficult," Kathy responded with disappointment.

"Brian is doing well," I said quickly in an upbeat voice as I returned to eating.

"Yes! I've talked to Beth, too."

I went on to describe my semester visit to Kent, including the mysterious girl that sat on my lap. Somewhere in the conversation, a loud commotion erupted in the kitchen. A small grease fire broke out on the grill, resulting in raised voices and clanging of pot lids as they smothered the flames.

"Seems like, when Mildred isn't here, the place goes up in smoke. Let's go," I said. We settled the tab by my paying but promising that we would do something similar again, and then Kathy could pick up the tab.

As I pulled into Kathy's drive, her dog—a collie—bounced off the porch and barked in protest at the strange car. Kathy rolled down her window and called out to the dog, "Hush, Sparkles, hush!"

Sparkles came up to Kathy's door, and Kathy reached out and patted the dog; and it went back up on the porch to watch us.

I didn't want to linger, so I immediately got out of the car and came around and opened Kathy's door.

"You're a gentleman, Mike. A fine person and a gentleman," she said as she got out, and I closed the door behind her. "Amazing what a difference a few months can make," she said in a whimsical fashion, "all of us have been hit by reality. Some of us have been able to take the hit better than others."

I assume she was speaking of Wayne and herself, so I spoke up. "Well, you and Wayne have had the biggest challenge and are doing great. Two months have already gone by, and the rest will fly past."

Kathy began to walk up to the porch, and I walked beside her. "Oh, we're doing fine, all things considered. But it's been a hard transition for some of us, and we all need to help each other."

Kathy was making a pitch for Susan again, and I didn't want to hear it; so I spoke bluntly. "As I said before, Susan will get through this. And she certainly doesn't need any help from me."

Nothing more was said as we walked the last few steps to the house.

Up on the porch, Sparkles sniffed at my sleeve and paced in circles while Kathy and I exchanged quick comments about Mildred's being different in the evening; then we said our goodbyes.

"So tell Wayne that Brian and I are rooting for him. And as for you and I, we will be bumping into each other in a couple months. I'll be home the end of May."

"I'll tell him, and I want you and Brian to know you've made life wonderful for Wayne and me."

Before I could respond to her exaggerated sentiment, she gave me a quick kiss on the cheek, opened the door, and called to the dog. "Come on, Sparkles. Time to come in. Goodnight, Mike!" She gave me a little wave.

"Bye!" I called to her, "see you in the summer!"

Later while driving home, I was in a fret. Having made just those few emphatic remarks about Susan made me feel like an old poop. But there was no place in my life for Susan now. Time had passed; space and distance had opened up enough such that I could clearly see a life beyond Susan. It was unfortunate Kathy had gotten involved, but that wasn't my fault. I had to watch out for myself.

Sunday morning, the Dog Bus groaned and wallowed its way west on Interstate 90, taking me from Buffalo to Cleveland. There, I caught a bus south to Marietta. The bus was comfortable enough with an air vent I could turn on and off. This helped because a chain smoker sat a few seats from me.

Out the window, I watched the omnipresent trees that were yet to bud leaves, and the familiar frame houses, barns, and farm equipment stream past. Riding the superhighway bypassed the villages and towns, which, themselves, got to seem identical after a time.

To pass the time, I fantasized staying on the westbound bus all the way to the Pacific Ocean. Or I might stop out west, get a job on a ranch using a different name, and work for room and board. I'd be a draft dodger like George Felton. I hadn't heard anything about Jeff. What a jerk, what a sorry-ass jerk.

But I went on back to school. There were only eight weeks left to the semester, and then I'd be a quarter of the way to my goal. My goal was going to have to change. My schoolwork was still on the ragged edge of chaos, and I'd decided to change my major to something in the humanities. If my grades stayed low, my draft board would get me. The school sent my grades to the draft board, as well as to my parents; and the draft board only gave deferments to serious students.

After visiting Brian at Kent, I had considered transferring to another school, but my low grades made that a pipe dream. There was no choice; I would have to pound it out for three more years on the banks of the muddy Ohio River.

Chapter 6

The End of School

Two words describe my spring semester final exam week: "fatigue" and "chaos." The demons of testing conspired to give me a combination of hot weather and a cramped test schedule.

The normal, but random, spring heat wave started just before finals and lasted the whole week. I had a hard time finding a place to study in the evenings. Only the newest buildings on campus had air-conditioning, so those buildings became overrun with squirming, whispering, sneezing, candy-wrapper-crinkling, and inconsiderate fellow students. I bounced between old classroom buildings for a couple evenings before finding a room, where enough breeze came through an open window to make it close to comfortable. My dorm did not have air-conditioning and became an ivy-covered brick oven during the day and held the heat through the night, making sleep difficult.

Then there was my test schedule. An ideal schedule would have had one subject a day or, at worst, an easy subject and a tough subject on the same day. But no, the finals for my two hardest subjects—and so, lowest grades—Math and Chemistry were on the same day, Wednesday.

That miserable day had passed, and it was Thursday, the last day of judgment. Just two relatively easy tests remained before freedom. I finished my American Literature test that morning and was on my way from my dorm to get lunch and to study an hour or so in the library. I took my "poli sci" final in the afternoon.

Students, who had finished finals, were packing up to go home. The lobby of my dorm was a madhouse as students and parents loaded cars to escape for the summer. As I walked past the telephone switchboard office, the switchboard operator called my name above the noise and commotion.

"Collins! Hey, Collins, you got a call from your parents this morning."

I pushed past kids carrying travel trunks and armloads of clothes to pick up the call slip at the office window. My father had called at 10:30 a.m. that morning but left no message. My mother was to drive down the next day, Friday, and we were to pack and drive home on Saturday. I speculated that there was a glitch with those plans and feared I might have to stay longer in what was rapidly becoming an empty dorm. But I was in a hurry and decided I would call home later in the afternoon, after my exam.

Relief—complete relief—that my last test was over. In all my years of schooling, I had never felt so relieved that a school year was over. I was depressed though because I knew I hadn't done well and that I had merely survived a battle in a long war. But I could relax now, for a time.

Final exams for freshman subjects with large enrollment were given on the canvas-covered floor of the field house basketball courts. Leaving the field house after the political science final, I joined the group of friends I studied with, who had also taken the test.

"So what do you think?" asked a tall guy named Johnson, who was from New Jersey, and in my class.

"Pretty much what we thought," I replied, "I think I did well. I better have. I need a good grade to raise my GPA."

Joyce, my fickle female friend, suggested we celebrate at the student union since it was the last test for all of us.

An unusually large crowd packed the union, and I realized many people were saying goodbye for the summer, just as we were doing. We found room at the end of a long table, pulled up extra chairs, and dumped our books before going to get a snack or a drink.

"Hey, I've got to make a phone call. It's my parents. Probably something about coming to get me tomorrow," I said to the group, "I'll only take a minute. I'll get something when I get back."

I moved past groups of happy people and into a long hall that connected the cafeteria to a large game room. A cluster of pay phones hung on one side of the hall. I would make a collect call as usual, but then, I didn't phone home often.

"Hello," I heard my father's voice. I hadn't expected him to answer the phone, and his voice sounded tired.

"Hi, it's Mike. I got your message. What's up?"

"Mike. Mike, I'm so sorry to have to call." His voice became weak and trailed off.

"Sorry? What's going on?"

"I've got bad news, Mike. Sad news." His voice continued to deteriorate, becoming broken and strained to the point where I might not have recognized him. My mind raced to anticipate and deflect whatever the bad news was, and I knew the news involved a death.

"Mom?" I blurted out, "is Mom okay?"

"Oh, yes, yes. Your mother's fine. Well, she's okay. I mean, she's fine. It's not your mother."

"Ben?" I shot another urgent guess over the phone. My brother worked around jets, and I feared his being sucked into a jet engine or burned by the exhaust.

"No. Ben's fine, he's fine. Just let me get this out please." His voice was firming up and was sounding closer to normal. "It's Wayne. We've lost Wayne. We've lost Wayne," he repeated.

"What do you mean we've lost Wayne?" I demanded emphatically.

"He's been killed. Killed in action. The soldiers came and gave his mother the news yesterday. I'm sorry to have to tell you."

He paused a moment to let me respond, but I couldn't. My mind drifted, and I became confused. I had to be in a nightmare. This couldn't be real. Wayne had said he was safe.

My father continued, "Your mother and I thought we should call you. We thought we should tell you since it will be so long before we see you, and we didn't want anyone else to tell you before us. We're just devastated. Everyone in the village is in shock."

"So Wayne's gone?" I questioned in an empty but calm voice.

"Yes, I'm so sorry. We don't know the details."

I didn't immediately respond, and my father didn't say anything more for a moment. I reached out and touched the phone. It felt real. I took a quick look around. I knew where I was, and I didn't wake up. "Does Kathy know?" I asked.

"Yes, Wayne's mother went to her house immediately. Oh, it's so sad."

"How are they taking it?"

"They're all grief-stricken, devastated. Your mother and many other mothers have been at the Peterson home constantly. I took your mother to the doctor around noon today, and the doctor gave her sedative pills. She is asleep now. That's why I called."

"So Wayne's gone," I declared in resignation. I wanted to sit down, and the phone felt heavy in my hand.

"Will you be okay?" My father asked.

"Sure, sure," I answered out of habit, "I guess I'll have to be. There is nothing I can do."

"Maybe you should get some help. Is there anyone you can talk to?"

I had the urge to change the subject, so I ignored his question and told my father that my tests were done and that I would begin packing. I felt slightly better talking about getting home. "I'll be able to do the lawn for you for the rest of the summer. I bet you had to cut it a few times already." I was talking rapidly because I didn't want my father to talk about Wayne anymore. I rattled on until my father wised up.

"I think you should take it easy, Mike. Find your friends. We'll both be with you as soon as possible tomorrow. Are you going to be okay?"

"Yes, yes," I said while desperately trying to avoid thinking of whatever it was that was upsetting me. We said goodbye to each other, and I hung up the phone.

I hung up the phone but then just stared at the beige, cinderblock wall in front of me. A moment passed before I turned and walked a few paces back toward the cafeteria. People crowded the hall, streaming past me in both directions.

Then a thought struck me, and I stopped, stepping aside and letting others pass me. The military makes mistakes. Both Wayne and my brother had talked about how situations were normally all fouled up. Besides, I had talked to my father, not my mother; and he probably didn't understand what was going on.

With relief, I turned back and grabbed the same phone I had just used and called home again.

My father answered again, disappointing me. "Dad, are you sure of all this. The government screws things up all the time. Maybe he's just missing in action, you know What do they call it? Absent— AWOL."

"Mike, take it easy. Try to hang on until tomorrow, and we'll be there."

"But, but . . ." I tried to think of something to say to make it not true. "Let me talk to Mom. You said she's been to Wayne's home. Maybe she knows it's just a screwup. Where's Mom?"

"Your mother is sleeping. I told you that. She's very upset. Now try to get a hold of yourself," he said sternly.

I didn't respond, and after a brief silence, my father continued. "Mike, listen to me. Go to the campus dispensary and tell them what has happened. They can give you something to help until we get there."

"Yeah, okay," I said in a tired, defeated voice.

"Mike, I'm calling the school administration and your dorm resident. Someone will be getting to you. Do you promise to go to the dispensary right now?"

"Yes, you're right. I'll go there right now. They're always open."

We said goodbye again, and I hung up the phone. This time I didn't stare at the wall but turned and leaned back against it, and I stood for a moment as people walked past.

Exhaustion overcame me, and it was hard to concentrate. Gradually, I just let myself slide down against the wall until I sat on the floor with my legs stuck out.

People walked around my legs, and other people stepped over me; then a group came along that was in high spirits and talking loudly. One of them began to step over me at the same time I pulled my legs in, and I tripped him up.

"Hey, man, don't block the way!"

They stopped—one on each side of me, and a tall one in front of me. I just looked up blankly at the one that spoke to me. "You should apologize," he said to me.

"Oh, go on. Just go on," I responded lamely.

"This guy has started to celebrate summer early," the tall fellow in front of me said to the others, and then he gave the bottom of one of my shoes a firm kick. "You should be more polite."

I noticed all three of them were Chi Beta Upsilon, the jock fraternity. Each wore something—a T-shirt or a windbreaker—with Greek letters on it.

"Oh, you guys," I said in recognition of the fraternity as I scrambled to my feet and stood with my back to the wall.

"What do you mean by that?" questioned the jock in front of me as he stepped closer. He was at least two inches taller than me and looked like he was on some varsity team. "And who the hell are you anyway?" he demanded.

The three were members of the same Greek tribe, and they were out maneuvering among groups of the other tribes. There wouldn't have been an issue if I'd been in their tribe. If I had worn the jacket of another fraternity, they would have had a clue how to deal with me. But I presented the worst case: I had no tribe, so they demanded identification.

"I'm nobody," I shot back, "but my buddy was somebody, and I've just been told he's dead, killed in Vietnam." And I nodded toward the phone beside me. "He wore a uniform. Only, it didn't have Greek letters on it." And I pointed to the embroidered Greek letters on one of the guys' shirts. "My buddy's uniform said 'U.S. Army,' and now he's dead."

The expressions on all three of the fraternity brothers' faces changed; and they, ever so slightly, relaxed and moved back. "Come on. This guy is out of it," said one of them to the others.

Their moving away emboldened me, and I verbally lashed out. "You know, we aren't shit here at school! Not you. Not me. None of us. We read books, drink beer, and chase women. My buddy couldn't do any of that, and now he's dead," I swallowed deeply and continued, "well, I'm not going to do this anymore!" And I waved a hand in a broad sweep in front of myself. "This is all bullshit, and I'm not going to do it anymore! I'm not going to do it!"

As the three stunned Chi Beta Upsilon brothers walked out into the cafeteria, one of them looked back at me as if to confirm that I was real. A small knot of other people moved past me. I was out of breath from my tirade, and a sense of claustrophobia came over me; so I hurried into the game room and ducked out an emergency exit.

I walked out onto a small triangle of lawn between the student union and the library. The lawn sloped down to the sidewalk, connecting the two buildings. I sat down on the grass with a plop; my legs spread wide in front of me. The sidewalk was busy, and I just sat there for a moment. I felt as though I was in a theater, watching a vibrant movie with excellent sound, color, and even the tactile feel of grass under my hands.

After a moment, I saw the Chi Beta Upsilon brothers I had confronted a moment ago as they walked along on the sidewalk with more of their brothers. The tall one noticed me on the grass, and though I could not hear, I saw him alert the rest of the group and point to me up on the grass. They were all amused.

In a moment of clarity, I spoke aloud to myself. "God wouldn't take Wayne and leave that conceited, swaggering asshole. God wouldn't do that. Why would God do that?"

∞

BOOK THREE

∞

CHAPTER 1

Chautauqua

"Son of a bitch. Damn," I muttered in a low, strained voice. The damned ants were back, and they were biting and stinging me under the bandages on my right foot. Worse was the sensation that ants were inside my foot tunneling through my flesh.

I sat up in bed, raised my foot, and reached down to fluff and reposition the pillow my foot rested on. When I let my foot down again, the false sensation of ants changed to a mild prickling as though I had a cheap wool sock on my foot.

Brian was sleeping on the floor, beside my bed, on an air mattress, under a bundle of blankets. He woke, sat up, and looked over at me.

"Have you got it?" he asked as he rolled off the mattress, got up, and stepped to the end of my bed.

"Yeah, it's fine. Thanks. I'm sorry I woke you."

"Where's your scratching stick?"

"It's here." And I raised the three-foot long, quarter-inch dowel my father had gotten me so I could easily scratch my foot.

The world had turned upside down and fallen apart in the last three years. I ditched school after hearing that Wayne was gone. Immediately after my father gave me the news, I walked down from campus to Marietta's main post office, where all the recruiters had offices and signed papers to join the army. I packed up my belongings and returned home with my parents the next day. I told no one and asked my parents not to talk about my enlisting because the village was still in shock from the news of losing Wayne. Three days after enlisting, I was off to the Induction Center. I joined as a combat engineer, nearly as dangerous as the infantry. The V.C. hunts combat engineers whereas the infantry hunts the V.C.

My combat tour ended on December 3, 1967, when I stepped on a land mine a month before I was to return to the US. The explosion shattered my right foot and riddled it with bacteria-drenched shrapnel, as well as putting other holes in me. I'd spent the last seven months in hospitals in Vietnam, Japan, and the United States. The doctors discharged me to home recuperation in mid-May with periodic visits to a V.A. hospital for checkups. I was an invalid struggling to recuperate.

Now—Saturday, June 29, 1968—seven months after being wounded, Brian and I were in the attic bedroom of an 1890s guesthouse on the grounds of Chautauqua Institution. My mother was working for the Institution again through the summer; and she wanted me near her since I was only moderately ambulatory, and my father was out on construction jobs. She had a room on the lower floor of the guesthouse known as "Exeter House."

Brian had driven over from Conklinville on Friday evening, and we had an enthusiastic reunion. I had seen Brian only once since my enlistment. That visit was while I was on leave during the Christmas of '66. We spent a few hours talking at my home during that visit and parted with cheery handshakes and wishes of good luck to each other. I left for Vietnam after the holiday. Since then, Brian and I had only exchanged letters once.

As I demonstrated my scratching stick to Brian, the deep, melodic tone of Westminster chimes drifted through an open window. Two stanzas rang out from the tall red brick bell tower down by the lake's edge. It was eight thirty in the morning.

"Damn," I said after looking at my bedside clock, "let's get some breakfast."

Unlike the hotels on the Institution grounds, guesthouses like Exeter House provided a large kitchen; and the guests brought in their own food and prepared and cleaned up after their meals. Our kitchen had three refrigerators and two stoves and a large table and chairs. Most guests ate in a large communal dining room decorated with antiques.

I was slow in getting dressed. I was slow at everything because of having to take care not to bump my foot. We made it down the three flights of narrow, creaky, and steep stairs to find no one in the kitchen.

"What do you want to do today?" Brian asked later as we sat at the table in the kitchen. He had stirred up a plate of scrambled eggs for himself, and I had a bowl of cornflakes.

"I'd like to take a drive. I don't care where," I answered, my voice muffled by cereal.

"Great! I was looking at a map, and the state highway that runs past the Institution goes on over to Lake Erie. It crosses the Thruway, so we might recognize the towns since we both took the Thruway to get to Ohio"

"I only went back and forth a few times compared to you. But that sounds fine. We can see what Lake Erie looks like compared to Ontario."

Other guests had come into the kitchen and were preparing breakfast when my mother came in. "I was going to make your breakfasts, but you beat me to it," she said after greeting us. We chatted and had coffee as she prepared her breakfast. We told her we were going over to Lake Erie.

"Oh, you have to try some smoked whitefish," she suggested. She then cautioned me to take some pain pills with me. "And don't get your foot wet. Lake Erie water will certainly infect it."

Eventually, Brian and I made it up and out of the main entrance of the Institution to the parking lot, where Brian had parked the Falcon. "How's the Falcon been treating you? It's been two years."

"Okay," Brian said as he drove the car out onto the highway, and we headed west. "I had both a valve and ring job done last summer. It had gotten to be a real tired motor."

"Did you have Crankshaft do the work?"

"Yeah, sure. He asked about you. I told him what I knew. Not saying goodbye pissed him off."

"Yeah, I left in a hurry," I said as I rolled my window down and hung my elbow out. The cool morning air washed around in the car, and Brian looked over at me. "I feel free," I said in response to his glance. "Chautauqua is a wonderful place, but I don't like the walls. They remind me of the fences and wire around an army post."

We drove along the shore of Lake Chautauqua. Neither of us had ever taken the route since our trips to Chautauqua ended at the Institution. I studied everything intently: the boat marinas, the lakeside cottages, the girls on bicycles. Everything seemed fresh and new, clean and organized. There were no rice paddies, no duck herder with a long stick to guide the flock. The cars were real cars, not tiny three-wheeled, two-cycle contraptions blowing smoke with a dozen people hanging on them. Best of all, there were no drab olive diesel trucks on the road with sad-ass-looking GIs in the back. I had returned to my home planet.

From Chautauqua Lake, we went over a ridge and down a multi-mile-long grade to Lake Erie. "Sunshine Superman" was playing on the radio, and the sun did come softly through my window; but I didn't have a girl to make mine.

"Westfield. I've gotten off the Thruway here to get gas," Brian commented as we went through the village, where the state highway crossed Interstate 90. Further along, the state highway ended in the village of Barcelona on the shore of Lake Erie. The army corps of engineers had built breakwaters there, forming a harbor for small boats.

We parked in the lot, next to the boat launch ramp. A concrete deck topped the breakwaters, making it possible to walk out on them and fish or to just enjoy the wind and water.

"Hey, it would be easy to get blown off this thing," I said when we had gotten halfway out on the breakwater. A stiff wind blew off the water and pulled at our clothes.

"Well, for Christ's sake, stay away from the edge!" Brian griped in return, "if you go in the dink, your mother will have my ass."

"And she would dump me back in the hospital."

"Did they have any good-looking nurses in your hospitals?" Brian asked.

"Sure, but only doctors interested them. They were wonderful to us, considering we were an endless stream of worthless GIs with no luck and no future. Hospital love stories are in the fiction section."

We looked out at the slate-gray lake from the end of the breakwater. I could see only one sailboat and no large Great Lakes freighters. While looking out at the water, I said, "I swam in the South China Sea once," I spoke to rhetorically, "this isn't the South China Sea."

"So was it nice?"

"Yeah, like a tropical paradise. Sandy beaches, surf rolling in, gorgeous, warm water, spools of concertina wire stretched out, and guard towers with machine guns. The USO was on the beach. They trucked us over there one Sunday afternoon. We skinny-dipped or swam in our underwear. You don't bring a bathing suit to combat. That was the only time I got to the USO in my entire tour."

We stood shoulder to shoulder, looking out at the lake. A duck glided low over the water and landed; then in a stern voice, I said, "I'd like to get back to that damn place."

"That must have been a great beach."

"Oh, not for the beach. I want to get back there and kill some of those little shits. I never whacked one. I might have. I tried like hell on two occasions, but I doubt I hit one. Now I'm back here, and I'll never get a clean shot on a dink in the open, right in my sights, and see my rounds snap him off his feet into a bloody heap." I was talking to empty space.

Brian didn't reply, and I realized it was a stupid remark. There was no way he could understand.

"Let's get off this thing. The wind is cold," Brian said as he turned away from me and started back off the breakwater. He stayed a step or two ahead of me until we came to the crude concrete steps back down to the parking lot.

"Want to get lunch?" I asked Brian as we approached the Falcon.

"Sure. I saw a place up on the highway, selling the smoked fish your mother spoke of."

After a short drive back along the shore road, Brian pulled off into an unpaved parking lot dotted with rain-filled ruts. A large sign on the roof of an old wooden building read "Billy's Bait, Beer and Smoked Whitefish."

Surprisingly, the parking lot had a view out over the Lake. A field stretched about a hundred yards to a cliff, and beyond was the lake. Four picnic tables sat on the lawn behind the building.

"Well, this seafood restaurant has a water view," Brian remarked

"I'm not wearing a tie. I hope they serve us," I replied.

We found the building divided between a fishing equipment shop and a typical lunch counter. There were no tables or booths, just a counter with a row of stools and the kitchen equipment behind the counter. Since there were six people—all men—eating at the counter, we figured Billy must serve up a reasonably good fish fry.

An old man with a three-day beard and dressed as a car mechanic, not a chef, took our order. "What do you want?" he demanded, sounding like customers were a nuisance.

We both ordered the smoked whitefish, french fries, and a beer. "You eating here or taking it out?" the old man asked.

"Want to eat at the picnic tables?" I asked Brian.

"Yeah, sure."

I turned to the old man. "We'll eat at the picnic tables out back."

"Well, put your mess in the trash barrel, else the raccoons will be all over the place."

The scruffy cook served up our lunch quickly. The fish and fries came on paper plates, and we carried it all out to the picnic table. "This is better than eating in a bait shop," Brian said as we sat down.

We ate and sipped our beers and looked out across the field to the Lake and the horizon, where the gray of the Lake met the slightly lighter gray of the sky.

"Let's see. Canada must be fifty or seventy-five miles over there," I said and then continued, "what's the word on George Felton. Anyone heard from the chicken shit draft dodger?"

"Not that I've heard."

"Nothing?"

"Not a word. And my mother would have told me if any news hit the village."

"I suppose the Felton family has kept quiet since Wayne has been gone."

For a moment, neither of us spoke; and then Brian unloaded a heavy question on me. "Why didn't you talk to me before you enlisted?"

The question startled me, and I turned and looked at him. "I didn't even talk it over with my parents. If I had talked about it, everyone would have tried to talk me out of it."

"Damn right! And I think you can see why."

I took another swig of beer. "I have no regrets, and I've spent hundreds of hours laying in hospital beds thinking about it."

"Well, all of us have regrets. We feel guilty we couldn't change your mind, talked some sense into you."

"That's silly. It was all my own doing."

"Your mother asked me over to your house after you left. She asked me if I knew you were going to do it. She was distraught."

"She shouldn't have bugged you."

"Well, you don't live in a vacuum. People care for you. Your parents love you. You owe them. We all owe someone."

The lecture insulted me, and I barked back at Brian. "It's my life, and I can do what I want with it."

Brian responded forcefully, "Pull your head out of your ass. You know that's not true."

"I couldn't help it. There was Wayne." I let my voice trail off, and I looked at the lake again.

"Don't you think I cared for Wayne? You two were close, but losing Wayne broke us all up. We are still broken up. You have an obligation to other people in your life."

"For Christ's sake, it's done now." I drank the last of my beer and smacked the bottle back on the table.

"Well, you still owe your parents."

"Do I owe you?"

"That's for you to decide."

"Okay, okay, you're right. Honest. You're right. We owe each other, all of us. Yet we must live our own lives. I made a decision, and that's the end of it. Wayne would be here if he had decided to go to community college."

Brian dropped his fork and wiped his hands with a napkin. "Come on, let's get out of here," he said.

We gathered up our trash and walked over to the barrel the old man told us about.

"Got anything for the raccoons?" Brian asked as he's scraped leftover fries and fish onto the grass beside the barrel.

"Not much, but they are welcome to it," I said as I dropped the overcooked fries on my plate on the grass with Brian's contribution, and I put my trash into the barrel with Brian's.

We drove ten minutes without speaking; then I spoke up, "When's the wedding?"

"June, the first Saturday after we both graduate."

"You've got to be engaged first."

"I'm giving her a ring for Christmas."

"It won't be a surprise."

"Yeah, I've got to dream up a clever way to give her a ring. But, obviously, it won't be a big surprise." Brian glanced over at me. "Did I ever talk about marriage to you?"

"No, but it's been a done deal for years." I paused then continued, "You're lucky. My girl ran away."

The Falcon had climbed back up onto the ridge between the lakes, and we were passing a large cornfield. "The corn looks good. Right on schedule," Brian commented.

I regretted the remark about Susan and was glad Brian changed the subject. "Right," I replied, "just enough rain. Give it a month, and there will be corn on the cob."

Later, as we approached Chautauqua Institution, Brian asked me about my future. "I know it's late in the year, but maybe Marietta would be willing to make an exception for a vet. Do you think you'll be healthy enough by fall if they did?"

"I wouldn't go back there if they waived the tuition and begged me. No, that place was a big ass mistake for me. There's nothing but rich, conceited preppies on that campus."

"What? When you came up to Kent at semester break, you talked about a group of friends."

"There were other fools like me that ended up there. No, if I do anything this fall, it will be at a community college." I waited a moment and continued, "I'm thinking of some unusual alternatives. I've lost my chance at a normal life, so why fight it?"

"Like what?"

"Photography. Maybe I'll be a newspaper photographer."

"Well, as you said, unusual."

I had pulled the photography idea out of thin air, never having considered it before; however, my comment about normal life was accurate.

Brian pulled up to the curb of the passenger dropoff lane at the main gate. "Remember, Thursday is the fourth of July," he said.

"Right, but as I said, I'm not going to be a drag on you and Beth."

Earlier, Brian had told me that his family and Beth's were going to spend the fourth of July on the Chautauqua grounds. Both families were staying the night at a motel near the Institution. "So you guys play tennis, swim, and whatever. And it will be enough just to stop by and say hello."

"Well, we will at least see you for the fireworks and flares Thursday night," Brian said.

"Okay," I said as I opened the car door and maneuvered my crutches out. "See you on the fourth! Thanks for coming over. It's been great to see you. I missed you, buddy." I reached over, and we shook hands and I got out. Brian beeped the horn and waved as he drove away.

The Institution had a system of small buses, and if I had been patient, I could have taken one to my boarding house. Instead, I walked the three quarters of a mile. It would have been an easy, pleasant walk, except for the crutches and the July heat and humidity. My bad foot was throbbing when I got to the house.

My mother greeted me on the front porch of Exeter House, and I gave her a quick description of the trip with particular detail of the fish lunch. When I was finished describing the afternoon, my mother asked me a question. "Do you remember we're going out for dinner tonight?"

"Sure, I remember. Six o'clock, right?"

The day before, we had agreed to go out for dinner that night; and I had forgotten.

"Yes, six o'clock. I've put a pressed dress shirt in your closet along with dress slacks."

"Fine, I'll be ready."

I didn't like wearing any of my old clothes; it felt like wearing a stranger's clothes (a stranger or a dead man). I was a dead man walking.

After that chat, I went up to my room to take a pain pill and catch a nap.

While lying on my bed, I looked around the room. The ceiling (actually the roof) sloped down to make a half-height sidewall to the room. My bed was under the low part of the ceiling. The room had the usual, for Chautauqua, porch off the front of the house; and since it was on the top floor, I felt like I was sitting in the maple trees when out on the porch.

The furniture was bought before the First World War, but the wallpaper was as recent as the Truman administration. It was quiet in the room. Very quiet. All I heard was the wind in the maple trees outside my open window. I daydreamed and wondered how many couples had screwed while in the room. There was a number, but no one would ever know it. My foot gave a sharp shoot of pain as punishment for my pornographic mussing. If I'd had a sidearm, I'd have splattered my brains on the ancient wallpaper.

My right foot was a mess. Doctors used it as a training exercise, cutting it open and rebuilding it twice since the initial wound. Infection had set in at the start caused by the little bastards smearing cow shit on whatever the explosive device was. I often regretted that the explosion hadn't blown the foot clean off. The foot was still with me because a day or so—maybe a week—after being wounded, I was in a medevac hospital in Vietnam when a group of doctors huddled around my bed and explained to me what had happened to my foot; then they gave me a choice. They could cut the damn thing off or try some experimental techniques to save it. They seemed keen on the idea of saving the foot and told me the work on me would help them help other GIs. I told them to go ahead and try to save the foot. They put the noble twist on it before they told me it would be months—maybe a year—of painful work. The Tet Offensive hit a month later, overflowing the hospital wards with the wounded. I wouldn't have been given the option to keep my foot if I'd been part of that mess.

The past two years had been hard for my mother. She said many of the same things Brian had just said to me. Fortunately, my father understood better. I made no attempt to explain to my parents or anyone else why I had enlisted. The discussion I had that afternoon with Brian was the first time that I had explained my motivation to anyone. If I had to explain to someone, then they wouldn't understand my explanation.

Unknown to my parents, I had saved them some grief after being wounded. I, like all shit-faced combat soldiers, was told to sign a waiver when they got to Vietnam that said that I did not want my family notified if I was "lightly wounded." I stayed conscious during the explosion that blew me thirty feet onto my ass. I told everyone, who worked on me—my squad medic, the dust-off chopper crew, and the staff at the medevac hospital—that I didn't want anyone notified of my wound. As a result, I was able to tell my parents personally that I had been wounded during a phone call from a hospital in Japan. I played the situation up as great news that it was a minor foot wound like having a toenail ripped off and that I would be coming home. They did not suspect anything until I had to tell them I was being dumped in a big army hospital near Denver for an undetermined stay. They came all the way out to Denver in February to visit me and were not happy when they discovered my deceit. They didn't appreciate (they couldn't have appreciated) that I had spared them the confusion and anxiety of not knowing my exact condition when I was first wounded.

Now, I lay in bed contemplating the flowers in the wallpaper pattern. My bed had a new firm mattress that was a relief from the sagging army hospital beds I had been sleeping on and was heaven compared to what I slept on in Vietnam.

The sound of the bell tower chimes came through the window again as it had that morning. I looked at the clock by my bed and realized that I had been lying there half an hour, and so, I gave up on getting any sleep.

I got up, grabbed my crutches, and made my way out of my room into the hall. Rather than go down the stairs, I turned and went to the door at the end of the hall and out onto the porch. As I stepped out, a familiar sensation came over me. I felt exposed, vulnerable, and I panicked. I had no weapon and felt naked. I desperately missed not having my rifle.

After my initial hesitation, I continued out onto the porch and sat down on an old wicker chair I had positioned at the porch railing. I had set the chair so I could look over the railing and down at the street in front of the building. I put my bad foot up on a stool and pillow I had also set in place. Situated this way, I looked over the railing and watched for people on the street.

The panic subsided, but a guilty feeling replaced it. Here, I sat on my lazy ass in a bizarre, leafy green world of intellectual tranquility while the shit was going down back in Vietnam. Getting wounded was a damn dumb thing to do. I had gone over the incident a million times since it happened. We had swept the road half an hour before, backing a 5-ton truck the entire five miles in reverse.

By doing this, the rear wheels of a truck would detonate a land mine, blowing them off, and giving the driver a better chance of coming out of it with just a temporary speech impediment. Our truck did not hit a mine. How, then, was there a mine a few minutes later when I was walking back along in the truck's tire track?

My squad leader had visited me at the twenty-seventh Surgical Hospital in Chu Lai before I was shipped to Japan. His explanation was that the Gooks had been watching us sweep the road. When we were gone, they came out of cover and quickly planted the mine. They had screwed up and buried it too deep or laid it in crookedly. He said I was damn lucky, and I should stop thinking I'd made a mistake. What he said made sense. Most mines blew people to all mighty hell whereas I only had one foot pulverized and a bunch of shrapnel. It was still stupid of me. I assumed we were safe when we were never safe.

Another houseguest was on their porch below me and was playing a radio. The music filtered up to me, and the song took me to an imaginary world, where my imaginary date wore blue velvet; and love was ours, and the flame burned brightly until now when I saw it all through my tears.

Chapter 2

4th of July

A young waitress, wearing a black uniform with a white collar and a white lace-trimmed apron came up to our table. "May I help you this evening?" she asked in a professionally perky voice. Her blond hair, blue eyes, and fair complexion gave her a Scandinavian look that fit the occasion since we were eating at the Edelweiss, a German restaurant.

"Yes," my mother responded and ordered one of the evening specials: pork chops, vegetables, and rice pilaf (although the name on the menu sounded much more appealing). It was pleasant to get out and have dinner even if it was with my mother. The communal dining at the Exeter House became tiresome.

I ordered one of the evening specials also: schnitzel. Fortunately, when the waitress left our table her, path toward the kitchen was in my line of sight; and I watched her closely as she walked away. It was a pity I could not have her for dinner.

"Will the Institution ever allow wine to be served on the grounds?" I asked my mother after I took a sip of ice water.

"Never, and it's a shame because there is no harm in it. Wine is part of church ritual." My mother paused and changed the subject while I continued watching the waitress. "I called your father this afternoon. He will be here Wednesday night and go back Saturday afternoon."

My father was coming to Chautauqua to spend the fourth of July with us.

"Great! How's his job going?"

"Oh, the usual equipment breakdowns and confusion over the plans, but he says they are making progress and are on schedule."

We talked about my father's work and of the problems my mother had in the Institution's finance department. As the waitress served our dumpling soup, I confirmed she had no ring on her left hand.

"Did Brian tell you he and his family are going to be here at Chautauqua for the holiday?" my mother asked as we sipped her soup.

"Yeah, he mentioned it, and that Beth and family are joining them. It's great they will be here. It will be special"

"Oh, yes! And there are other families from the village coming down for a long weekend. They are all staying at the Whitmore Inn at Stowe Point."

"Who else?"

My mother went on to say that the minister and family, as well as other families from the church, were coming.

During our main course, as I was cutting my schnitzel, my mother put the bug on me about church. "Will you be going to church tomorrow?"

"No, I'd rather not," I said without hesitation and continued to eat. I hadn't been to church since coming home. At first, I used my foot as an excuse; but that was wearing thin as I got better.

After a few minutes of strained silence, my mother gave me another suggestion. "It's Saturday evening. The College Club has live music tonight. I'll help you down the hill and, later, come and help you back up if you'd like to go."

"Thanks, I appreciate that, but I'd feel awkward down there on crutches and not knowing anyone. Brian and Beth will be here on the fourth, and we'll stop in then."

"Well, the offer is open if you want any help getting there."

I thanked my mother again. The College Club was a building on the lake shore, beside the community beach and bell tower. The building may have been a boathouse once since the sides opened, providing a breezy venue for dancing. The College Club was the center of all the clean and wholesome activities organized by the Institution for (what they probably called) the older adolescents. It surprised me that the place existed and permitted kids to touch one another even if it were on a well-lit dance floor. I spent my "Rest and Relaxation" (R&R) week away from Vietnam in a drunken, debauched stupor at an army-approved (confirmed clean girls) hotel in Bangkok, Thailand. The College Club was a nursery in comparison.

The next item on my mother's dinner agenda was my future.

"I understand that Rochester Community College accepts applications up until nearly the start of the semester. Do you think that would be a good option for this fall?"

"RCC would be fine if I was going back to school, but I may not. I'm thinking about other options."

"Oh, may I ask what?"

"I'm not certain of anything. For now, I just want to get well."

"I'm not being nosy, but any good job requires education and training. You did fine at Marietta. I would hate to see you miss deadlines for applications."

"You're right. I understand. I'll decide soon and tell you right away."

Our waitress served dinner, and we ate in silence. We both finished our meal, and as we waited for the waitress to take our dishes, my mother asked about my health.

"You're getting around better. How is the pain?"

Her question interrupted my mental speculation on how to meet and seduce the waitress, so I responded slowly. "Better, better. Yeah, it's getting better."

That was my standard answer given with varying combinations of encouraging words whenever someone asked me about my foot. Truthfully, if I had a chainsaw, I would cut the damn foot off.

"Good," my mother replied in a less than convinced tone, "we'll see what the doctors say on the ninth."

I was scheduled to be admitted to the large V.A. hospital in Buffalo the Tuesday after the holiday. I would spend the day getting X-rays and an examination. My stomach knotted up when thinking of the hospital. There were just too many half dead people flopping around, moaning and groaning in the hospitals. The guy in the bed next to me in the Vietnam medivac hospital died one night. What a hell of a commotion! It was easier to ignore the racket when someone died at the other end of the ward.

"It's okay. My foot's better," I added to ease her anxiety.

My mother didn't respond, but her frown said enough.

She had cared for me since my coming home but hadn't given me unqualified sympathy. Obviously, my enlisting still pissed her off. As Brian said, my enlisting affected more than just myself. But what would the difference have been if I had been drafted and wounded?

My sweetheart waitress cleared our dishes and returned to ask if we wanted dessert. She stood with her order book next to my mother, and she was directly in my view. Her waitress uniform was of no use since I knew every anatomical detail about her.

We declined dessert; and the waitress, pleasantly thoughtful or just good professionally, brought my crutches that were leaning against the wall. She was close enough for me to catch the scent of her perfume, a mild floral scent. I curse women's perfume. It's chemical warfare.

We left the hotel lobby by a rear entrance and took one of the many narrow public walking paths that crisscross the Institution. As we walked out into the cool evening air, I noticed a cluster of the hotel and restaurant staff in a tiny parking lot off to the side. They were leaning against a car, smoking and joking with music coming from the car radio. Now, I knew where I might meet the waitress.

According to promotional material, four hundred people lived permanently on the Chautauqua Institution grounds. During the summer, the population rose to multi thousands as the hotels and guesthouses—such as Exeter House—filled. Also, the summer gentry came to spend the summer in their vacation homes.

On Tuesday morning, I sat out on my high porch, looking down and watching new arrivals excitedly unloading their cars. The car license plates came from all over the northeast. Kids were everywhere, and many of them rode bikes. Entry to the enclosed and gate-guarded grounds required a pass. Cars were parked in a common parking lot outside the main gate and were allowed in only to load and unload. This made parents feel at ease in letting the kids do as they liked. Everyone walked or pedaled bikes along the narrow, shaded streets, adding to the unique communal atmosphere.

The street in front of the Exeter House was heavily used for strolling between the main park, Bestor Plaza, further up the hillside and the large park at the lake shore. The bell tower, small community beach, and the College Club were located next to the park. Since many of the walkers were girls, I spent time watching from my fourth floor porch. I could get a good but brief view of people and hear their conversations clearly. The best part was that they never looked up at me.

So I sat like a spy that morning, watching all this go on, when a laughing young female voice made me twist and look up the street to where the walkers came into view between the intervening leaves and tree limbs. A girl with shoulder-length strawberry blond hair appeared. Walking next to her was a guy about the same age but skinny and slightly shorter than her. The girl's face turned to her companion and so presented me with a profile. Even from a distance, and looking from above, there was no mistaking it was Susan.

"Damn!" I said as I jerked back from the railing. I listened and heard her voice even more clearly as they walked in front of the house. I snuck another peek at them when I was sure they would be walking away. I wasn't hallucinating; it was Susan.

For a moment, I stared at the aged white clapboard siding of the house and then, quietly, I asked myself aloud "What is she doing here?"

It was a dumb question; she and her family were part of the town group visiting Chautauqua for the holiday. Susan and family had come early; that's all.

It didn't matter what brought her to Chautauqua; I had to avoid her. I had been hobbling up to Bestor Plaza in the afternoons to visit the library and to have an ice cream on a café patio. I had also gone to lectures and concerts. I could do none of that while Susan was here.

I hadn't seen Susan since the New Year's Eve party, which was also the last time I saw Wayne. She had deviled me, though, by sending me letters. I received the first letter just after arriving at Fort Dix, New Jersey, for basic training. It was a sympathy card for Wayne, and her words were touching. My mother forwarded the second of Susan's letters to me two months later while I was training in the Missouri woods. Susan was a sophomore then, so she should have been past the problems Kathy had told me about. I didn't open the letter. She wrote me again a year later while I was in Vietnam. I flicked the unopened letter into a rice paddy beside a road we were clearing of mines and booby traps. My objective was to stay alive, and I didn't need an old girlfriend distracting me.

The latest letter from Susan caught up with me in the Denver hospital. I could tell by the envelope that it was a get well card. The entire village knew of my wound, and I was getting cards. They were all the same crap, so again, I didn't open Susan's mail. I was in constant pain and heavily medicated and didn't give a shit about anything. Not that I cared now. I have no idea what happened to the card.

A problem came up on the fourth of July morning; kids were already setting off firecrackers. The slightly muffled crackle pop of the firecrackers sounded like a distant firefight. I first heard them as I was creaking down the stairs for breakfast.

My father had joined us the night before, and we were eating breakfast in the big, common dining room when another string of firecrackers went off. The noise rippled through an open window in the dining room.

"Did Brian say when he might be coming by?" my mother asked as she stirred her tea, and my father concentrated on his newspaper.

"No, he didn't say," I answered as I pushed back from the table. I got up, and by hopping and leaning on chairs, I made it to the window on the other side of the room; and with an effort, I slammed down the old window. "Why do those assholes have to start that crap so early?" I blurted out before remembering who was listening.

"Michael! Don't talk that way," My mother scolded.

Two old ladies at another small table in the room gave me a scowl as I hobbled back to my chair. "Pardon me," I said in a less than apologetic tone as I sat down.

"Ask me, and I can do things for you. You might have fallen," my mother told me. My outburst had my father grinning from behind his paper

"I told Helen they could relax on our porch anytime through the afternoon or evening, and I have drinks and snacks in the refrigerators to offer them." Helen was Brian's mother. "And Rev. Baxter and his wife may stop by also. I've told him where we are and that we hoped to see them."

Other houseguests came out of the kitchen, carrying their breakfasts. They sat at the other end of our table, and after all of us exchanged good morning greetings and comments about the holiday events, my mother continued.

"The concert is at seven o'clock, and the fireworks and flares are at ten o'clock. Other than that, I thought we'd just relax here." She paused and looked at me. "Will all that be too much for you?"

"No, that's fine. I'm feeling okay today," I answered. My foot had given me only a few light twinges that morning.

The concert was a special holiday music festival at the amphitheater with patriotic songs, John Philip Sousa marches, and Aaron Copland mixed in. The Institution's own symphony orchestra and a large amateur chorus put on the show.

At ten o'clock, the entire community went down to the lakeside with lawn chairs and blankets to watch fireworks put on by an amusement park just across the lake. At the same time, lakefront property owners observed an old Chautauqua Lake tradition by igniting strings of red road flares at the water's edge. The Lake was over twenty miles long and about half a mile wide, so there were thousands of flares lit at once. Red dots of fire ringed the entire lake for a few minutes.

"More scrambled eggs?" my mother asked as she nudged a large bowl across the table to me. My plate was empty, and I was finishing my coffee.

"No, I'm full. I've had seconds already."

"Well, then I'll get your pills."

I took three pills every morning: two antibiotics and an antidepressant. The antibiotics prevented a recurrence of infection, and GIs in the hospital called the antidepressant the "happy pill." The happy pill kept us from thinking about how crapped up we were.

I had no pain that morning, so I didn't ask for a pain pill. I hated taking pills. It reminded me of the hospitals. In the hospitals, the nurses would sweetly sing out "pill time." Those poor nurses took a lot of crap from us: wisecracks and an occasional quick grab.

I especially hated my foot. Once, a few weeks before when I was first home, I was alone for a moment at the dining room table. My brain boiled up as I thought about my situation, and I took my fork and reached down and repeatedly jabbed my foot through the bandages. The pain made me queasy. When my mother changed my bandages, she saw the odd patterns of five swollen red spots and got upset. I lied up a whopper about similar spots turning up while in the hospital, and the spots simply went away.

I lied a lot now. I was impressed with how well I lied. Before all this, I never lied—least of all to my parents. It was easy to lie about things other people knew nothing of. My letters from Vietnam were full of lies of omission. I wrote happy letters saying I was fine two hours after half a dozen mortar rounds plopped in on us. At the moment I wrote the letter, all was quiet; so I wasn't lying. I also told my parents that I flew in and out of landing zones by helicopter. I didn't say our pilot often flew up deep mountain canyons through blinding monsoon rain while I sat in the back, watching trees whiz past the open door.

After breakfast, I took my pills and made the slow climb back up to my room. With luck, it could easily to excuse myself from all the goings on my mother had planned for the day. I would lie, saying that my foot hurt. What the hell, it would hurt by that time of day.

I flopped on the bed; looked up at the odd, sloping ceiling; and thought about Susan for the million and first time. What a damned wimp I was. Nearly three years, school, a war, a weeklong drunk in Bangkok, damn near getting whacked a number of times, and finally months of pain . . . All that separated me from her. But the scent of her perfume, the touch of her angel-soft cheek, seemed only hours in the past.

My mind drifted, and I remembered being in the back of a dump truck in Vietnam. I was with three others; one of them was the M-60 machine gunner. He had the M-60 sitting up on the headache board over the driver. The rest of us had our M-16 rifles and were carrying extra belts of ammunition for the M-60. We had gone through this routine so often that we rode along in a dull silence. Traffic snarled the road, and our driver had to blow the horn and nearly run over Gooks to get them to let us through. Our truck could easily have crushed the stinking little pushcarts and small three-wheeled scooter trucks that surrounded us. The only car was a weird black French car that I had heard was called a "traction avant." It looked like something out of the 1930s.

Our truck pushed through until we came to the wide, deep round hole that was causing the traffic jam in the middle of the road. The V.C. had crawled inside a culvert and out to the center of the road and planted a hell of a big explosive charge that cratered the road. Our truck and others behind us were to fill the hole and get traffic moving. We all got down off the truck and herded the angry crowd away from the hole so we could work. Kids were climbing in and out of the hole, which made us feel better since that meant that the V. C. hadn't planted booby traps around to blow us up when we repaired the hole.

But we were nervous that someone in the crowd would start shooting at us or toss a grenade. I had a great urge to flick my rifle on to full automatic and spray the crowd like a garden hose. Another guy and I pushed the people back while the other GIs shoveled dirt and chunks of pavement into the hole.

Despite the intense heat and humidity, I wore my flak jacket and helmet and carried the extra M-60 ammunition, extra magazines and clips of M-16 ammunition, two canteens of water, and a couple of C-Ration cans for lunch.

I had already drunk most of one canteen and was thirsty. "Damn, I wish we had more water," I said to another GI, "and I need to piss."

"Go over to that McDonald's." he told me and pointed to the side of the road.

I stared in disbelief at a McDonald's restaurant, where rice paddies should be. I could even smell the hamburgers and french fries. The parked cars were all normal American cars like Fords, Chevys, even an old Studebaker and a red Mustang fastback.

But I didn't go. I just stood there cursing the Vietnamese while getting thirstier and thirstier and worrying I'd pee my pants.

"Mike! May I come in?" I heard someone ask me. I looked around; but everybody in my squad was shoveling dirt, and another truck had pulled up to dump its load; then I heard a sharp, mechanical clicking, and I panicked thinking that some Gook had locked and loaded his weapon and was about to blow me away.

"Mike, come on, guy. Let's go. The holiday is passing you by."

I jerked awake and flung my arms out, searching for my weapon on the bed. "Easy, guy. It's just me," Brian said. He had let himself into my bedroom.

"Damn, son of a bitch! Geez, I'm sorry. I was sleeping and didn't know where I was. What time is it?" I asked as I swung my legs over the edge of the bed and rose up to a sitting position.

"It's one thirty. Come on, we've pooled our money and rented a rowboat. We're going to take turns paddling around the docks and swimming from the boat."

"God, I can't believe I've slept this long!" I said in confused disbelief as I stared at my watch.

"Hell, yeah, it's late! Come on, let's get rolling. They're waiting for us."

"Hang on, man. Just hang on a second. I'm sorry, but I've got to take a piss something terrible."

Brian grabbed my crutches and helped me stand up. After I returned, he started in again.

"Okay, you look fine. Keep going. We paid for the boat already, and they are down there having fun."

"No, no way. I'm a mess. I feel like hell."

I flopped onto the old easy chair. I wasn't kidding either. I was still trying to figure out the dream. I felt like a time machine had snatched me from Vietnam and plunked me down in front of Brian.

"Bullshit! Take a pill and get your lazy ass in gear. I'm sick of hearing you whine."

Brian came up to me and pulled my arm with one hand and pushed the crutches at me. He was right, just like a drill sergeant. I was damned lucky to have him as a friend. I put a couple of pills in my pocket, and we left the house and started down the street.

"These people are fanatic patriots. Every house has a flag," I mentioned as we walked.

Every house on both sides of the street had a flag displayed from the front porch. The scene created an odd sensation as though Brian and I were in a parade, but there were no spectators.

We walked down the hill into an iconic Norman Rockwell summer lakeside scene. We crossed the park and went over to the dock beside the College Club. The sun sparkled on the blue-green water, where sailboats with white sails competed for right of way against chrome and mahogany speedboats that pulled water skiers. On the small beach, between the dock and the College Club, girls lounged in bikinis showing almost all of what you wanted to see.

Beth was out on the dock with a cousin of Brian's named Charlie, whom I had met years ago, and another girl. We exchanged greetings and Charlie, a chunky and clumsy guy, introduced his girlfriend Gail, who was too nice-looking for Charlie. An old dented aluminum rowboat bobbed at dockside.

"We tied up next to the ladder." Beth pointed out. "We can help you make it down into the boat."

I noticed the wooden ladder leading a couple of feet down to the boat, but I also noticed that at least an inch of water covered the bottom of the boat. I knew they were using rental time to get me in the boat, so I was direct with them.

"I'm sorry, guys, but I can't risk getting my foot wet. It would be hard to get in, and I'd have to keep the foot propped up. All of you go, and I'll watch from the dock.

"We can beach it, and you could step in from the front." Charlie suggested.

"No, the water sloshes around, and I can't risk getting my foot wet. If it becomes infected again, they'll have to cut the whole foot off," I said (which was true). Beth and Gail recoil at the thought of amputation, so they all quickly agreed to go without me. Everyone clambered down into the boat and shoved away from the dock.

The girls squealed with every tip and roll of the boat while Charlie and Brian each tried to be captain and tell everyone what to do. They were all laughing, and off they went with the oars flailing at the water.

After a moment, watching the comedy cruise, I started to walk off the dock. The dock creaked and swayed with each swinging step I made with the crutches, so I looked down and watched carefully as I went along; then I heard a familiar voice call my name.

"Michael! We both missed the boat!" It was Susan.

I froze in place and then looked up. "Yeah, it looks that way" was my brilliant reply. I felt trapped: water on three sides and Susan in front of me.

"Welcome home!" She put a hand on my shoulder and gave me a kiss on the cheek. "I heard you were doing better." She reached out and put a hand on my arm, but I didn't respond to her touch. I was looking at a woman now, not the teenager I last saw at Wayne's party.

"Thanks! Yes, I have improved a lot since being back. You're looking well," I added in a flat tone of voice.

"Thanks," she replied. For a moment, we just looked at each other; and then Susan spoke up. "I sent you mail. Did you get it?"

"Yes, I got a letter just after I began training. I appreciated your remarks."

"I sent other letters while you were in Vietnam. Did they get to you?"

"Yes. Yes, they did. Thanks." I was feeling ill at ease and hoped she would forget about mail, so I made an excuse for not answering her. "I was in odd situations that made it hard to write anyone."

"And the card I sent to the hospital in Colorado?"

"Yes, I got it. It was nice of you to take the time to write."

"You're welcome. Was it hard for you to write then, too?"

"Yes. Sometimes. When I was all doped up."

"Could a nurse have helped?"

"Oh, well, I don't know," I responded with a stupid look on my face.

She looked skeptical but didn't say anything more about mail. "I've heard you're here at Chautauqua with your mother for the summer."

"I hope not the whole summer. As soon as I'm more mobile, I'll be able to get along by myself back at Conklinville."

"Have you heard I'm here for the summer? I'm taking classes at Syracuse University Extension."

I twitched in surprise, and I'm sure she noticed. "Really! Good! You do like the place. Now, you'll be able to enjoy it all, not just the weekend concert."

"I have to work though. I'm working at the Athenaeum Hotel."

"But you'll still have time for evening concerts and all the weekend attractions." I then inserted my escape. "I'm sorry, but I can't stand for long. I'm sure we will see each other again, but for now, I had better be moving on."

We exchanged sociable farewells, and Susan turned and walked off the dock, into the park while I hobbled after her. I watched her until I lost sight of her among the people.

"Damn!" I muttered, frustrated that I had run into her. She was with the gang naturally; Brian had just kept quiet about it. What in hell had I done to deserve hopelessly falling in love, losing a close friend, and then having my foot blown apart?

I hobbled off the dock and over to the College Club. I went in one of the wide sliding doors, sat down at a table, and looked out at the water to find the intrepid rowers. They were out of view. I considered getting something to drink at the snack bar but decided not to since I would have to ask someone to carry it to the table for me. Instead, I just sat, watching sailboats. Those were lucky kids on those sailboats—rich kids that didn't have to worry about the draft.

I never saw a lake in Vietnam. I saw the South China Sea all the time, flying in and out of Chu Lai. The sea was gorgeous like a Lowell Thomas travel log. My battalion and company headquarters were at Chu Lai. We engineers were just a small part of Chu Lai. The American Division HQ was there and also a large marine air station. The lucky paper-pushing bastards that sat inside the wire at Chu Lai only had to worry about an accessional mortar or rocket attack. The USO had round-eyed girls, too. A traveling group of USO girls called Doughnut Dollies did fly into a landing zone I was on once. They put on a vaudeville show and passed out packets of sundry items like toiletries that didn't come with C-rations. They flew black to Chu Lai before it got dark. And it did get dark out there in the mountains. It seemed always to be a moonless night when I had guard duty. Guard duty was a real bitch when it rained. Even with some kind of cover, like a bunker, the rain leaked in. And there were more rats out on the perimeter. The rats lived well out in the guard bunkers because we always brought crap along to eat, and no one bothered to clean up the bunkers until it got really bad. The bunkers stank, too, from everyone taking a piss near the bunker. It smelled better after a monsoon rain.

I came back to reality, and watched a thin, bony young girl— maybe a freshman in high school—wearing a blue bikini, come in from the tiny patch of sand and go up to the snack bar.

"Shit!" I thought. Why didn't I say something ironic or witty to Susan? Why was she so concerned that I got her mail? There was no damned reason for her to send me a get well card. There had been no reason for her to send me those letters while in Vietnam. She wanted to torment me. Why would it give her pleasure to torment me? What the hell would I have written in response to the get well card? "Thank you for your kind thoughts. I'm doing fine. My body is rejecting the quarter pound of rods and screws in my foot, and the pus oozing into my bandages smells divine. And how are you? What are the latest hairstyles? Who is your latest boyfriend?"

I stood up, leaned on one crutch, and looked out among the boats for the gang. They weren't back yet.

I was a damn fool to be spending a beautiful holiday afternoon, pouting about crap that went down years before. So I took up the other crutch and started to walk over to the Holy Land.

The Holy Land was a section of the lakeside park, where the devout founders of Chautauqua had landscaped a relief map of the Holy Land into the lawn. Mounds of earth representing the different mountains surrounded a 25-foot-long depression in the shape of the Dead Sea. A cluster of small bricks with a name inscribed represented the cities and villages with Jerusalem being the largest. Each significant place had a small engraved brass identification marker with a text from the Bible. It reminded me of the map of the Holy Land in the Bible given to me in Sunday school.

Shuffling my way from Jericho to Bethlehem, I wondered if I still qualified as Christian. There was a good possibility I was a killer. I tried damned hard to be one. I fired my weapon carefully during an ambush, concentrating on the tree line across the rice paddy. There was no target, but I fired for effect, not randomly. I mixed tracer rounds with standard ball ammunition in my magazine so I could adjust my fire. During another incident, I was radio telephone operator for the squad; and using a sweat-soaked relief map, I talked a Cobra helicopter gunship onto a target. We had taken sniper fire, so I directed the gunship to use its mini gun to chew up a bamboo thicket. A deep humming sound came from the gunship above us; then, after a short delay came the heavy patter of thousands of copper bullet casings raining down around us. It was hail from hell.

My hatred for all Vietnamese posed a worse threat to my soul. VC, NVA, or friendly are all subhuman to me. Trash people. I felt a glimmer of sympathy for the kids, but that was all.

The misery of the Vietnamese amused me. I was in a helicopter once as it skimmed low while the pilot searched for a place to land. The rotor wash blasted down on the thatched roofs of a cluster of hooches. Dinks came running out, waving and shaking their fists. The blast of air flattened their rice, too. Everyone on the helicopter laughed and enjoyed seeing the little shits waving their arms and running in circles. I smiled remembering that ride. I wished I'd whacked a few of them.

Nice thoughts to have while walking through a model of the Holy Land. Two, little, old ladies were talking softly while looking down at Bethlehem. They gave me a sympathetic smile as I made my way back to the sidewalk on the crutches. They probably thought I was praying for healing.

I moved along under the maple and sycamore trees back toward the College Club when I saw Brian and the others coming off the dock. They had tied up on the opposite side of the dock, and I hadn't seen the boat. They saw me and waited in a patch of shade at the end of the dock.

"So I see the 'good ship Lollipop' brought the crew back safely," I said to Brian as everyone began to walk up the street through the park.

"A U-boat fired a torpedo at us, but it bounced off our hull. A dud." We exchanged other absurd comments, and then Brian asked if I would join him at the table, where all their parents were spending the afternoon. "Lots to eat!" Brian promised.

"No," I answered, "I'll go on back to the hotel and check with my mother. She probably thinks I've fallen overboard." We were about to go our separate ways when I mentioned seeing Susan. "I met your tardy passenger on the dock after you shoved off. She surprised me."

Brian kept walking but turned and said in a raised voice, "You may see a lot of her. She's here for the summer, taking classes at Syracuse University Extension."

"Yes! She told me!" I replied in a raised voice as Brian walked away. *What a mess*, I thought to myself.

The Exeter House had a small redwood patio deck accessible through a door off the kitchen. Tall landscaping surrounding the deck gave the area the feeling of a pleasant grotto. I found my parents and the village minister and his wife, sitting around a compact rectangular table on the deck.

I saw the Rev. Cunningham as I came through the kitchen, so I stopped in the doorway and greeted everyone but did not go out onto the deck. The minister jumped out of his chair and stepped right up to me and began pumping my hand and arm.

"Michael, you look great. It's wonderful to see you. What a blessing! The Lord answered our prayers, and you're back with us again."

He went on like that, and my only response was "Thank you, thank you."

Eventually, he paused slightly to catch his breath. I quickly cut in before any conversation could start and began making excuses to leave. "Please excuse me, but I've been at the beach and gotten a lot of sun. And I think I should get up to my room and take a rest." I retreated through the kitchen, but everyone followed me.

"It's wonderful you get around so well. Truly, the Lord has answered our prayers," Reverend Cunningham went on.

My mother filled a plastic jug with ice cubes and added water. "Go on, Michael," she said finally, interrupting the agonizing small talk I made with the minister and his wife.

"Thank you very much for stopping by," I said to the Rev. and his wife as I shook their hands at the bottom of the stairs before starting up to my room.

Rev. Cunningham gave me a parting shot. "I'm looking forward to giving prayers of thanksgiving together when you get back home," he said, shaking my hand.

I had mastered the stairs and knew just how to maneuver my crutches, so I disappeared up the stairs relatively fast.

Up in my room, my mother poured a glass of ice and water for me and started a fan on the bureau. I sat on the edge of my bed, drinking the water when she said, "Rev. Cunningham's enthusiasm is catching and makes us all feel better. Wasn't it nice that he stopped by?"

"Yeah, sure," I said while looking straight ahead at a crack in the ancient lath and plaster wall across from me. "He's great. He must have an inside track with the Big Guy. Too bad he didn't pray for Wayne."

My mother's response came quickly and effectively. "God's will be done and with no questions from you. Furthermore, your father and I could quickly name half a dozen of our friends that didn't come back from the war." She left immediately, closing the door sharply behind her.

So I had crapped up again, just as Brian had scolded me about over the weekend. I had hurt someone I loved. But the cocky, self-assured minister pissed me off.

I pulled out the two pills I had put in my pocket before leaving with Brian and took them both. Taking two pills at once would make me slightly nauseous, especially since I hadn't had any lunch, but I needed them. Walking with crutches left my foot swinging, and I had bumped it a number of times. Now, it felt as though someone was sticking a ten-inch pin in my foot every once in a while. I needed to kill the pain quickly so I'd be able to get to sleep. The last thing I wanted to do was lie in bed and think of Susan, but that's what I did. I envisioned we were making love—slow, patient, enthusiastic love. I kissed her all over. I dreamed she lay naked on her tummy, and I stroked my hand over her buttocks and then slip my hand up between her thighs; and she responded, squirming with delight.

Reality destroyed my daydreams as the daylong firecracker firefight intensified and rolled back and forth through the entire Institution. I half expected to hear gunships come flapping in over the trees.

Closing my windows was out of the question on a hot day; so, using one crutch, I hopped over and repositioned the 1930s era table fan to point at the bed; then I laid down, put the earphone of my radio in one ear, turned on the radio, and began reading a car magazine. The radio was playing "Hot Rod Lincoln." If I drove my parents to drinking, it wouldn't be from driving a hot rod Lincoln.

I didn't go to the concert that evening. The pills made my foot feel better by six o'clock, so I went down for dinner. We had a holiday dinner of hamburgers, German potato salad, and watermelon.

"Are you going with us tonight?" My mother asked.

"No, you both go. I don't want to stir up the demons in my foot again."

"Don't talk of demons," my mother cautioned.

Dinner came off well. We talked of my brother and when he would be home. We exchanged memories of holidays, fourth of July at my grandparents', my father's parents, Christmases and birthdays, and all pleasant times. We didn't talk about politics.

My mother and father went into the kitchen to get the strawberry shortcake. While sitting alone at the table, I thought about my fourth of July holiday the year before, in Vietnam.

I looked around at the patio table, the deep green foliage beside the deck, and listened to my parents' voices in the kitchen. This was supposed to be reality, but I wasn't convinced. So I rewound my life, tracing backward to convince myself that what I saw and felt was reality. It only took a moment. I thought of where, supposedly, I was, Chautauqua, then back to being brought home, then of hospitals, being wounded, Vietnam, enlisting, losing Wayne, studying at Marietta, being in love the summer after graduation, and then back, back, back to being a happy kid running through fields and pastures with my dog in bright summer sunshine . . .

The details I recalled gave me the odd sensation of remembering a movie, not my own life. Maybe it had been a dream. It had to have been a dream. If I concentrated, focused, prayed, then I would stop remembering the dream; and it would be good again.

I shifted in my chair to avoid a shaft of sun flickering in my eyes. The movement triggered a twitch of a mild pain in my foot. The pain was real, not a dream, this was reality.

My mother brought out the delicious summer dessert, and we sat enjoying each other's company.

My parents left for the concert early and fully equipped. They left early because the amphitheater was open seating, and early birds got the best seats. They each took a book to entertain themselves, and they took seat cushions because of the hard slab pews at the venue.

After they left, I sat on the first floor front porch to watch the great migration of people move up the street to the amphitheater. Many carried the same accessories as my parents.

Later, after watching *Ironside* and *Bewitched* on the communal television in the sitting room, I went back out on the front porch and found I could clearly hear the more rousing portions of the concert, drifting down on the night air. So I sat and enjoyed "Yankee Doodle" and "The Battle Hymn of the Republic."

While sitting alone on the porch, I wondered what the reaction would have been had the American Forces Vietnam Network (or the AFVN, the GI radio network in Vietnam) played martial music. Maybe we would have marched off to the war every day, whistling "Yankee Doodle." Actually, for all I knew, they had played the music because I seldom listened to the radio while in Vietnam.

As one thought led to another, I wondered why I hadn't listened more to AFVN. The reasons came quickly and depressed me. I hadn't bothered with a radio because, first of all, batteries were damned near impossible to get; and most of the time, I was not on a big base, where electricity was available; then I'd have to lug the radio around. Even if it was small, it would be more to carry when my unit changed locations; and we constantly moved. I had to carry every stinking thing I owned in a duffel bag and be able to toss the bag onto a truck (ounces counted). Anyway, when I was out on an artillery firebase for a few months, radio reception went from crackling static to nonexistent. Now, just like that, I was back in the world, watching TV and listening to AM and FM; and I could buy a stereo, albums, and all that stuff.

I looked at my watch and calculated the time change from New York State to Vietnam. It was the morning after the fourth, but then, maybe Vietnam didn't really exist. Nothing around me indicated that Vietnam existed. The news talked about it, but the news talked about a lot of places.

The concert ended, and I watched the narrow streets fill again with a stream of people, this time, coming back down from the concert.

Many were going on down to the lake to wait for the fireworks and the lighting of the flares.

"How was the concert?" I asked my parents from my wicker chair on the porch as they came up the steps.

"Wonderful! I'm sorry you missed it," my mother answered.

As my parents came onto the porch, I noticed Brian, Beth, Charlie and Gail following them up the steps.

"Oh, I heard quite a bit of it. I could hear the best parts even down here," I commented to my mother.

"Well, that's at least something," my mother responded as she stood next to my chair. "How are you feeling?"

"Oh, okay," I answered as I got up from the chair and gripped the railing in front of me and looked past my mother and smiled at Brian.

"Fine," she said and then turned to the group now on the porch. "May I get anyone something to drink?"

Everyone declined, and Brian stepped up to me. "So are you going to be able to make it down for the fireworks? We've got extra chairs."

I nearly didn't answer him because, looking past him, I had seen Susan come into the light at the bottom of the steps and come up on the porch. With her was the same skinny guy that had been with her when I saw her three days before.

"Gee, damn. I don't know," I answered Brian haltingly. I was trying to think fast, a near impossibility for me even when I wasn't taking medication. So I reverted to a mix of lies and truth. "I'm pretty tired out." That was a lie. "And the old foot starts to hurt when I'm tired." That was true. "You guys go on down, and I'll join you later if I can. Where are you sitting?"

Brian told me where they were sitting relative to the bell tower. We talked and joked more, and I spoke to Beth and greeted Charlie and Gail. Beth and Gail, who had been in our high school band, joked about how they had played some of the same music they had heard at the concert. Susan and her friends stayed at the back of the group.

I urged the group to leave, or else, they might miss something at the lake. Everyone walked down the steps and into the dark, except Susan. She spoke to her friend, who left with the group, and then she came up to me. She made a motion with her hand, and we walked away from the front door to a dark corner of the porch. I leaned back against the railing, holding my foot up, and looked at her.

"Hi," she said after turning to me, "look, would you please forgive me for greeting you with a lot of cold questions this afternoon on the dock?"

She said nothing more. She just looked at me, waiting. A slight breeze brought her perfume to me. I remembered the perfume from years before.

"Oh, there is nothing to forgive. I understand that not hearing from me would make you wonder. But the letters confused me. I couldn't see why you would bother to write me."

"Writing to you made me feel better. Don't you think I worried about you?"

"I suppose, but I don't know why. Let's just forget about it."

She turned away and looked out at the people walking down the hill with folding chairs and blankets to watch the fireworks; then she turned back to me. "We can talk about it some other time." She smiled and continued, "Well, what a surprise that we're both here at Chautauqua."

"Yes, fate is playing games with us."

I could have gone on and asked her about what classes she was taking, what she had studied the last two years, and what she had planned for after school; but I wanted to get the interview over. I shuffled back to the steps. "Well, the gang is waiting. I suppose we'll see each other here and there around the grounds."

We said goodnight, and she went on her way.

I did go down to the park later and found Brian and Beth sitting on lawn chairs next to their parents. There were many groups of people; so I couldn't tell, without obviously looking, if Susan was anywhere close. It was pleasant talking to Brian, Beth, and the parents. They had stopped by to see me just after I had gotten home, so I brought them up to speed on how I had improved since early May.

Soon, I couldn't keep up the small talk. The same problem I had that morning—firecrackers—was worse than ever.

"Damn!" I snapped, interrupting someone else speaking. "Where the hell do they get those things?" I had twisted in my chair and was looking back into the park. "I thought fireworks were illegal in New York."

"People get them down south when they vacation, and Chautauqua people can afford nice, long vacations," Beth's father answered.

"Well, crying out loud!" I said in a strained exasperation.

The noise made me feel vulnerable and helpless. I had nothing—no weapon—to defend myself with. I couldn't see who was shooting, and there were crowds of ordinary people milling close around me.

I came to my senses enough to realize that I should make excuses and get the hell out of there. The situation would get worse when the amusement park fireworks started. They probably included artillery or at least mortars.

I considered cooking up a story (maybe an upset stomach from too much holiday food,) but I decided to skip the fiction. "I'm sorry everyone," I said as I stood and fumbled with my crutches, "these fireworks spook me. It sounds just like small arms fire during a firefight. Please excuse me. I'll go back up to my room away from the crowds."

Everyone stood and began consoling me, just what I didn't want. I continued speaking to the group. "I know this is melodramatic, but I guess I'm still fresh from being over there. I really enjoyed talking to you tonight, but I've got to go."

Hands reached out and patted me on the back, and sincere words of sympathy were spoken; and Brian walked with me for a ways back through the park. "We are leaving tomorrow, but remember, Beth and I are coming back for that concert at the end of the month— the last Friday— whatever date that is. You're going, too. No arguments. So, hang in there, buddy. Maybe by August, you can come home for a few days, and we can go up and hang out at U. R."

"I'll go to the concert. I'm looking forward to seeing you again. You're a great pal. You've been super. I'm sorry about tonight. I feel like a damned jerk."

"Forget it. Everyone understands."

Brian went back with the group, and I went on up the hill. Walking with crutches up a grade is slow work since your stride is much shorter because the pavement comes up to meet your foot.

Later, in my room, I was glad I had left the group. The fireworks from the amusement park across the lake sounded like a night fire mission from a distant artillery support base. The hollow thump was similar to hearing 105-MM howitzers firing from a distance of about three kilometers.

The noise from fireworks that evening was Mickey Mouse stuff compared to what Wayne lived through. I wondered how Wayne slept when he was off duty and a 175-MM gun cut loose. I had experienced just that, and it woke me up every time.

"I've got to get out of this place" was my reaction to the fourth of July holiday. Brian and all the other folks from my village had left by Saturday. Susan was still lurking around though. Her speaking with such sympathy impressed me. But I didn't regret not having answered her mail. Nothing made sense, and I wasn't going to bother to figure it all out.

The problem with getting out of Chautauqua was *where would I go?* Years before, I had read *Travels with Charley* by John Steinbeck. In the book, Steinbeck circles the country in a truck camper, just him and his dog. That was the kind of escape I longed for, but it was so far out of reach.

If I went home and lived alone during the week, I'd see more of Brian; but that might be a bad thing. We were definitely getting on each other's nerves. The past two years were radically different for each of us. Time and circumstance naturally change people. Hell, for that matter, my mother might soon kick me out as a blasphemer. And then there was a visit to the VA hospital coming up next week. I daydreamed a doctor would tell me I could start walking immediately, and I could drive, as well. If I were as lucky as to get that good news, I had been speculating on wild ideas like reenlisting. As bizarre as it sounds, civilian life bored me. I'd been medically discharged, but maybe by some miracle, I could get myself back into the army. I had been a damned good combat soldier and could be again. Most importantly, I had to get back to Vietnam to kill some Gooks. I wanted to catch some little bastard planting a mine in a road and blow his shit away as he squatted down. I thought up a scheme of camouflaged observation posts that covered a stretch of road in both directions. Each observation post would have a 50-caliber machine gun so they could reach out at long-range and touch someone, really touch them. I imagined looking down the 4-foot barrel of the big Browning and seeing a skinny, little shit squatting down. (They always squatted when digging a hole for a mine.) I could feel my right thumb press down on the butterfly trigger and the beast spitting out a half-inch diameter, 3 ¼-inch-long supersonic missile that blows the leg off the Gook. And the second round would rip his arm off at the shoulder. I'd have to enlist in the infantry since the engineers didn't deliberately hunt down the little shits.

My ridiculous imagination was so full of bullshit that I could smell it. I was a joke, sitting like a child worrying about what would become of him. With my luck, the VA doctor I would see the next week would pull out a dull knife and amputate my foot without anesthesia. And what the hell if he did?

Chapter 3

VA Hospital

The VA hospital looked as much like a military prison as a hospital. It was a dull, institutional gray brick building with all the standardized Federal building signage telling you where to go and what to do. The military atmosphere made me tense. Although technically a civilian and inside a building, I worried about not saluting a uniformed officer. I expected to get my ass chewed out at any moment. My mother had gotten me to the hospital early, which was fortunate because casualties from the Tet Offensive overran the place. Beds lined the halls, and lines of guys in wheelchairs waited in front of every examination room.

After dropping me off, my mother had gone to spend the day shopping; there was no point in her waiting around. They X-rayed my foot at 9:30 a.m., but I didn't see a doctor until just after four o'clock.

A surly orderly wheeled me into a small, drab examination room painted in the usual two shades of green and left. Half an hour later, the doctor came in.

"Can you get up on the table, or do you need an orderly to help?" the doctor asked as he took my envelope of X-rays. I said I could make it and, with some effort, got my ass up on the end of the leather examination table. The doctor, who didn't look much older than me, stuck the X-rays into the light box reader on the wall, studied them, and made marks on them with a grease pen.

"You are Collins?" he asked with his back turned to me.

"Yes, sir," I answered out of habit. While he looked, he made grunting noises as though talking to himself; then after about three minutes, he turned to me.

"Lift your leg up."

I lifted my right leg up, and he pulled out a support contraption from the end of the table; and I let my foot and leg back down on it; then the doctor sat on a stool and did one badass push, pull, squeeze, and pinch exam of my foot. I suppressed my urge to winch and pull my foot away when the probing hurt, but I doubt I fooled him since my muscles twitched involuntarily.

"So two of the four incisions are still draining," he said as he pushed back from me and snapped off his examination gloves. "That's not good." He then looked at me and asked, "Have you been trying to walk?"

"No," I said mildly surprised at the question, "the damned thing hurts."

"Okay, well, the bones haven't fused as thoroughly as I would have expected. Let's see." He looked at my charts. "Wounded just before Christmas, seven months, but infection complications in Japan. They had to open you up twice." He spoke with a hollow indifference; then he dropped the chart on a small table and gave me a blunt unsympathetic prognosis. "You've had a bad one. It's getting better but slowly. Keep trying to get exercise without putting pressure on the foot. You're going to have ups and downs. The muscles are healing, but there is hardware in the way that complicates the normal process. The foot will feel strange when you first put weight on it, don't worry about a little pain. Take your meds and be back here in a month. If it changes significantly like you feel the metal moving around inside, or it gets infected— whatever— Get back here ASAP. Any questions?"

"Yeah, I've a hell of a time sleeping."

"Okay, sure," he turned to the table and took up his prescription pad and scribbled on it, ripped out the sheet and gave it to me. "This will put you out. But, be careful! If you get drunk and take a few of these, you'll never take another drink, you understand?"

I said I did. An orderly came in and bandaged up my foot in a flash, and then he let my foot down and helped me back into my wheelchair. He pushed me through a maze of halls back into the lobby. I'd spent a whole day to get an X-ray and a fifteen-minute exam.

While waiting in the lobby for my mother, I was reminded again of how damn lucky I was. Many of the guys being wheeled around were missing legs, arms, or hands. I saw one, white, bandaged mummy all trussed up in bed in what was probably the burn ward. I saw the same scene in Japan and Denver. "Carnage" was the best word to describe what was around me. I thought of a football game, wherein the players took their positions to snap the ball and froze in place for a second, and then there was a great release of energy. Bodies smacked into each other and tumbled through the air, coming to rest in a twisted and tangled heap. Just like when a squad of GIs is ambushed or hit by a mortar round. Chaos erupts. But in a football game, the guys untangle themselves, shake the cobwebs out of their heads, and return to the huddle; GIs weren't so lucky. Some were zipped up in bags and carried away while others ended up like me and the guys around me.

I wondered if the village minister I ridiculed had visited a VA hospital. An even better learning experience would be to take the holy man on a search and destroy operation, where often the pious come back in bags, and agnostics go out on another mission.

An orderly interrupted my daydreaming and asked if I would like a drink of water. I said I would, and he pushed me down the hall to the water fountain; then he pushed me back to the lobby and gave me a magazine to read. He was a good guy.

CHAPTER 4
At The Library

Chautauqua Institution's library would be a credit to a small city. The two-story red brick building stood prominently at the end of Bestor Plaza, the center of the community. White columns and wood trim gave the building a colonial New England appearance. Wide stone steps lead up to the main entrance; however, there were no sculptures of lions in repose beside the doors.

The library was a quiet escape for me. I mostly read periodicals and Civil War history books. Usually, I was at the library in the afternoon; but on Thursday, two days after my hospital visit, I spent the entire evening at the library. Just before closing, an announcement asking all patrons to check out their books to avoid the rush at closing time came over the public address system. I decided to begin my slow walk out. I wasn't carrying any books, so I took the wide central stairs down to the main floor. As I carefully worked my way down the stairs, Susan came zipping up the stairs.

"Oh, hi!" she greeted me as though we were old friends.

"Hi," I said with an automatic smile, "well, we knew we would see each other again."

"Wait. I mean, I need to get my books." She took another step up the stairs but then looked at my crutches and the other people coming down the stairs on either side of me. "You go on, but please wait for me on the benches out front. I'll just be a second."

I agreed, and she bolted up the stairs.

There were benches everywhere on the sidewalks surrounding the Plaza. I had just sat down on one in front of the library when Susan sat down beside me with her books in hand.

"Thanks for waiting," she said as she put her books aside and settled herself. "Brian mentioned you were going to the hospital Tuesday. I hope they had good news for you."

"Yes. Yes, they did." I gave my robotic response enthusiastically. "Everything is fine. I should be walking in a few weeks." Adding an extreme exaggeration didn't hurt.

"Oh, that's great! You must be sick of the crutches." She glanced at me, but sitting side-by-side in near darkness made it impossible to judge a person's facial expressions.

The last of the library patrons had filed out of the building and dispersed in all directions. I could have cut the conversation off there, excusing myself, and the two of us would have gone our own ways into the dark. But it had been polite of her to ask about my condition, and I was curious about her.

"So," I said, "what classes are you taking?"

"Oh, it's nice of you to ask," she responded as though she had wanted to tell me, "I'm taking a very interesting class that is just on Hamlet. An entire class on one play. The other class is as boring as the Shakespeare class is interesting. It's a class on teaching grammar. But the Hamlet class is a jewel taught by an old guy named Herring, who knows how to stimulate a class and is teaching us that, as well. The class title is 'Teaching Hamlet.' I wish there were classes like it at Albany."

"So you are going to teach?" I asked.

"I hope not, but I'll have teaching as an alternative. I want to do something more exciting. Journalism, broadcast media . . . I don't really know."

I didn't respond. My life was so crapped up that I couldn't give anyone career counseling.

Susan continued, "It's a busy summer for me with school and work."

"No doubt," I answered, "is the Athenaeum as stuffy as it appears?" The Athenaeum was the largest and most elegant hotel at Chautauqua. Presidents stayed at the Athenaeum when giving speeches at the Institution.

"It has to put on a stuffy appearance, but the staff is nice to work for, just regular people. They have been nice to me, letting me work only in the afternoons, one o'clock to six."

"Doing what?"

"I work in the business office, helping the bookkeeper and doing general secretarial work. But when there are staff problems, I fill in waiting tables in the dining room or making up rooms."

"Still, it is a dream come true for you."

"Oh, I do as much as I can. I don't get to the activities during the day, the lectures, and many of the speakers . . . But I make the better concerts and all the weekend events. I love it! It's been wonderful, and I had to make up transferable hours this summer to graduate next spring. I got way behind in credit hours at Albany. Did you know I was sick a number of semesters?"

I hesitated and considered mentioning the long ago conversation with Kathy; but I didn't want to mention either Kathy or Wayne, so I played dumb. "That's too bad. I'm sorry to hear that. Digging out of a hole is hard work."

Susan went on to describing having a touch of pneumonia during both her freshman and sophomore years and having to reduce the number of classes she took. As she talked, I could hear a symphony playing at the amphitheater not far from the library. The sound of her voice and the distant music mixed in the evening air reminded me of the summer of 1965 and our dates at Chautauqua.

"Well, I've got to be going," I abruptly cut her off and stood up. "If I don't get back to the room, my mother thinks I've fallen, and the wolves or something will get me."

"Oh, I bet she does worry. I've got to get along, too."

I said goodnight politely. As I made my way back along the dark narrow streets, I resolved to go to the library only in the afternoon when she was working.

Chapter 5

The Explanation

On Monday afternoon, I went alone to the Edelweiss restaurant. Fortunately, the hostess sat me at the table served by my favorite waitress; and I didn't need to ask for specific seating. I was the youngest person in the dining room by multiple generations although being on crutches helped me fit in.

My honey waitress came up to my table. "Good afternoon, Sir, may I bring you something to drink?"

I gave her a wiseass answer. "Yes, a draft beer please."

"Oh, I'm sorry, Sir. The Institution does not allow alcoholic beverages served on the grounds." There was apprehension in her voice, and I realized I'd been a dumbass and not a wiseass. She continued, "We have tea, iced tea, coffee, sodas, and sparkling water."

"Excuse me. I apologize. It was just wishful thinking. I know you can't serve beer. I'll have iced tea." I smiled up at her. She smiled in return and didn't seem offended.

Moments later, she returned with my iced tea and asked if I was ready to order. "I'm conflicted," I told her, "what is your favorite dish on the lunch menu?"

My question flattered her. "Well, my favorite is the knackwurst. It's like a giant hotdog but tastier, and the potatoes have a funny French name but are just large french fries."

"So do you and the other girls get to taste test what the chef cooks?"

"Yes, and sometimes, there are great leftovers. It's a benefit of the job." She smiled.

I complemented her black and white lace uniform.

"Oh, thank you sir!" And she squirmed a bit.

I ordered the knackwurst and watched her work the other tables while I waited. I brought a copy of the Institution's daily newspaper to read. I deliberately exchanged smiles with the waitress as I was reading. She was thinner than I remembered. Maybe her uniform was tight.

"Here you are, Sir," she said as she placed my plate in front of me.

"Oh, thanks!" I said and turned and looked up at her. "You don't need to call me 'Sir,' and by the way, what's your name?"

"I'm Eileen." She smiled and gave a shallow curtsy and then leaned down to me. "They like us to be formal here."

"Yes, I suppose they would. My name is Mike, but we can be formal in here." She smiled again and went on about her work. The crowd had thinned with only one other table occupied.

Later, when I had finished eating, Eileen came to my table. "May I take your plate?" she asked.

"Yes," I said in a normal voice but then added in a softer tone, "Eileen, what do you have planned for the fall? Going back to school?"

"Of course," she answered as she collected the silverware.

"So where do you go to school?"

"At Chautauqua High. It's just across the state highway from the Institution. I'm a senior this year!"

I'm certain my eyes opened wide. I immediately became ill at ease, expecting to be handcuffed at any moment for molesting a minor.

"Terrific!" I blurted out, "the best year of high school. You'll have fun. Do you plan to go to college?"

"No, my boyfriend and I are getting married as soon as possible. We think having a wife and maybe a baby will save him from the draft."

"Sure, sure. Certainly, it will." I was fishing in my wallet for a tip and trying to get out of there fast.

"Oh, I was wondering. How did you hurt your foot?" she asked as she put down the bill.

"A motorcycle accident. Nothing serious."

"That's good. Motorcycles are fun! I love them."

I put down a generous tip, said "Good afternoon," paid in the lobby, and got out of there. A bright sun and huge puffy white clouds greeted me outside. As I walked along, I went over and over in my mind how I could have been so far off estimating

Eileen's age. My guess was that the uniform fooled me, or I was just damned hard up.

My girl situation was becoming absurd. I simply wanted to find a moderately attractive, intelligent, self-confident girl who was friendly. On Wednesday evening, I hobbled down the hill to the lakeside College Club for their live folk music night. I knew the worst I might do was hustle a new high school graduate because the Club required proof of being at least eighteen to enter.

The rowdy atmosphere of a monastery prevailed at the College Club when I got there soon after opening time. A low platform against a sidewall provided the stage while small round tables with chairs gave a coffeehouse atmosphere. I took a table about halfway back from the stage. I would be exposed but have a better chance of talking to people at adjoining tables.

As I looked over the thin audience, it occurred to me that the kids from the well-off families simply took the old man's Mercedes or Cadillac and went to the lakeside nightclubs outside the Institution, where they could booze all they pleased.

Two guys in black turtleneck sweaters and carrying guitars took the stage. A slim girl with long, blond hair and wearing what I called a "granny gown" joined the guitarists. Later in the show, they would comment on their stereotypical folksinger image.

The crowd was, as usual, mainly girls in groups of two or as many as four. There was only one table of three guys, and they looked and acted like new high school grads. But the same old problem presented itself: how to approach a girl cold.

The performance was better than I had expected. The group called "The Wanderers" sang some of the usual folk songs, but mostly sang songs from what they called Carl Sandberg's "The American

Song Bag." The songs were work gang tunes sung to relieve the monotony of hand labor.

The College Club was a poor venue for performers with the entrance and refreshments vending area at the side of the performers. Soon after the program began, Susan and her odd duck boyfriend came in and sat at a table. She had not seen me.

Susan's being there didn't make any difference as far as my hustling a girl; there wasn't a chance of that anyway. I was trapped in a weird environment and being haunted by an old relationship gone bad.

There were no easy ways out of the room, and I didn't want to wait for intermission since Susan might approach me as I left. So, while the group sang, I collected up my crutches as quietly as possible and went out the normal, lighted entrance in view of the audience.

Working my way back up the hill to the hotel, I considered leaving Chautauqua and going back home. But then, I remembered a remark my mother made in June when we decided I would join her at the Institution. If I went home, she would quit work here to be with me. I was a damned nuisance to everyone.

I had more to worry about than getting through the summer; there was the rest of my life to figure out. Everyone assumed I would go back to school. If I did, it wouldn't be to Marietta. And what would I study? What would I do to earn a living?

An oddball alternative had come to my attention after reading about a civilian company doing business in Vietnam, as well as Africa. I might hire out as a security guard in a war zone. I wouldn't be a soldier of fortune but more like an armed thug. I might even train troops in the army of the new countries that had been colonies. I was going to research the possibility, read, write letters, and make phone calls. Shit, I knew more about light infantry weapons than anything else.

My fun night out ended with the daily ritual of washing my foot and changing the bandages. I could do it myself but had to report the condition of the wounds to my mother. I concluded my foot had improved since the evaluation by the VA doctor the week before. There was no drainage; the bandages were dry. The incisions were all of pale color, indicating no infection. It was foolish to be optimistic, but I wasn't pessimistic either.

That night, the demons came again. My dreams were a vivid horror that transported me into a surrealistic world, where the sights, sounds, and smells were alive: a transposition in reality.

In my dream, I was on an unnamed, besieged landing zone. Clearly, it was the siege of Kah Sanh. I had seen brief news reports of Kah Sanh on the TV that winter and spring while in hospitals.

The dream took place in a nearly blacked out bunker used as an aid station. There were two treatment tables—each with a wounded soldier on them and each being treated by a surgeon. The place was in complete chaos with people yelling and screaming while incoming shells exploded outside, shaking the place and raising dust.

As at the real siege, it was a marine unit in my dream. There was no explanation why I, an army soldier, was on the landing zone; but the marine officer I reported to accepted me without question. The dream got odd when the officer told me to change into a tuxedo. I acknowledged the order without surprise.

Then, just like a movie, the dream changed scenes. I was still on the besieged landing zone but was outside of the bunker, bent over running and stumbling along in a trench as mortar rounds thump in around me. I looked up and saw Susan ahead of me, standing and smiling. She wore a tartan pleated skirt and a snow-white blouse. It was the skirt she had modeled for me in her dining room three years before. I was stunned and ran to her and knocked her flat while yelling that she was nuts to be standing up. I didn't question her being there, but rather, we talked excitedly about the situation as if she were another GI.

The realistic sensation of touching her, hearing her voice, and smelling her perfume startled me awake. I jerked and thrashed in bed and then came to my senses. As usual with my extreme dreams, I awoke mad as hell and pissed off at the haunting. The worst part of the dream was touching Susan; she was so real it hurt. I felt unjustly persecuted, punished. I wanted to bust something, shoot someone; I wanted to know why I was a victim. I had done my duty but was having my sanity slowly stripped away.

I sat up in bed and reached out for my glass and took a drink of water. A thunderstorm had passed through that evening. It was still windy, and I could hear the wind in the trees and a branch slapping the porch outside my window. I read a car magazine to stop thinking of the dream. The Le Mans 24 hour sports car race in France was postponed until September because of the student riots.

I was in a funk all day on Thursday and only went downstairs for meals. My mother immediately picked up on my bad mood. "Are you feeling okay?" she asked me at dinner.

"I am now," I responded deflecting her inquiry, "I had a hot dog at the College Club Wednesday night that must have been left over from last summer, but I feel much better now."

By Friday, I had cabin fever and was ready to do anything. At breakfast, I checked out the daily schedule of activities in the newspaper and decided to go to an interesting lecture entitled "The Coming Czechoslovakian Revolution" to be given at the Hall of Philosophy that afternoon. The Hall of Philosophy was an open air venue with seating for about three hundred people. The Hall resembled the Parthenon in Greece, having the same classic proportions as that building, just much smaller. Bright white Doric columns held up a beautiful, heavy wooden frame and red tile roof. The building sat in a grove of trees with winding brick sidewalks leading to it. From one end of the building, it was possible to look out over the lake. The building was a shrine to the intellect.

The lecture started at two o'clock, but I was ten minutes late. I still had not learned that walking with crutches takes longer. I came in at the back of the audience and stood for a moment to pick out an easy seat to get to. I always had to consider my damn crutches; then I saw Susan. She sat a few empty seats in from the aisle near the back. I maneuvered into the row and sat one seat away from her.

Susan was startled but smiled at me. I leaned towards her and whispered, "How have you been?"

"Fine," she whispered back.

While I listened to the speaker drone on about Czechoslovakia, I wondered what had possessed me to sit next to her. I could have sat well out of her sight or simply walked away since I had no serious interest in the lecture; then I recalled the dream.

I wasn't superstitious, but I had never experienced such disturbing, realistic dreams as I had since coming home. It was preposterous to think that Susan would somehow end up in Vietnam. I might get back there, if I were lucky, but not her. She had to stay alive.

I sat straining to see as much of Susan as possible while still appearing to be looking at the speaker. She wore denim shorts, canvas shoes with no socks, and a white pullover blouse with narrow horizontal dark blue stripes. A stack of books sat on the chair next to her.

The speaker, who had a heavy Eastern European accent, explained how during the previous fall, a protest by students, faculty, and industrial reformers had snowballed. It led to Alexander Dubček, a reformer, to become the First Secretary of the Czech Communists Party. I was vaguely aware of problems in Czechoslovakia, but a war and a mutilated foot distracted me. After half an hour, I couldn't sit still; so I got up. But before I left, I leaned over and whispered to Susan, "I'll talk to you after."

I walked along the garden paths behind the Hall and looked out over the lake. I could see a farm across the Lake and just make out the speck of a tractor as it crossed a smooth green field. It was an ideal scene for a landscape artist.

I came back to the Hall of Philosophy when I heard the audience applaud the speaker. "So what did he conclude?" I asked Susan, who stood beside the path as people streamed past.

"He says the Russians will invade like they did in Hungary in 1956 and that, this time, we and Western Europe should help them."

"Easy for him to say," I replied, "would you like something cold to drink at the Corner Café?"

The Corner Café was a small combination of a bakery and a coffee shop with a few tables. It occupied the end of a large brick building on the Plaza. The same building held the post office and a bookstore.

Susan was happy to go along to the café, and we walked with the crowd past the amphitheater and down the length of the plaza. As we walked along, making small talk, I wondered if I had a fixation for Susan the way Gatsby had for Daisy. Gatsby was a dope. Was I a dope, too?

The ice cream parlor (also on the plaza) was crowded as usual, which was why I hadn't suggested it. We passed the institutional-looking post office with the bookstore in the basement and came to the Corner Café.

We found it crowded, too. Susan quickly saw our predicament. "Pardon me," she said, "how about if you find us seats, and I get the drinks?"

"Oh, right," I replied, "I'm no help carrying anything. Here. Let me give you a couple bucks." I began to fumble with my crutches to get my wallet out.

"Silly, go get us a place before all the seats are taken." And she pushed me along and went to get in line.

Later while sipping our drinks, Susan mentioned the program at the College Club. "So you didn't care for 'The Wanderers?'"

"Not particularly."

"That's good to hear. I worried that Frank and I made you uncomfortable."

"Oh, no, not at all. I was bored with the College Club, and you've got to admit the group wasn't great."

Susan didn't reply but glanced over at a couple our age sitting at a table near us. They were repeatedly laughing and reaching across the table to touch each other's hands.

"So is Frank one of your summer classmates?"

"Yes, and he's in my classes at Albany, too."

"Well, Chautauqua is convenient for both of you." I had taken the paper wrapper from my straw and twisted it into a long, tight string with small knots.

"Frank is from New York City and would have had a hard time here without me."

"Sure. Summer is a long separation."

Susan turned and looked at me with a crafty smile. "No, Frank is different. Frank likes other boys."

I looked like I had been slapped with a wet fish. "Oh, well, that's his business. He goes his way, and I go mine." I squirmed in my seat.

Susan's smile grew larger, and she leaned back in her seat. "Have you heard from Brian lately?"

"Not since the fourth of July," I replied and mimicked her by leaning back in my seat and looking directly at her. "We had an argument the weekend before the holiday. We got along okay fourth of July, but I feel like hell about the argument."

"What was the argument about?"

"We quibbled about why I ditched school and enlisted, eventually getting this." I slapped my leg.

"Brian doesn't understand?"

"No."

"Too bad. It's obvious."

"Obvious," I responded with a slightly sarcastic tone.

"Sure, you and Wayne were great friends. He joined a band of brothers and never came back. You wanted to join the same band of brothers as a tribute to him. Shakespeare described it in Henry, IV."

"Well, sounds like you've got it all figured out."

"Do you know the scene?"

"No, I haven't read the play."

"I'll look it up for you."

I took a deep breath and changed the subject. "I have another problem you can help me with."

"Well, I do know a few things about life," she said defensively in response to my tone.

I looked directly at her and gave her a verbal shock. "The problem is I don't know what happened to us at the end of the summer before we went off to school."

Susan's smile transformed into a serious look, and she glanced again at the couple near us. "Let's take a walk," she said.

We left the café and stepped back out onto the busy sidewalk. She led the way, and we walked out onto the grass of the plaza. Dozens of grand old maple trees ringed the plaza, so we sat under one and leaned back against the rough bark.

"I've thought about that August a great deal, and you deserve to know what my feelings were," Susan said as she plucked a rouge dandelion from the grass. "Remember that I had just turned eighteen." She continued after a pause, "I didn't plot anything out. I wasn't thinking so much as I was feeling, and I felt that I couldn't commit unequivocally. And if I couldn't commit to you, then you shouldn't have to commit to me. I understand it appears I didn't think you worthy." Again, she paused. "That isn't what I was thinking. I was young and afraid of making a mistake. The future frightened me. I wasn't able to describe my feelings then, but now it's clear. I was immature. It's unfortunate, but it was the right thing for me to do at the time."

For a moment, Susan and I watched the plaza. A young mother pushed her baby stroller across the lumpy lawn near us, and small children squealed and splashed their hands in the fountain. Old couples enjoyed the view from park benches.

"I knew I'd miss you, but keeping in touch would have been hard, taken time, and just complicated our lives. I want you to know I wasn't planning on looking for someone else."

Susan spoke from her soul as she always did, and I loved her for it.

I leaned back and looked up at the tree limb spreading out above us with its deep green leaves fluttering. "Okay, enough said. I get it. That was years ago, and we'd better get back to the present." I shifted myself, trying to find a comfortable position against the tree; then I continued on a different subject, "Brian and Beth are getting married after graduation next spring."

"Yes, it's wonderful! Beth has been planning for years. Every time I see her, she has new plans for the flowers or gowns or the reception. I'm a bridesmaid, her sister is maid of honor."

"Brian had better have a grad school slot. Shit will still be going down in Vietnam a year from now."

"Oh, God. I hope not."

I didn't reply, and after a silence, the conversation went in the wrong direction. "Kathy is engaged. The wedding is the end of October."

"Oh, that's great. I'm glad," I responded dryly. I was sincere, but it hurt to hear the news.

"She met a guy in her night class. He's from Rochester. He's a couple years older and has a medical deferment."

"That's all swell, but let's skip it."

Susan looked at me with surprise. "Okay," she said and began talking about the next weekend, "Did Brian tell you he and Beth are going to be here next weekend?"

After a moment searching my brain, I responded, "Oh, yeah. He did. He said he and Beth were coming back at the end of the month."

"Did he mention the dance band concert?"

"He mentioned a concert but didn't say anything more than that."

"Well, Beth wants to see this particular band. The band is special for some reason. She took a music appreciation class so knows the history of the dance bands around the time of World War Two."

Leaning back against the tree was getting uncomfortable. A fly buzzed around my ear. Susan had moved away from the tree and sat cross-legged in the shade.

"Would you care to be my escort to the concert?" Susan asked while not looking at me.

"Escort?" I replied.

Susan turned to me and playfully slapped my leg, the good one. "Yes, Silly, would you take me to the band concert? There's no charge."

A shaft of sun broke through the shade of the tree and flickered in her hair.

"Oh, come on. I am on crutches. Couldn't Frank take you?"

She turned away and looked out over the park. I continued my evasive stuttering. "And what about whoever you're dating? You'll have to make excuses eventually."

Susan looked over her shoulder at me with a scowl; then she squirmed around to face me. "Dating? You know I'm not dating anyone."

"I just assumed," I said defensively.

Still scowling, Susan launched into me, "You didn't read my get well card did you? That's why you didn't write back as I asked. You didn't even read it. I asked you to answer me because you hadn't answered the other letters." She stood up, slapped her hands together brushing off the grass and dust. "Did you read any of my letters? You looked like you were hiding something when we talked on the dock!" She looked down at me with disgust, as I looked up at her with a blank expression.

She immediately walked away. I started to scramble to my feet but was fooling with my crutches while she kept walking. "Hey, help me here!" I called after her, "I'm a poor, wounded vet!" She didn't stop, and I suppressed the urge to curse a blue streak. "Hey, a little help here!" I yelled again. I was about half standing when an old man stepped off the sidewalk and gave me a hand. Susan must've looked back because, when I was up and had my crutches positioned, she was a few paces from me. I thanked the old man, who smiled when he saw Susan and went on his way.

"Helpless like hell," she said and turned and began striding away again.

"Okay, I'm a rat that doesn't read his mail!" I called out and began to swing out after her on my crutches. She didn't turn around, and I knew she would keep on going. "Hey, I want to go to the concert!" I yelled, "go to the band concert with me please!" Ten yards separated us when she stopped and turned around.

She raised a hand as I approached. "Don't strain yourself any further. Okay, we can go to the concert, but I'm damn mad." She turned and took off again at a fast pace toward the school and her dorm.

"What the hell just happened?" I muttered to myself as I began the walk back to the Exeter House. The letters must have been some kind of true confession. I should have let her walk away and ended the whole thing. Supposedly, I was a hard ass combat vet; but actually, I was a jackass. Throwing the letters away was the right thing to do. Now I was messing up big time. Agreeing to go to the band concert was stupid.

Confusion and anger pushed me to a fast pace as I approached the steep downhill part of my walk. As I walked, my right crutch snagged in the grate of a storm drain along the curb; and in a flash, I was in trouble. As I pitched forward, my right leg—and so my bad foot—instinctively stepped out in front to prevent me from smacking my face on the pavement. My foot came down hard landing crookedly, half on the curb. The foot twisted and slid down into the gutter as I crumbled forward into a heap. The palm of my right hand took much of the force of the fall.

My foot didn't hurt immediately, and for a short moment, I thought I might escape the stupid stunt with no serious problems; then the pain came in throbbing pulses as though a giant invisible hand were squeezing and then releasing my foot, only to squeeze it again. No one was near me to help; so I untangled myself, collected up my crutches, and started out again. As I walked, I alternately grunted from the pain and then swore as though I were back in the army.

Fortunately, my mother wasn't home from work yet; and I went directly up to my room and took a double dose of pain pills from my secret stash. That left me with only six tablets, and I knew that wouldn't be enough. I would have to ask for a double dose every other time I asked my mother for a pill.

I flopped onto the bed and just stared at the ceiling until the pills eased the pain, and I fell asleep. Sleep was an escape as long as I didn't dream, and that afternoon, I didn't dream.

"Well that was a good nap you took," my mother commented as I sat at the kitchen table while she prepared dinner.

"Yes, and I needed it, too," I had to explain my foot hurting. My mother was telepathic, and my wisest action was to voluntarily confess to a less serious condition. "I have pain and if I swing my foot too fast and it's sensitive to the touch."

"When did this start?"

"I bumped it on a street curb as I was coming back this afternoon. It's no worse than some other times." I was truthful as long as I didn't say when it had been worse.

My mother gave me two pain pills that evening when I asked for them. I took one immediately and held out until 3:00 a.m. before I took a double dose.

The needle-sharp pains continued by Saturday morning. By the afternoon, the possibility of having to go back to the VA hospital began to haunt me. I was a big blowhard when thinking to myself that I would let them take the foot. I wanted to get well and be as normal as possible.

I only remembered generalities of what the doctors said at my visit ten days before. My pain didn't worry him, just anything unusual like another infection. The pain was the same as other times, and I didn't feel broken bones or screws pulled loose. I decided to hang on until Monday before pushing the panic button.

On Saturday afternoon, I walked down to the park and found a bench in the shade, where I could spend an hour or so. I needed to get out of my room to avoid my mother becoming suspicious. I could see the beach from where I sat, and even at a distance, it was nice to see girls in bathing suits. One good-looking girl wore a daringly skimpy two-piece suit that nearly qualified as a bikini. She was caring for two small children, so I suspected she was a nanny for one of the well-off families summering at the Lake. Fat chance I would have at meeting such a girl. Why would she care for a busted up college dropout with no money? As I sat on the bench, the clouds gradually crowded together and turned deep purple; so I hiked back up to the Exeter House before it rained.

On Saturday evening, my mother and I watched *Gunsmoke* in the communal living room. During a commercial and after other guests had left the room, she spoke up, "Would you do me a favor tomorrow?"

I hesitated slightly and took a deep breath. "I don't want to go to church."

My mother stood up quickly. "You're losing your way," she said and left the room.

My mother didn't come upstairs to check on me or say goodnight that evening. I took care of my foot as usual and went to bed. My foot felt nearly pain-free, and I hoped I might get through the night without another pill.

I needed a sleeping pill, but I didn't have one. A hammer would do the trick, too. I could whack myself in the forehead with it and go to sleep instantly.

Since I had neither pills nor hammer, I listened to the radio and read John Steinbeck's *Cannery Row*. It was one thirty when I last looked at the clock.

A dream jolted me awake at three o'clock. In the dream, I was standing knee-deep in the fast running water of a mountain stream in Vietnam. I was looking at a smoldering, wrecked helicopter further out in the water. I had been in the chopper and was the only survivor. I looked around at the dense green bush along the stream and up at the steep slopes, where wisps of fog hid the ridge line. Oddly, I didn't feel remorse for the dead GIs in the wreckage but went to work, checking my rifle and counting the magazines and clips in my flak jacket pockets. I waded out of the water and sat down in the high grass on the bank. It was quiet, and as I sat there, the reality swept over me that I was the last GI in Vietnam. Everyone was being evacuated, and mine was the last helicopter; and now I was alone. My stomach tightened, and my hands shook. If I wanted to get back to the world, I would have to wade down the stream until it hit the Song Tra Khuc River and then steal a boat. With a boat, I could go down through Quang Ngi and paddle out to an aircraft carrier in the South China Sea.

I felt as though I had suddenly moved a million miles further from home. It was a death sentence.

Watching both banks carefully, I moved on down the shallow stream; but my legs splashed the water loudly no matter how slowly I walked. I became more and more tense, just as in a good movie until the shock of hearing Vietnamese shouting in the bush woke me up.

A long minute passed as I struggled to identify where I was. Nothing made sense, and I slowly worked through the possibilities until I caught up to reality. I wasn't back in school, in the dorm; I wasn't in a barracks, in boot camp; I wasn't out on a mine sweep on a dirt road in Vietnam, and I wasn't in some hospital with busted up GIs around me. I was in a strange but safe place. I wouldn't be killed or captured.

The dream ignited my anger. I sat up in bed, found my crutches, and hobbled out of my room onto the porch, my usual escape. I was in my underwear and sweating, so the mid-summer night's breeze gave me a chill. I had been the last GI in Vietnam in other dreams but with different settings and not as intense as this dream.

As I calmed myself, depression replaced anger. In a serendipitous moment, I realized dreams of Vietnam would haunt me for the rest of my life. The revelation was that ghosts didn't wear a silly Halloween mask. The ghosts haunting me came vividly in my dreams but not as the talking, chain rattling characters depicted by Dickens.

I objected at first, protesting that I hadn't whacked any Vietnamese that I knew of. But I had directed helicopter gunship fire when ambushed. And I was part of a monstrous killing machine.

I sat on the porch, swatting mosquitoes and remembering how the killing machine worked. I witnessed a napalm strike from a mile away. My unit had not called in the strike but enjoyed watching the show; if the Gooks were that close, we wanted them dead. A small spotter plane buzzed around a steep hill, flying at treetop level. It shot smoke rockets to mark the target and then dived away, revving its engine to get out of the way; then from out of low billowing clouds came the hammer of Thor. An F4 Phantom dove, down at a steep angle, released two black tanks from under its wings and streaked away. An orange and yellow mass bursts out of the green hillside and then turned into a churning black oil fire.

The show delighted us, and we yelled enthusiastically. The entire act was repeated at another spot on the hill with the hammer coming in from a different angle. But we didn't bother watching the encore. We were on a mine sweep and had to watch the bush close to the road.

The haunting would continue till I died; and the sooner I died, the better.

After an hour of thinking about Susan, taking exams at Marietta, nearly insane army drill sergeants, incoming, outgoing, body bags, and back to Susan . . . I went to bed. Mercifully, I fell into a dreamless sleep and didn't awake until late Sunday morning.

Chapter 6

Talking In Circles

On Sunday, a few minutes past noon, I was in the kitchen preparing my breakfast. New houseguests that had arrived on Saturday were in the kitchen, and I had been asked about my foot. I gave them the BS about a motorcycle accident. That story simplified and shortened the conversation; they just thought I was a dope.

"Good morning. How do you feel today?" My mother had come up behind me, having just gotten back from church. I turned, and she put a hand on my shoulder and smiled at me.

"Good, good. Much better," I said, returning her smile. Actually, my foot felt the same as the day before. I sounded optimistic because it wasn't worse.

I took my plate of scrambled eggs and sat down at the table. I had become good at moving short distances using one crutch and carrying a plate in the other hand. My mother sat with me and poured hot water into a cup and dropped in a tea bag. "I'm having the minister of the summer congregation for coffee at three thirty. I'd appreciate it if you came and sat with us for a few minutes. He's a young man, newly ordained, so you might have more in common than with our minister back home."

I had dusted too much pepper on my eggs and had my napkin up to my face as I stifled a sneeze. "Okay, fine. I'll try to keep track of the time and come down. Come and get me if I don't show up. But I'll probably only stay a few minutes," I responded in a muffled voice. My last comment about not staying long was a mistake.

"Talking to a minister is time well spent," she replied curtly.

I didn't reply, and after a moment, she began a conversation about the entertainers booked for the Friday night concerts through the summer. We also talked with other houseguests as they filtered into the kitchen to prepare lunch.

On Sunday afternoon, I came down to the communal living room at two thirty and watched a baseball game. My mother was busy setting the table out on the front porch. A thunderstorm had passed through during the night; but it had cleared off, leaving only the humidity.

The minister arrived on time as a good minister should. He greeted my mother, and they talked for a time; but even though the window was open, I couldn't hear the conversation. Soon, my mother came in and asked me to come out and meet our guest.

The table was set with woven straw placemats and a matching set of pitcher, tumblers, and plates, all decorated with a daisy pattern. A plate of cookies sat in the center of the table, and our glasses were filled with lemonade. A cool breeze blew up from the lake, making an ideal summer setting.

When I saw the young minister, my first thought was "basketball player!" He was about six feet and four inches tall, and he was the tallest, thinnest minister I ever met. My mother introduced him as the Reverend Thomas Allenby. He greeted me enthusiastically, "Mike! It's wonderful to meet you. Just call me Tom. Thank you for spending some time with us. You're getting around well."

"Yes, better and better every day." I tried to sound convincing.

After the introductory chat came the awkward explanation of how I was wounded and the gory details of the wound. People desperately wanted to know but were polite enough not to ask specific questions. As a result, they searched for safe ways to talk about my wound.

"Are you seeing a local doctor?" he asked me.

"Not unless it's an emergency, an infection flare-up, something like that. I go to the VA hospital in Buffalo for treatment."

We talked on about the hospitals I had been in and that I had repeated infections during recuperation. I spared him the details of how cow shit on the land mine compounded the problem. Eventually, he asked the question that I had anticipated but didn't have an answer for.

"Well, since you're going to be back to normal soon, what are your plans? What do you want to do now that you're a decorated veteran?"

My mother was still at the table, so I couldn't be a wiseass and say I wanted to go back to Vietnam to hunt and kill as many of the little shits as I could. Neither did I want to talk about what my mother wanted to hear—that I was going back to school.

"I am not sure. Maybe travel, see the peaceful parts of the world. Maybe take a camera with me and take nature pictures and simply live. I'll be getting a small disability pension. Europe is cheap compared to the US. I could live there."

"If you're unsure of your future, I suggest prayer. You see, God has a plan for your life. The Lord takes care of each of us."

As if on cue, my mother stood up and said, "I'll refill the lemonade." And she took the pitcher to the kitchen.

I didn't reply to the minister but just nibbled on my cookie and sipped lemonade. The preacher was on a roll and eagerly leaned forward, putting his hand on my right arm as if to demand my attention. I didn't like strangers touching me, minister or not. I frowned at him, which he interpreted as confusion about what he was saying, so he launched into more detail.

"You will find the good news in many places, in the Scriptures. Jeremiah 29:11 and Psalms 139:16 are just two. God and the Lord Jesus know us and love us and so have laid out a path for us, and all we need to do is follow."

I responded with a nod of my head, but my face remained blank. I was thinking this minister was the same as our minister back home. I didn't want to argue with him, but then, I also didn't want to hear a repeat of what I'd heard for years.

"You see," he continued, and I knew it was time for a testimonial. "I had doubts, too, but I let the Lord take control, and my life turned around. Do you understand?"

I couldn't resist. "So the Lord only drafts heathens?"

"Oh, it doesn't work that way. It's impossible to understand why life is difficult for us. But if you ask, you will receive."

"It's a pity. About two hundred GIs a week forget to ask. And those dinks we kill, they are asking Buddha, so the message doesn't get through."

"Well, they are Communists, not Christians."

"I'm thinking of the kids that get fried when the napalm hits off target," I snickered and smiled. "Or on target."

"I want to talk about you, from where you are now, about your future. You should ask for guidance. You should let the Lord direct your life."

I had to stop being a fool and just agree with him. He was right; logic didn't apply. "Pardon me, Reverend. You're right. I'll try to be better. I haven't been sincere enough." I stood up and grabbed my crutches. "I'll go see if my mother needs help. She's been gone awhile."

I went inside and looked in the kitchen. My mother was slowly stirring a pitcher of lemonade. "Everything all right?" I asked.

"Oh, yes!" she answered in surprise, "go back out and chat. I'll be out soon."

Back at the table, I immediately asked the minister a question to get the focus off me. "Where did you go to seminary, Reverend?"

"Boston College Department of Theology," he replied, "but let's talk more about you. It's normal for a person who's been through the trauma you have to lose faith. What your mother and I want to do is help you back. Help you believe again."

"Reverend, it would be best to leave me alone."

"No. No, we can't take that chance. We must work with you to find out what helps you. We don't know what will work, but doing nothing is not an option."

I couldn't shake him, so I spouted off. "I'm not up to it, Reverend. I don't want to talk theology, philosophy, or speculate on how many angels can stand on the head of pin. The crap I went through doesn't seem so bad now. I believed in my weapon, Reverend. If I kept it clean, and I had enough clean magazines, I was okay. Nothing kept the Bible readers from getting blown to hell any more than the cursing potheads."

"But maybe they went to heaven, not to hell."

"Yes, and I heard you say 'maybe' because you have no idea."

My strained voice alerted my mother as she came up behind me.

"What's the problem?" she asked as she set the pitcher down.

To my relief the minister spoke up. "Oh, Mike and I are just having a good, spirited conversation. It's invigorating and reminds me of school."

"Yes, Tom was saying he went to seminary at Boston College."

"That's where I met my wife," Joe added.

"Oh, how interesting," my mother said in a questioning voice as she looked at me skeptically; then she turned to Tom, "Was she a student, too?"

"Yes, and she got better grades than me."

"Is she ordained?" I asked.

"Yes, but she hasn't a church, yet. Women ministers are still unusual."

"Well, wonderful. It will work out," my mother said.

"Yes, and good luck to both of you," I stood up and continued, saying "Reverend, please excuse me. I want to check on the score of the ball game I started watching."

The minister stood, and we shook hands. "God bless you, Mike! You will be completely recovered soon. I'm sure. I hope to see you in church!"

"It's possible. It's possible," I replied.

"Couldn't the ball game wait?" my mother asked, looking up at me with a frown.

"Mom, I didn't see a TV for a year, and this is a color TV." I then turned to the minister and said, "Pardon me, Reverend. I missed the simple pleasures."

I went back to the ball game, knowing I hadn't been a good host. It was a dull game, and the Indians beat the Yankees, 4-1.

My comment about watching TV wasn't a stretch. Even the car commercials were interesting. I'd missed the introduction of all the 1968 models and was catching up on what the new cars looked like.

After a time, I heard the raised voices of my mother and the minister as they said goodbye to each other. So I hobbled out as my mother was clearing off the table. "Sorry, I can't help clean up." I then added, "He was the tallest minister I've ever seen."

"Yes, and you worry him. And I don't think you have any intention of going to church."

She carried dishes and glasses into the kitchen, and I went back to the ball game.

I didn't have dinner with my mother that evening. Instead, I went to the kitchen late in the afternoon and made a couple simple sandwiches and took them and a couple bottles of soda up to my room for the evening.

CHAPTER 7

The Black Ass

My attic bedroom was warmer than usual on Sunday evening. The fan stirred the air but was no relief. I was reading a new *Road & Track* magazine and listening to my bedside clock radio. The stations kept fading in and out. One station, WOWO, was as far away as Ft. Wayne, Indiana.

The Fort Wayne station began to fade, and I could hardly hear the DJ (a guy named Bob Sievers) announce the records. I decided to go out on the porch and see if there was a breeze.

It was cooler sitting in my chair outside. The dark quiet around me immediately gave me the urge to go back inside. I fought the urge, convincing myself I wasn't on guard duty and didn't need a weapon.

The minister's visit put me in a crappy mood. I fell into the mood whenever I screwed up royally; it was my guilt mood. The mood had come over me after denting the family car and during my first night at the army induction center.

This time, I was guilty of not keeping my mouth shut, of not going with the flow. What the hell difference would it have made if I had just been congenial to the minister? And joining my mother at church was a simple thing to do for someone who loved me.

I had gone to church dozens and dozens of times. Why was I a dipshit now?

I had gotten my foot blown off because I hadn't gone to church enough, and my prayers were insincere. But Wayne wasn't worse than me; he wasn't evil, so why was he whacked? And I knew George Felton wasn't nearly as decent a person as Wayne or I. He was a pompous ass sitting in Canada, working for businesses that would make him rich like his parents. Were Wayne and I given divine punishment, or was it just simple luck? Random chance?

What the hell difference did it make? The world would blow up soon. Humanity escaped annihilation during the Cuban missile crisis, but there could be a conflagration over this Czech revolution. Everyone had more bombs—bigger bombs—and more missiles now. The world would end up as in the Gregory Peck movie *On the Beach*. I'd seen the movie and read the book.

I treated my mother poorly. I wasn't a good son. Other parents had children in law school or med school or getting a teaching certificate. I tossed my future away to go kill Gooks. Other parents had grandchildren. I couldn't get a girlfriend even before my wound. Now, I was a mess—a mess for life—and always dependent on others.

But I could fix it. I could stop being an unappreciative drag on everyone and escape the devil spirits of Vietnam, as well. I'd blow my brains out. I should have died in Vietnam anyway. Some celestial plan screwed up, and I survived. But I could fix it now. I could fix it right that night.

I hobbled back into the bedroom, feeling relieved I had solved the problem. But what a jerk I was! Did I think I'd take a .45 pistol from the desk drawer like in the movies? Where the hell would I get a large caliber handgun? It had to be a large caliber to do the job right. Shit, a weapon, would take days to wrangle up. How else could I do the job? There were no bridges to jump off, and I swam too well, and the lake was too small to swim out past my ability to swim back. That, again, was movie theatrics.

I would hang my worthless neck if I could find a rope. I looked at the sheets, but they would get you out of jail, not strangle you.

I sat on the edge of the bed, listening to WOWO, which was coming in strong again. Ivory Joe Hunter sang about life since he met his baby; then a jackass started selling used cars on Washington Street. After more thought, I decided to look for a rope in the hotel cellar. The proprietor had a workshop down there. He did all the maintenance on the building and might have a rope.

It was nearly one o'clock in the morning when I crept down from the fourth floor attic to the cellar. I had been down there to chat with the old fart, who seemed to like me; but I hadn't paid attention to where he kept anything, let alone a rope. Fluorescent lights lit the cellar, and a neat worktable sat in the middle with shelves along the walls. I walked around, looking at the tools hung on peg boards and pulled open drawers. In one drawer, I found a coil of heavy cotton clothesline. It was at least 100 feet long, and I could double it up to be sure it would hold my weight.

I was in a sweat when I got back upstairs and out on my porch. The next problem was a proper noose. I'd quit Boy Scouts before learning any knots, so I doubled up the rope at one end and fashioned a noose around my neck with a tight makeshift knot at the back. It was so tight I could hardly swallow.

I had to work fast. If I paused and thought about it, I'd chicken out. Next was figuring out the length of rope. After I stretched out fifteen feet of doubled up rope, I began to look for a tie off point. I tested the simple wooden railing, which was probably last repaired when Lindbergh crossed the Atlantic. It was all dry rot and loose. I gave a porch post a firm push, and it creaked and began to split.

Frustrated, I sat down in one of the old wicker chairs and looked around. Solving one problem after another tired me out. After all the fuss, whatever contraption I came up with would leave me in the rhododendron bushes below my porch with a broken leg, cuts, and bruises. I'd end up in the nut ward of the VA hospital and be a worse drag on everyone. I was too incompetent to kill myself.

Chapter 8

A Long Talk

I was up early on Monday morning, having set my clock radio early so that I could see my mother before she went to work. I took a "happy pill" the night before, after taking the noose off my neck.

"Good morning! You're up early," she said with surprise as I entered the communal kitchen.

"Right, nothing is wrong. I just got hungry early, I guess."

"So is your foot better?"

"Yeah, it is. Friday's problem wasn't serious," I answered her as I muddled around the kitchen.

"What's this on your neck?" she asked as she reached up and pointed under my chin. "It looks like a rash."

The rope had left an irritated, red line. "I don't know. Bug bite, pimple, or rash. Maybe it's a reaction to soap in my shirt collar."

We said nothing more about the rash, and we had a cordial breakfast. I had decided I would go to church next Sunday, sort of turn over a new leaf and be human. My mother left for work, leaving me with another boring day.

The Institution was well into its summer program. The rush and urgency of the start of the season had mellowed, and a lazy routine had taken over the colony of intellect seekers. After breakfast, I looked at the calendar of events and lectures and found nothing of interest.

Since my foot felt better, and I had stopped dwelling on my life situation, I returned to thinking of Susan. I told her I would go to the dance band concert, so I wasn't going to back out. The mystery was why she was being so pleasant to me. And why the flap over my not reading her letters? Also, she wanted me to know she wasn't dating anyone. I felt a change in the currents as a canoeist would feel when approaching rapids.

The best way to meet Susan would be to bump into her in a public place so the meeting would appear coincidental. But that would take some arranging, so I decided to meet her on her own turf and be assertive. Besides, I did need more details about the concert.

That afternoon, I took a mini bus over to the Athenaeum Hotel, figuring I might catch her as she left work. As the bus bounced its way along the narrow streets, I ridiculed myself for still dreaming of an old girlfriend who had dumped me. Her explanation for shutting me out made sense, but then, a moonstruck fool like me would believe anything. The bus ride was better than riding in an army duce and a half truck, but as always, I missed having my M-16.

The Athenaeum was the center of "class" on the Institution grounds. It was advertised as the largest wooden structure resort hotel still in use and was in impeccable condition despite being eighty or so years old. The hotel's name, Athenaeum, was a reference to classical places of learning or libraries. The building had large meeting rooms used for weddings, lectures, and commercial conferences.

The main entrance was on the side of the building so as not to spoil the idyllic view of the Lake from the front of the building. As I got off the bus, I stepped into a busy cluster of well-heeled guests and the bellboys carrying their luggage. I anxiously hobbled away from the commotion as fast as possible. I didn't belong there. After the cars were gone, and the guests and bell boys had gone inside, I came back under the red awning and looked into the lobby. Antique furniture and appointments decorated the lobby in simple elegance. Large bouquets of fresh flowers graced the ball and claw-legged tables. I expected to see Cornelius Vanderbilt and J. P. Morgan sitting, smoking cigars, and reading the financial times.

I built up my courage and went in. The lobby was in an "L" shape with the main desk, where the lobby changed direction. I went past the desk and turned and went out the front entrance onto the grand porch that faced the Lake. People had tea or whatever at small tables, so I had to turn around before some waiter accosted me. As I went back past the desk, it was obvious the reception staff had noticed the handicapped bum in the lobby. As I made slow progress back out the way I had come in, I heard a voice behind me.

"May I help you, Sir?" It was Susan teasing me.

I turned and responded, "Yes. Yes, you may. I'd like to take lodgings here but find myself short of funds. Would the hotel consider giving me a room gratis?"

Susan strained to keep up the charade. "Yes. Yes, we would. But we would need some token of security to show your willingness to pay us eventually."

"Would this priceless, five-dollar Timex watch be adequate? It takes a licking and keeps on ticking."

"Oh, yes! That's quite satisfactory!" She broke out laughing. "You're looking great. What's up?"

"Oh, I just came by to talk about the band concert, how to dress, and things like that."

"Wonderful! It's good to see you." She moved off to the side and continued, "Wait a moment, and I'll tell them I'm leaving. You can sit if you like." She motioned to a chair beside the fireplace.

I sat down and watched her walk across the lobby and go through the door with "Private Office" stenciled on it. She wore shorts, and I could swear shorts had gotten shorter while I was in Vietnam. Her chipper mood surprised me. She had been downright pissed off the last I saw her; but it was as if she either had forgotten or hadn't really been mad.

When she came out of the office, she was carrying a couple of schoolbooks and notebooks. "Let's go out the front and sit on the lawn," she suggested.

We went out through the front porch and down one side of the horseshoe-shaped double stairs and out onto the lawn. There were numerous green park benches set to provide a view of the lake.

"How's the working and studying going?" I asked as we sat down on a bench.

"Very well. Much better than I expected. I've been lucky. But how about you?"

"Fine, fine. Getting along." In a reflex reaction, I touched my throat, where I had tied the knot to hang my worthless ass.

I turned and looked back up the sloping lawn to the hotel. "Wow, the hotel has a terrific view of the lake! The front rooms must be expensive."

"They are, but the whole place is expensive. The money people have is incredible."

In front of us was a grand panoramic view of the lake. The bell tower, community beach, and College Club were off to the left. A white Cape Cod style building sat at the water's edge. This was the "Sports Club" and was where you could rent a small sailboat or rowboat.

We talked about the dance band concert, and she assured me I only needed to look neat to get in. Susan said that there would be a lot of old people our parent's age, but that young kids were getting into swing music.

Two squirrels chased each other across the lawn in front of us and zipped up a tree. "Well, that's he chasing she, or he chasing he who was chasing she." Susan was polite and chuckled. I leaned forward and put my elbows on my knees, clasping my hands in front of myself.

"About what you said of my not writing you, I'm sorry I didn't read the letters. I apologize."

A moment later, she responded, "Well, they were mostly personal, self-serving letters anyway."

"I read the first letter about Wayne. Thanks. Sympathy helps. I knew we were all hurting, and I should have thought of you and other friends, not just myself."

"Now that you say it, my other letters were a kind of request for sympathy and understanding."

"Just so you know, Kathy told me you had a difficult second semester. I dropped the ball on that. I should have encouraged you."

"Well, I didn't welcome any contact from you. My later letters tried to make amends for that, but I understand your feelings and why you didn't answer."

"Neither my first nor second semester were worth shit," I said, leaning back on the bench. As I spoke, I realized that it was the first time I had sworn in her presence. "Pardon my military vocabulary."

"No harm. I'm a long way from high school. Looking back, I realize my first semester was abnormally easy, and I hit a wall in the second semester. It's easy to dig yourself a hole, and I'm just now getting out of it. I got behind in the number of hours to graduate."

"Well, Kathy said you got sick. You couldn't help that."

"Oh, I was sick, but there were other personal reasons. You might say I was sick at heart, too."

I didn't respond, so she continued, "Sorry," she said while turning her head from me. "I shouldn't be talking to you about disappointment."

"That was then. This is now," I said which meant nothing but sounded good.

"You're polite."

"What happened to you is none of my business."

"I tried to make it your business."

Neither of us spoke, and I realized how quiet it was even though there were people around. All I heard was the wind and the birds in the tree above us.

"I've learned a lot in school that isn't in textbooks," Susan continued as she picked up one of her books, thumbed the pages, and put it down again.

"Oh, congratulations," I replied.

"Don't be mean. I wasn't talking about sex."

"Look, I don't know how I can help. I've got my own problems," I said as I squirmed on the bench and took a deep breath. I didn't want to hear about the guy, who replaced me.

"So you still won't listen, just the same as with the letters." She got up abruptly and walked away but only a few yards and stopped beside another tree.

I stood up and leaned on a crutch. "We learned the last time I can't come after you even when I want to, and I want to."

Susan came back with a frustrated look and sat down.

"Forgive me. I've developed a crust over the last couple years. I want to help but feel helpless," I spoke to her in a conciliatory voice.

"Listening helps."

"Okay, I wish I could do more than that, but go ahead."

"I've learned there are a lot of fakes, a lot of selfish and mean people."

"True," I said to encourage her.

"There's a reason why I'm telling you all this. You see, you've haunted me these past two years. You haunted my relationships with other guys. I always compare them to you, and they come up short."

"I'm sorry you've been hurt. Truly, I am. The best I can suggest is that you keep on trying. Now, you know what to look for. You'll spot the selfish collectors quicker."

Susan didn't respond to my comment but took a deep breath and continued, "Tom helped me with class notes while I was sick. We dated through the spring of my freshman year, and he came to see me twice during the summer."

As she spoke, I remembered being in basic training at Fort Dix, New Jersey, that summer. I didn't interrupt her but watched the sailboats.

"But when we got back on campus in the fall, he was definitely cooler towards me. Then he told me he was taking someone else to homecoming, and that was that."

I surprised myself by blurting out, "Asshole!"

"That's accurate," Susan responded with a laughing tone, "I think the commitment frightened him. But maybe, he just found someone he liked better. But you see, I always felt I could trust you that you knew yourself and wouldn't be false to me."

"Polonius," I said without looking at her.

"Yes, obviously. And as true now as then." After a pause, she continued, "I mentioned this in my first letter to you. Anyway, I swore off men for quite a while. I had many friends that were boys. Just no boyfriend."

Susan stopped speaking and looked over at me. "I shouldn't be talking to you about this. Are you sure you don't mind?"

I did mind, but I wasn't going to admit it to her. "No, no, continue if it is helping you."

"It is. I've talked to Kathy and a couple close girlfriends at school. It does help." She looked back out at the Lake and continued, "I saw the two of them on campus. She was better-looking, sexier, more extroverted than me. But this is an important part. I was more upset at being rejected than with losing Tom. Kathy said that I didn't really like the guy, which wasn't true. I liked him, but just liked him and that's all. Does that make sense?" She turned and looked at me.

"Sure, absolutely! I knew a number of girls at Marietta just as classmates, friends to talk to. And we went out as a group and had a good time."

The sun had moved around, and our shade was getting thin. I suggested we walk a bit and then find another bench. We got up and walked along the sidewalk and passed a large white Greek revival style house. Four, tall columns with Corinthian capitals graced the front. A large, blue sign with white lettering over the double door entrance announced "Chautauqua Women's Club."

"Impressive," I said.

"Yes, but let's sit down again. I've only explained one of my letters to you."

This time, we sat close to the water, at the end of a dock. We could hear the small waves slapping against the boats and the quacking of ducks swimming under the dock.

"I need to tell you about Allen," she said anxiously as she turned to me, stretching out an arm and gripping the bench near my shoulder.

"All right," I said flatly.

"So the difference with Allen was how he changed. I met him through a roommate the spring of my sophomore year. I know it's terrible of me to run on like this, but since I started, I have to give you the whole story. Allen fooled me, and that scared me. I seriously question my judgment of men after he changed."

"Sounds like you were serious about him."

"I was. I was. I thought he could be the right person for me. The relationship became serious last September. By October, he offered me his fraternity pin. I thought pinning a bit immature, like a high school ritual. But he was so charming, and I accepted."

As she went on, I thought of the Elvis song about wearing a ring around your neck. Listening to her was beginning to sound like a soap opera. I was in a monsoon, and sleeping in trucks mired in mud while Allen was putting a pin on her. "Yes, I understand," I said automatically so she would know I was still listening, even if I didn't understand.

"So after that, he began to change and not just a little. I became his prize, and when we went to a fraternity party, he would show me off. You would think that flattering, but he began to order me around and criticize how I dressed and even simple things like how I crossed my legs. Would you believe! I put up with it for a few weeks. But homecoming was no fun at all. He wanted to pick out my dress. The worst was he assumed that getting pinned was the same as getting married, so he expected me to be his sex toy!"

I interrupted her, "You don't have to go into detail. I get the picture."

"Yes, you're right. Well, I gave his pin back and told him he had become obnoxious, and women were not going to put up with that kind of behavior."

"You probably weren't his first victim."

"No, probably not, but it's depressing. I don't know what attracted me to him. He wasn't like you. You've never been possessive. You treat me with respect, as an equal. You're passionate but not aggressive."

I squirmed on the bench. "Consider this," I said to cut her off, "you've had two guys very interested, so you've got what it takes. And it's just a matter of time."

She ignored my comment. "Now you know why I wrote you."

"I wouldn't have been much help given the situation I was in. But I should have answered. I have no excuse."

"I worried about you. I cried when you enlisted."

"Cried?" I responded turning to her, but the bell tower chiming five thirty drowned out my voice.

Susan stood up abruptly and spoke over the chimes. "I've got to be going. I study in the evenings. Can you make it back to the Exeter House?"

"Sure, I just take my time." The chimes had stopped.

"Fine, then, I'll go up to the hotel and catch a bus. It's been great talking. I'll see you Friday night if not before." She strode off across the lawn, carrying her books. Out on the lake, a beautiful antique mahogany and chrome motorboat purred rapidly past pulling a guy and girl on water skis.

CHAPTER 9

Reconciliation

Walking back to the Exeter House with crutches should have taken no more than half an hour, including a long rest. The walk took me over an hour because, each time I stopped to catch my breath, I thought of Susan and the mess I was in. So Susan wanted to relight our fire. After years of singing the blues over Susan, I was worried instead of thrilled.

Susan had compared the person I was in high school to her boyfriends. She didn't know who I was now. I wasn't the nice boy I was in high school; nice boys don't spend days in a drunken stupor with a whore named Gypsy. Gypsy didn't know what a gypsy was, but then, I may have been the first to ask about her professional name. The military made sure she was at least sixteen. Gypsy knew her business and taught me how to make her happy, which made me happy. I wondered if I should tell Susan about Gypsy.

As I walked along the edge of the lake, I watched old folks playing shuffleboard at the courts beside the Sports Club. They were old as dirt but were more mobile than me. One of the old farts wore red and white stripes that reminded me of a barber pole.

After another fifty yards, the crutches began hurting my hands and armpits; so I took a break and sat on a bench by the landscaped model of the Holy Land. I looked over at the dock, where I had run into Susan while the rest of the gang rowed their boat. The gang hadn't set up a meeting, but they knew she and I would bump into each other and kept me in the dark.

I fell into a trance while sitting on the old green wooden park bench. I didn't see the calm lake, blue sky, and white clouds in front of me. I would have preferred to hear a helicopter, a "slick" making its flap, flap, flap sound as it skimmed a few feet over the Lake. I wanted to see the stone-faced door gunner look down at me as he draped one arm over his M-60 machine gun.

Susan didn't know how bad my foot was and what that meant for the future. The past months of slow recuperation convinced me I would never walk, run, or play like others my age. Susan was an active girl. What if she wanted to ski?

Susan telling me about her boyfriends pissed me off. They were wimp shits, and I hoped their draft boards got them as soon as they graduated. I'd take them on 10-mile mine sweep in ninety-degree-heat and pouring rain and then ambush their sweet asses. We'd do something like that every day for a year and see how nuts they became.

I would like to wake them up with incoming mortar rounds for three or four random nights a week. They would have to drag their sorry asses out to the bunker line and get eaten by mosquitoes for an hour while they wondered if Charlie was done with them for the night; then do the mine sweep the next day.

After a few months, I bet they would be as crazy as I am now. I bet they would have those sweet dreams I have, and they would be nervous, walking in the open without a rifle and maybe even try to hang themselves. If they got home, they might confuse themselves by wanting to go back to Vietnam and finish business by blowing away a few little shits. Susan didn't know who the hell I was now.

A happy all black cocker spaniel, dragging its leash behind, bounced up to me and sniffed at one of my crutches. I smiled, wishing that I were as happy as the dog. A woman's voice called out from behind me. "Skipper! Come here, Skipper." Skipper took off toward the voice.

I was getting hungry, so I got up and continued on toward Miller Park, where the College Club public beach and bell tower were. As I began walking through the park toward the street leading up the hill to my rooming house, I noticed a covey of four girls lying on towels in the sun near the public beach. I sat on a bench from where I could inconspicuously watch them. They appeared over eighteen, but after my waitress incident, I didn't trust myself. They had a radio, and I could faintly hear the Beatles singing "Hey Jude."

Watching the girls led me to think of Susan. It was easy to imagine being with her again, talking, loving the way we had those few months. I could start my life over again, go back to school, and lead a typical collegiate life. I would get credit for my freshman year even if the grades were mediocre. The hard part would be deciding what I wanted to do for a career and what to study.

But all that was silly thinking. I'd be three years behind Susan, an impossible gap. But, was my imaginary life as a war correspondent or photographer any more realistic? The reality was that I was a mess and shouldn't involve anyone else in my mess.

The bathing beauties left without my noticing. The sun was much lower, and I was hungrier than ever, so I went up the street to the Exeter House, leaving my future until after dinner.

On Tuesday evening, I was at the library, hoping to see Susan. The more I thought about our talk in front of the hotel the day before, the more I felt I had to come clean with her. She had compared the person I was in high school to the guys she met, not the person I was now.

I situated myself on the first floor, in the periodicals section so I could watch the main entrance. I was reading a New York City newspaper mounted on a long stick. On the second page, a headline reading "Landing Zone Mary Ann Overrun by Enemy," snapped me to attention. I knew of an LZ Mary Ann in my area of operation in Vietnam, but I hoped that this was another with the same name; then I read that the LZ was in Quang Tin Provence, and I knew it was the same one. I remembered a helicopter operations clerk telling me that the chopper I was to get on would land at my LZ and then go on to Mary Ann and then LZ San Juan Hill. I never saw LZ Mary Ann, but I knew it had to be similar to mine and all the others. The landing zones reminded me of forts in western movies, isolated, surrounded by hostiles, and millions of miles from home.

I managed to read the entire first paragraph of the story. Thirty-three GIs were K. I. A., and many were wounded. The attack came on a foggy night, and the sappers had a complete run of the place. Being overrun made gunship and artillery support confused and ineffective. It wasn't a battle as much as it was a deadly bar brawl: person-to-person, face-to-face, hand-to-hand killing. If they could overrun Mary Ann, they could have overrun my LZ any time they had wanted. I felt hollow and cold inside as I hung the newspaper back on the rack. I hadn't seen Susan come in, and now, I didn't feel like talking to her. I would have to catch her the next day.

The news about LZ Mary Ann crapped up my sleep that night. I had two short dreams, each unrelated to the other. A common theme in the dreams was confusion and anxiety. In one dream, I was riding in the back of a truck taking me back to a night defensive position after working on a remote road repair. My truck broke down, but the other trucks kept going. My dreams were not rational since a small group, as in my dream, would not be left behind. But in the dream, the squad and I set up a perimeter and spent the night straining to decipher every sound and every shadow. I woke from that dream, made my way to the bathroom and back, took a drink of water, and (fortunately) promptly fell asleep.

Around dawn, I had a second short dream. I was on guard duty on an LZ under attack. A flickering white arc light from parachute illumination flairs turned the scene into a black and white terror movie. There were Gooks clearly visible, trying to get through the wire in front of my bunker. I fired on them, ejected an empty magazine from my weapon, but dropped the loaded magazine as I tried to slam it up into my rifle. I groped in the dark, trying to find the magazine; and the anxiety woke me up.

On Wednesday afternoon, I took one of the small blue and white buses to the corner of the Institution, where Syracuse University had classrooms and a dormitory. After missing her at the library, I hoped to find Susan at her dorm. I had gotten there before Susan would arrive from the hotel, which gave me time to walk around and look at the buildings. After a few minutes of walking, I realized there were more students on the sidewalks, carrying black music instrument cases than on a typical campus. A tall attractive redheaded girl, carrying a violin case, walked past while a talkative guy, carrying a trumpet case, trailed along beside her and yacked in her ear. The trumpeter was trying to get into the violinist's pants, but from the blank expression on the girl's face, he didn't have a chance.

Students walked in and out of several buildings, but I had no idea what the buildings were: dorms or classroom buildings. Sidewalks crisscrossed every which direction, and I realized that finding her dorm wouldn't be easy. I walked along Palestine Ave. and came to the Fletcher Music Hall, took another narrow tree-lined street, and walked past the rambling multiple buildings of the Chautauqua School of Art. Nearby was Lincoln Dormitory, but across the sidewalk was a building called a residence hall. I became pissed and decided to hike back to where I got off the bus and forget what I was going to talk to Susan about. On the way, I passed the school of dance and a separate building dedicated to drama. Many of the facilities were named for their rich patron. I suspected one. Sheldon Hall of Education might be where Susan took classes.

After more confused walking, I inadvertently found myself back at the bus stop. I was tired and found a bench nearby in the shade of a tree that was much older than me. I was sore from walking and deep into a sour mood. At first, the buildings impressed me; but now, I was resentful that I couldn't be part of such a wonderful place. My only talent was for killing Gooks, which I hadn't done enough of. I couldn't blow a trumpet, but I could blow a booby trapped dud 105mm artillery round with det-cord and C-4 explosive. While I sat on the bench in Chautauqua, New York, there was a good chance a GI was bleeding to death on the floor of a dustoff flying over Vietnam. I had gotten my ride in a dustoff. None of the lucky shits I saw around me could say that. And whose fault was that? The draft board would have left me stay in school. My grades were good enough.

I heard and then saw a bus coming, so I got up and made for the curb. The bus pulled up, the door opened, and Susan stepped out.

"Oh, hi!" she said with a smile as she stopped beside me.

The bus driver left the door open for me, so I waved for him to go on and turned to Susan. "Hi! Well, you've had a long day."

"Yes. Yes, I have. It's a pleasant surprise to see you though," she replied with a tone and look that demanded I explain myself.

"So I thought that it would be a good idea to come over here and see just what this part of Chautauqua looked like and maybe—and if you didn't have to hit the books right away—you could show me around this island of the fine arts." My rapid chatter put me out of breath, and I grinned at Susan.

"Wonderful! I'd be happy to," Susan responded with a smile. "First, let's go to my room, and I'll change."

I noticed that she was wearing the same white blouse and blue skirt she had at the hotel, and I assumed it must be some kind of uniform. We walked across a small open park area and came to the back of one of the buildings I had seen previously. It was Lincoln dormitory, a small two-story masonry and glass building. We came into a lounge area furnished with comfortable chairs and a TV. "Would you mind waiting here while I change? You can come down to the room after."

"No, fine, take your time."

While I waited, both guys and girls came in and went to their rooms. "A coed dorm. What a great idea," I thought to myself, "Marietta will have this next century, maybe."

Susan came back down the hall dressed in shorts, tennis shoes, and a T-shirt. "Okay, would you like to see my room?

"All right, I assume it's permissible."

"It is, and it's great. We are treated as adults."

"So there's no dorm mother?"

"No. No restrictions at all."

We walked down the hall and into her room. It was decorated in typical dorm quality modular furniture, desk and chair, dresser and closet, and two beds. One bed had a bare mattress.

"So no roommate?" I asked

"No, and that's great, too."

I didn't sit down but congratulated her on her good fortune, then said, "So let's go see where your classes are."

We walked along another shaded sidewalk to a single-story, wood frame building with a portico around three sides. The sign at the main entrance read "School of Theatrical Arts." Half the building was an open room with a stage on one side. "The dance school uses this room when they need extra space, but it's for rehearsals and acting classes."

Across the hall was typical classroom and we went in. "So this is where I learn about Elizabethan literature."

I manipulated my crutches and sat in one of the wooden desks, desks identical to the old ones at Marietta. "You sound like you enjoy it. That's good! Ever went to act?"

"No, never. I enjoy the literature, myths, and histories. Shakespearian characters are real and contemporary."

"They should be," I commented while looking at the graffiti on my desktop. "People still react to the same motivators. Love, ego, greed, fear of death . . ."

"Yes. Yes, that's true," Susan replied and then paused and turned to me. "Are you going back to Marietta this fall?"

"Oh, hell no!" I shot back without looking at her.

"It doesn't have to be Marietta," she replied with a slightly defensive tone.

"It doesn't have to be any school. Hell, I'm way behind. I'd graduate in 1971 and be twenty-five. You're graduating next spring."

"I've had a lot of GIs in my classes. It's changed since you were in school."

"I don't know what I'm going to do. This is a good point to consider all kinds of alternatives—both crazy and sane."

After a moment, she responded saying "Like a fresh start. Something different. I can understand that." Her voice was hollow, and she continued, "What crazy options have you thought about?"

I relaxed and leaned back in my seat. "The CIA has operations in Vietnam, Laos, Cambodia, all over. They need hired guns as much as spies. I saw them flying around on an airline that's a CIA operation, Air America. I'm well-trained and experienced. I'm only trained for war. My foot would have to get better."

"Sounds exciting," Susan's voice was not enthusiastic.

I ignored her deadpan. "Sure, the CIA's a long shot, but maybe, I could be a war correspondent, or photographer . . . something that would get me back into the action. I miss combat. I know that sounds strange, but combat is the big game. There are no bigger games and no higher risk. It's a big bad world out there with the emphasis on bad. It's strange that I'm drawn to it, drawn to the bad. There is an addictive, evil beauty to war. Vietnam is an exotic, oriental nightmare. Everything is different. Everything. The trees and plants, topography, farming, dress, culture . . . And the people are tiny, little shits you can't trust even while looking at them."

"You remind me of the characters in the James Jones book, *From Here to Eternity*."

"I don't expect you to understand what I don't understand. War isn't like a normal job. Combat cements camaraderie. Our lives depended on each other. If that book depicted men bound by the misery of war, it was accurate." I realized that I was rattling on like an overly dramatic TV announcer. "Pardon me. I'm getting carried away."

"That's understandable. You've been under immense stress. And you didn't mention your wound and all the time in the hospitals. Civilian life, especially life here at Chautauqua, must seem trivial, even bizarre."

I wanted to change the subject. Portraits of English and Irish authors lined one wall of the classroom. The drawings included Shakespeare, Dickens, two females that may have been Jane Austen and George Elliot, Dickens and the unmistakable James Joyce. While looking at the portraits, I asked Susan if she wanted to visit England.

"Absolutely!" she responded emphatically, "it will be hard coming up with the money, but I'll do it. I'll get there. I'm encouraged by getting here."

"You certainly have perseverance," I said as I stood up and gathered my crutches. As we left, a rehearsal was starting in the large hall. "What's the play?" I asked.

"Our Town."

"A great play," I replied, "I especially enjoy where the guy and girl talk between their bedroom windows. I bet the guy had binoculars to watch her."

"You're terrible!" Susan said jokingly. "I like the graveyard scene."

"Too spooky for me."

As we walked from the building, I checked my watch. It was five fifteen. I wished I could just keep walking and talking to Susan, but I hadn't been serious enough with her.

"Have you seen the opera house?" Susan asked before I could control the conversation.

"No, I'm already impressed, but I would like to see it."

We walked along Pratt Avenue, sharing the narrow street with bicyclists and other walkers. I realized that it was the route my bus had taken earlier.

After walking about 100 yards, I began to slow; and Susan slowed her step for me to catch up. "Do you like to ski?" I asked.

Susan glanced at me as we went along at a slower pace. "I've never tried it, but it would seem like fun if done slowly. I think I would enjoy gliding along, something like ice skating."

We came to the opera house, so I did not continue the conversation. The opera house, formally named Norton Hall, was a heavy-looking Art Deco building made of poured concrete and painted white. The impressions of the wooden construction forms were still visible in the solid slab walls. Four square columns connected by round arches created a portico at the entrance. Molded into the concrete of each column was a group of characters dressed in classical Greek robes and with ancient hairstyles. The characters on each column held symbols representing one of the four fine arts: drama, dance, music, and the visual arts.

We went up the steps into the cool shade of the portico and tried each of the five pairs of tall wooden doors, but they were all locked.

"Let's try a side door," Susan suggested.

"No, I'd rather not. If the front is locked, they don't want anyone in. I've used up too much of your free time. I should be going."

"Nonsense!" Susan replied sharply, "you appreciate the arts, and I enjoy walking around and showing you the place."

"Yes, but you have to study." We were walking back to the street.

"Not as much. Now, I'm working on a paper."

"Well, that may be even more work."

"Hey, I've got an idea. How about I cook dinner for us? The dorm has a small kitchen. I was going to cook spaghetti for myself. Want to join me?"

"That's tempting, but I need to get back to my room and get my pain pills. I've walked too far today. Can we do it another day?" I regretted the encouraging remark. Having dinner together would just be the start.

"Sure. Any day." After a moment of silence, Susan spoke up, "Why did you ask me about my liking to ski?"

"Because I'll never be able to ski. I'll never walk normal, play tennis, things like that."

"Will you be able to swim?"

"Yeah, I suppose so."

"And you'll drive a car and be able to walk normal distances?" she asked.

"Yes, but I'll be different."

"And different is always bad, and absolutely no one likes slightly different people."

"I don't live in a dream world," I said.

"And neither do I."

There was no point in continuing the conversation. We were almost to the bus stop. "So what is your paper on?"

"Shakespeare from a modern feminist perspective."

"Oh my!"

We came to the bus stop and stepped into the shade. We talked about her paper until we heard the bus coming. The approaching bus reminded me of why I'd come to see Susan. "Nuts, I meant to ask for details about the concert Friday."

"Well, come over for dinner tomorrow, and I'll tell you the details. Come around five thirty." The bus pulled up, and we walked toward it.

"No, I won't be able to make it," I said and stepped closer to the open bus door.

"Why not?"

"We'll end up in your bed. That's why." I stepped up into the bus and smiled back at her.

On Thursday afternoon, I resisted the temptation to go over to Susan's dorm and have dinner. I questioned my sanity, but trying to get her into bed—successful or not—wouldn't do either of us any good. My worthless life was at another major decision point. So far, my decision-making stunk. I had to be careful since she was not the girl I knew in high school any more than I was the guy she knew in high school.

The Jonathan Winters Show came on at 8:00 p.m., so I went down to the common living room early to get a seat close enough to see the television. My mind was blank as I watched the commercials when I noticed a figure come in the entrance and then come toward the living room. It was Susan. I jumped up and went over to her while using only one crutch.

"Hi! Well, this is a pleasant surprise."

"I'm returning your surprise visit from yesterday."

"Come on. Let's go out on the porch."

We went out onto the porch and sat in a pair of chairs hidden by shadows. The evening air carried the faint melodies of a concert at the amphitheater to us.

"Have you been working on your paper?" I asked, referring to a set of books in her hand.

"No, these are for you," she answered as she passed me two paperback books.

I held them up to catch light from a window and read the books titles. They were catalogs of classes at Albany.

"You mentioned journalism and photography yesterday. Albany has classes in both."

I paused and then said in a hollow voice, "Albany is an excellent school, and I'm sure the classes are top-notch. But we talked about this yesterday."

"And you said you wouldn't go back to Marietta but were considering both crazy and sane alternatives. A degree in the professions you mentioned would give you a better chance at a good job doing what you want, where you want. These class descriptions are just examples. You don't have to go to Albany."

"I wish I were sure. Sure of something, anything. I doubt that I could sit in a classroom for hundreds of hours, studying any subject with all these loose screws rattling around in my head."

After a pause, I lifted my arm and pointed to a house across the street and slightly down the hill. "See that? See the cigarette?" I asked Susan. The house was dark, except for one lighted window on the second floor; however in the dark, that was the front porch. A cherry red dot bobbed and, occasionally, held still while it glowed brighter and then continued its jerky movements. I continued, "If that guy were on guard duty, he'd be a perfect target. I was on guard with dopes that smoked and with dopes that smoked dope. It's no fun waiting in the pitch-black for the Gooks to shoot up your bunker. I was always aware, always ready, or tried to be. But something went wrong, and I got this." I slapped my bad leg. I realized I was going off my rails. "See, those are the loose screws rattling around."

"Sure, you're just back and still recuperating. You've gotten a lot better and will be fine soon."

"I don't know. I just don't know. School takes a lot of work."

"And you won't know until you try."

"You need to understand where I'm coming from, why I am the way I am. Vietnam, any war I suppose, is clean and uncomplicated. Kill the son of a bitch before he kills you. Wars are won or lost, just like a football game. What I'm saying is I still want to be in the game, to whack some V.C., and that kind of thinking is out of place here. I'm out of place. It isn't normal to sit on this porch, listening to distant symphony music while fantasizing about getting a scrawny, little shit in your rifle sights and cutting him in half with a long concentrated burst. In school, jocks dream of scoring a touchdown and getting a piece of ass off a cheerleader. I want to catch a squad of NVA, crossing a rice paddy and call in an airstrike to barbeque them with napalm." Susan didn't respond immediately, and I thought maybe I had finally gotten through to her.

Susan raised a hand and objected, saying "You know World War II vets around the village. There are lots of them, normal people. You've heard of all the vets that flooded the universities after the war. Some of our high school teachers were vets that went back to school. They adjusted and so will you if you have the guts for it."

Her emphatic challenge irritated me. "Oh, let's forget it. Whatever goes down goes down. It doesn't make a piss-ants difference what happens to me," I quickly continued before she gave me the typical encouraging reply, "what about the concert tomorrow? Where should I be, and at what time?"

"Bullshit!" she shot back, startling me as she stood up. "You won't change the subject that easy. What happens to you makes a world of difference to me, your friends, and your family. You're selfish with your life. None of us live just for ourselves. Your life isn't yours alone!" I looked up at her and remembered an elementary school teacher, who would tower over me. She continued, saying "Be at my dorm at five o'clock. We're all meeting there, and we will cook a simple dinner and then go to the concert."

Susan walked off the porch, and I stood up and took a hop to the porch railing. She turned and walked up the hill, back past me. I could see her shadow and hear her footsteps. "Good night!" I called to her in a conciliatory tone, "I'll see you tomorrow!"

"Goodnight," she responded flatly from the dark.

Well, shit, I thought while still standing at the porch rail. Whatever I do will be wrong to someone, to myself, to my parents, or to Susan. If I couldn't make everyone happy, maybe I should do something no one, including myself, wanted me to do. I could do nothing and become a drunken bum. There were men my parent's age around the village who were lost weekends. Some of them were likely war vets. In the army, many of the "lifers" were drunks. Some old movie claimed drunks were citizens of the world.

Instead of going back inside, I hopped back to my porch chair and got my crutches; then I hobbled down the steps to the street. I considered making it all the way over to Susan's dorm, but instead, I turned left and went down the hill to the park and the lake shore. The College Club was busy, and I heard Credence Clearwater Revival singing about a green river. I went behind the bell tower and walked out to the end of a small dock and sat on a bench. The lake was a dark floor stretching in all directions. A string of lights reflecting off the water marked the far edge of the lake. There were no boats out for a romantic cruise.

I had deliberately come to a quiet spot, hoping to get ahold of myself and make a decision about my future. The damn future. It was always just in front of you, demanding all your attention. People yelled at you about the future, but no one knew for sure what the future would be. We all speculated, made guesses, and based on flimsy evidence, gave each other advice. I asked myself a series of questions without answering any of them. "What were my dreams when I went off to Marietta the fall of '65? What were my dreams before the war, before we lost Wayne?" Finally, I thought to myself, *What would Wayne want me to do?*

I sat listening to the sounds of night birds, insects buzzing, and the creek of the dock as I shifted my position on the bench. No booming voice came across the water with the answers to my questions.

CHAPTER 10

The Concert

I didn't know when Brian and Beth would get to Chautauqua, so I went about my Friday morning as usual. After I cared for my foot, which was getting much better, I went down to the kitchen for a bowl of oatmeal. The Institution published a daily newspaper featuring a full schedule of events and background stories of the lectures and performances. I found a copy of the day's newspaper in the kitchen, and I read it while I ate. There was a story about the "Swing Revival Band" describing the band as bringing back the golden age of the big bands such as Glenn Miller, Tommy Dorsey, and other names I didn't recognize. My father often played Miller and Dorsey on our Hi-Fi at home, so I knew the music.

On that afternoon, I joined the usual crowd in the periodicals section of the library. There was a middle-aged woman I suspected of being a school teacher (maybe high school English). She was neat as a pin and took notes as she read magazines. There was an old man, who regularly fell asleep in one of the comfortable chairs. Every crowd had a similar cast of characters, just as every school class had a class clown and a dedicated student that was irritated by the clown. I always took on the character of the suspicious observer, who was afraid to comment.

According to the newspaper I was reading in the library, one hundred and ninety three G Is had bought the ranch the previous week in Vietnam. That was two companies and eight platoons, going home in a bag. Oh, Graves Registration gave them nice aluminum boxes. I saw the boxes on a C-130 at the Chu Lai Marine Air Station for the ride up to Danang; no flights to the world left from Chu Lai.

The other news was of the political conventions coming up, the Russians twisting the Czechs arm getting ready to stomp on them. I had changed my mind and decided that the US wouldn't help the Czechs since that would mean a two-front war for a new president. The best news was what hadn't happened; there were no assassinations in over a month, and no cities were burning, for now.

A thunderstorm was threatening when I came out of the library, so I moved along smartly going back to Exeter House for lunch. I came down the grade, walking in the middle of the narrow street when, just as I got to the steps to the house, a voice called out to me from the porch.

"Better hurry or you'll get that foot wet!" It was Brian, and he was sitting on the porch in one of the same chairs Susan and me had sat in the night before.

"You're early!" I said as I came up the steps. "Hi, good to see you," I said as I stuck my hand out, and we shook hands.

"Yeah, I gave up a day of work. We didn't want to rush down here. It's more relaxed this way."

"Swell. Good that you did. You've missed driving in the rain." I propped my crutches up and sat down in the other chair. Purple clouds churned overhead, and the wind blew the trees into a swaying dance.

"Hey, I hear you're taking Susan to the concert," Brian commented.

"Brian," I said in mock seriousness, "so far, women and war have defined my life. I can handle war better than women." I paused, and then continued, "Susan may not be happy about going with me now. She was here last night, and somehow, I irritated her. And I'm now on her shit list."

"Oh, that happens. Here. Have a beer." Brian took a beer and a glass off a small table beside him and gave them to me. "I met your mother just as she was going back to work, and she saw I had brought beer. She suggested we drink from a glass while out here in front of the house."

"Thanks. This is great. Yeah, it's true. Many people drink, but no one makes it obvious."

"You were getting along well, coming down the street. When will you be able to put some weight on your foot?"

"Yeah, it's feeling much better. I'll be told about walking at my August visit to the VA hospital."

After more small talk, Brian went in to get a couple more beers. When he got back, I put the screws to him about his future. "So are you planning on taking the GRE exams in the fall and going to grad school?"

"Yeah, of course. I think I'll get into a good school. Maybe stay at Kent. I want to get an MBA."

"Good. Because draft boards are stingier and stingier with education deferments, especially for people who've already had four years," I cautioned.

The first fat raindrops of the thunderstorm started to splash down, and the few people out on the street scampered for cover.

Brian spoke again, saying "It looks like the war's going to drag on and on."

"Damn right, and don't believe any of the presidential candidates. They won't stop the meat grinder." I turned and looked at Brian. "You know, I still think deferments are okay."

"Sure, I know where you're coming from."

"I understand both the guys that got caught like Wayne, and the guys like you and me, who got deferments. I especially feel sorry for the unlucky bastards that are both poor and slow whittled. They are sure to be ground pounding grunts getting their shit blown away."

"I'll be okay," Brian replied, and I knew he wanted me to skip the subject.

"Well, if you get in a jam, enlist for three years. That way, you can choose what you do in the army. And, obviously, don't choose a combat specialty."

"Three years. That's a shitload of time."

"You bet your ass," I agreed.

"You know, you should be proud of what you did. You stood up and put your ass on the line and so someone else didn't have to. Don't you feel good about what you did?" Brian was serious.

"Oh, crap. Come on," I replied, "it's all chance, all dumb luck. There are hundreds of thousands, eventually millions, of guys our age who'll get scooped up into the meat grinder—I like to call it a meat grinder—and it's dumb luck who is sucked in and who isn't. It's just luck that you've been able to avoid it and that luck could change."

"You're right. You're right. Still, you should be proud of what you did, what you've sacrificed."

I chuckled and gave Brian a string of bull about combat. "We had a truck driver in the company, who survived having three trucks blown out from under him. Other than a ringing in the ears and slurred speech, he didn't get a scratch. Then there was a Puerto Rican kid that got a load of shrapnel in his ass during his first week in country. He went down into a ditch to check and see if the Gooks had put a mine through the culvert, out under the road. The Gooks booby trapped the ditch. He tangled his foot in the trip wire and, instead of freezing and calling for help, he turned and bolted. Tripping the wire was bad luck. The grenade being under water and sunk in mud was good luck." I paused a moment and looked at Brian. "Go figure. Luck. It's just dumb luck I'm still here, just dumb luck."

The rain came down like a cow pissing on a flat rock, quickly forming streams in the gutters of the street. The rain cooled the air to the point of being chilly, and the air was fresh and clean and wonderful to breathe in. The thunder grew closer until the lightning flash and thunder crash were almost simultaneous. We didn't try to talk; both of us were enjoying the show.

The rain stopped half an hour after it began. Minutes after the rain stopped, the sun was breaking through, and the pavement in front of Exeter House began to dry. By four o'clock, the teenybopper girls came out to show off as much skin as their mothers would allow.

According to Brian, the girls were planning an Italian dinner for us. Brian was to drive the gang to the grocery store, so he left for Susan's dorm as soon as the rain stopped. I declined Brian's invitation to go with them and stayed in my room, deciding what to wear to the concert. I discovered that what few new civilian clothes I had were in the laundry, leaving me with three-year-old shirts from high school. I hobbled around the bedroom, opening drawers and looking in the small closet. The radio was playing "Sunshine of Your Love" although crackles of a faraway lightning interrupted the song.

The clothing situation frustrated me, and I flopped onto the bed. I was twenty-one; I could vote now, but I didn't have decent clothes to wear. I didn't own a car as Brian did. I'd accomplished nothing toward a future; Brian had three years of school and great prospects for more. I did have a crapped up foot and a set of small, blue leather-covered boxes. One box contained a trinket in the shape of a heart with Washington's profile on it. The other boxes had trinkets and ribbons and came with citations yacking about meritorious service. None of it qualified me for a job. A kid coming out of high school who learned how to weld a good bead in shop class had better qualifications than me. In the horse race of life, I was trailing the pack by many furlongs.

I fell asleep for a time. I had a series of short dreams, like flashing images across the screen of my mind. One image was of being back in high school, standing at my locker, watching the commotion in the hall between classes. I drove a car in another scene. There were other quick impressions, including one of being in the army,; and all the instant dreams had a similarity. I was anxious, nervous about something in each dream, but the reason for my anxiety wasn't explained.

A knock on my door woke me, and my mother came in with clean shirts and pants. They were the new clothes, and I wouldn't look like a dope at the concert.

A bus dropped me off near Susan's dorm at five ten. I hurried across the lawn that was still wet from the rain. The sun was still strong (though lower in the summer sky), and the heat and humidity reminded me of Vietnam. At least, I didn't have combat gear loading me down. Too many damn things reminded me of Vietnam.

I expected to see the gang in the lounge, chatting away. Instead, there was only one couple that I didn't recognize sitting on the couch. As I came in and looked around, the guy, who was tall and athletic-looking, stood up and stepped over to me.

"Hi, are you Mike?"

"Yeah. Hi, I'm Mike," I said as I reached out my hand, and we shook.

"I'm Tom and this is Teresa," and he turned to her and smiled. Teresa smiled at me and gave me a little wave. "We're friends of Brian and Beth. Teresa is Beth's roommate."

"Oh, I'm glad to meet you. Good. The more, the merrier," I commented as I made my way to an easy chair, sat, and put my crutches where they wouldn't be in the way.

"Everyone else has gone to the grocery store," Tom said as he sat down, "we thought we would wait for you so you wouldn't think everyone abandoned you." He was wearing a blue knit shirt with an alligator embroidered on it. He looked sharp with crisply pressed khaki slacks and penny loafers worn without socks.

Teresa wore stylish clothes, too. She was attractive but not stunning with shoulder-length, brown hair; and she wore wire-rimmed glasses. She looked slightly frail.

"Have you been to Chautauqua before?" I asked.

"Yes," they responded in near unison; then Tom elaborated, "We've each been here at one time or other, but this is the first time here together."

"Well, I'm impressed that they get big name attractions this far from a big city," I responded to make small talk.

Then Tom asked the usual question. "How did you hurt your foot? It must be serious."

"Oh, a silly accident," I answered, "it's nearly healed, and I'll be walking on it soon."

"That's good. The crutches must be a nuisance. Are you at Kent with Brian?"

"Oh, no. No, I'm not," I answered and twisted in my chair and looked out the front window. "I wonder what could be keeping them. I'll just go out and see if they are walking in from the parking lot." I gathered up my crutches and went out the main entrance.

After a few minutes of standing in the shade of the dorm's porch, the Falcon drove up, the gang piled out, and everyone began talking at once. Brian opened the trunk, and they hauled bags of groceries past me into the tiny kitchen.

Susan gave me an amorous smile as she passed and said, "I'm glad you've come!"

I took a deep breath and followed the group inside. A great commotion broke out in the kitchen as the three girls searched for pots and pans and utensils. After unpacking the bags and putting the beer and wine in the refrigerator, Brian spoke up. "I've got to take the car back out to the parking lot. So don't drink up all the booze before I get back."

"Hey, I'll join you," I piped up.

"Oh, why not stay here and help out?" Brian answered, while giving me a questioning look.

"I won't slow you down coming back in. I'm fast enough. Besides, I'm in the way here."

Mike looked at the group. Tom was completely involved with the cooking. "Yeah, fine, let's go," he said.

While we were driving out of the Institution, I thanked Brian. "I appreciate you getting me out of there. Crowds like that make me nervous."

"That wasn't a crowd," Brian replied, giving me a glance.

"Well, I don't know Tom or Teresa."

"You're going to have to work on social skills before going back to school."

"There's no damn school in my future. Fuck school. Everyone yacks about school."

Neither of us spoke again until after we parked the car and we started walking back. Brian had to park way out on a grass field since the Friday night crowd had filled the paved parking lots.

"Beth and Susan were chatting about you in the grocery store," Brian said as we stood waiting for a traffic light to let us cross the state highway at the main entrance to the Institution. "I think they are plotting something for you."

"Just my luck," I replied.

"Just good luck, I'd say. Bad luck is when girls don't talk about you," Brian said as we walked across the street with a group of old folks out for a hot night on the town.

The girls had made amazing progress on dinner by the time we returned. "Wow," I exclaimed as I poked my head in the kitchen. Cooked hamburger filled a bowl; the spaghetti and tomato sauce were steaming on the stove; and Beth carried the salad past me to the table.

"Wow?" Susan questioned me. "This is the simplest dinner possible. Here. Try this," She put a slice of french bread to my mouth.

I felt more useless than usual as everyone worked to set the table and bring the food out from the kitchen. Susan spoke to me often, making me feel part of the festivities.

"Come and get it!" Beth called out as she placed the last bowl on the table. We all gathered with our partner and crowded up to the table. It was a cozy feast since the table would have been small for four, and we were six.

After we sat at the table, and just as the guys were preparing to plow into the food, Teresa spoke up. "Hold on. Let me say a quick blessing."

Both Brian and I pulled our arms back from preparing to fill our plates, folded our hands, and bowed our heads.

"Thank you, Father, for our beloved friends gathered at the table tonight. We will remember this evening with fondness for the rest of our lives. Thank you for the food we are about to eat, and please provide for those who have none. Amen!"

Everyone thanked Teresa for the blessing, and we began the feast with wine pouring. The girls had chosen Italian Chianti and

Spanish sangria. I had vague memories of my parents serving one or the other of the wines, but like the other two guys, I would have been happy with a beer.

"We're going to need a candle for this bottle when it's empty," Tom said as Teresa poured the Chianti from its basket-weave-covered bottle. I chose the sangria for no particular reason.

As we began to eat, the slurping sound of spaghetti being pulled up into the mouth went around the table, eventually triggering a snicker. That got us all laughing, and laughter became more common as we drank.

A short conversation began about ethnic foods. "There are French restaurants, Italian, Mexican, and some German. But how come there are no English—that is, British—restaurants?" Beth speculated to no one in particular.

"Because English cooking is meat, potatoes, and vegetables. It's what we all eat. It wouldn't be unique enough to call it English, so we call it home cooking," Susan suggested.

As we ate, my knee bumped Susan's; but she did not pull her knee away, and I smiled at her. We remained in a knee embrace for the rest of the dinner. Sex was driving my better judgment.

Brian began a semiserious conversation with Tom. "What are you going to focus on this year? Finance? Banking? Maybe operations management?"

"I've put off business operations as a subject, but I should take a class. I'd like to get into financial markets and investing."

"So you want to get rich on Wall Street?"

"Sure!" Tom admitted.

I knew Wall St. was in New York City, and that's where the money was. Beyond that, my financial knowledge ended at my checkbook—when I had one, before the army. Discussing senior year classes and careers continued, with Teresa describing her plans. "My dream is to go to Paris and get into the fashion industry," she said.

Susan leaned to me and whispered, "She's a French major."

"Brian and I will be at a graduate school," Beth contributed in a happy voice, "hopefully, I'll be able to get a job at a local public school."

"Oh, wedding bells! That sounds wonderful!" Teresa blurted out, and at the same time, I noticed Tom look toward the ceiling. "Isn't it wonderful that we don't have to worry about getting pregnant like our mothers? That must have been awful." Teresa's face contorted in disgust.

My interest perked up as I wondered if there would be an admission of who was on the pill and so, who was getting it regularly? But, after all the girls raved about modern contraception, the discussion turned to the concert. "I'm looking forward to this!" Beth exclaimed, "I've heard this music all my life, and it's fun to dance to. I may sound old-fashioned, but I bet everyone will enjoy themselves tonight. Most importantly, this is not Lawrence Welk kind of music. It's fun. It's swing."

Someone noted the time, and we were late. The cleanup consisted of piling everything in the kitchen and sponging the table, so the lounge area didn't look like a dump. No one needed to change clothes, but the girls made a long visit to Susan's room to put on makeup.

Everyone filed out the door and began the walk over to the amphitheater. Susan had suggested she and I take the bus, but I had refused. The buses ran slow just before a major event because all the old folks took ages to get on and off. So Brian and Beth were to save room for us on the buttocks-numbing wood plank benches, and everyone walked on ahead of us.

The sun was low, the shadows were long, and the summer evening air was delightful. "Dinner was great. I enjoyed it. That was the happiest meal I've had in years, honestly," I said to Susan as we passed the opera house on our way to the main plaza.

"Thanks. Beth and I, and I assume Teresa, enjoy doing that once in a while." We took a few steps and Sue continued, "why did you tell them you had an accident that injured your foot?"

"Oh, to save pointless gas bagging. They wouldn't have understood what happened, however I explained it."

"You seemed cool to them. They are nice people."

"Absolutely, I'm not criticizing them. They are lucky people that haven't shared my experiences, and it's hard to talk to— to communicate with them."

"I haven't been in a war. Am I hard to talk to?" Susan asked as we approached the plaza and blended into a steady stream of walkers headed for the amphitheater.

"No!" I answered positively and glanced over at her. "You sincerely care. You want to know me, as hard as that is."

"I'm glad you realize that."

"So," I said with emphasis, "did you tell them what happened to me?"

"No, Brian did. Both Tom and Teresa were sympathetic, even humbled."

"And probably pissed that I snubbed them."

"No, they weren't. As I said, they are nice people."

I was anxious to talk about the pill after Teresa mentioned it at dinner but couldn't think of how to start a conversation. Finally, I just blurted out a comment. "I wonder if Teresa is Catholic. If so, the Pope will disappoint her when he forbids the pill."

"Yes, I've heard he will. Teresa might be Catholic. I could ask Beth. What Teresa said is true about the pill creating other problems."

I immediately wished I'd kept my mouth shut, but I went ahead and responded to her prompt. "Such as?" I asked.

"If sex becomes so casual, how will couples demonstrate the depth of their feelings for each other? Having sex will be no more a demonstration of love than a kiss."

The sidewalk became crowded as we neared the amphitheater, and I hesitated to say the word "sex" for fear of getting a dirty look from some old maid. "You're right. I agree the problem is getting worse, but then, there has never been certainty in love."

Susan didn't reply, and we continued moving along with the flow of concert goers.

We came to the amphitheater and entered through a gate and walked to the back of the top row of seats. The semicircular venue was below ground level, and steep ramps lead down to additional seating on the level area at the bottom. An orchestra pit and stage were at the focal point of the curved seating. An impressive array of glistening silver organ pipes covered a wall behind the stage.

Open seating created competition for the best viewing locations. Columns holding up the amphitheater's roof created blind spots, and so, the audience jockeyed to avoid those places.

Susan and I walked along the top perimeter, looking down into the seated crowd, trying to find the gang and our seats. We spotted Brian waving to us, and we went down to them. The seats Brain saved were on the end of a row so I could set my crutches alongside my seat, and we didn't have to interrupt people with my awkward mobility.

"A lot of gray heads in the audience," I whispered to Susan as we sat down. She suppressed a chuckle and nodded her agreement. This was the largest crowd I'd been in for years, so I twisted in my seat looking in all directions, watching for any threat. Not having assigned seats led to milling around, shuffling, and squeezing to find an open seat. People saw my crutches at the end of our aisle— and maybe my bad foot—and so, latecomers didn't try to crawl over us.

As the band took their places onstage, old farts continued creaking around, looking for seats. Precisely on time, an attractive blonde woman in a flowing, sequined evening gown stepped on the stage and approached the microphone. "Ladies and gentlemen, good evening! I'm Constance Pardee, and I, Jimmy Rose and the entire 'Swing Revival Band' is happy to be with you this evening. So let's go! Swing it, Jimmy!" She turned, and the band leader gave a wide downbeat with his baton. The saxophones, followed by the trumpet section, belted out a rousing flurry; and then the entire band exploded into "In the Mood." The beat lifted the audience into a roar of approval. I grinned in pleasant surprise and immediately started bouncing my good leg to the music. Susan lit up, too, and we smiled at each other. A hardworking bass player stood in the middle of the band and thumped the beat. The band also swung their instruments in choreographed unison: up and down, left and right.

The song ended in a final blast of trumpets, and after the applause calmed down, the bandleader encouraged the audience saying "You are in the mood!" And everyone cheered. Jimmy introduced the next song, "Bugle Call Rag," and the tempo didn't slow. Later, the lovely lady who started the program came onstage accompanied by two other attractive women and they sang "How Deep is the Ocean." The other women wore floor-length gowns, too, but with bare shoulders. All three wore large bouquets on their left wrists. Seeing the flowers reminded me of the corsage I gave to Susan for our prom.

Next, they sang "It's Been a Long, Long Time." It was then that I realized World War II inspired many of the songs played and sung that evening. I blamed my ignorance on my youth. After the trio sang "kiss me once, kiss me twice, kiss me once again," I leaned over and surprised Susan with a kiss on the cheek. She took my hand and whispered, "It *has* been a long, long time."

Intermission came as a relief since the evening was still warm and muggy, and sitting with hundreds of people made it worse. It seemed as though the entire crowd wanted to leave to get refreshments. I took up my crutches and got, as quickly as I could, up and out with Susan behind me. Teresa volunteered to hold our seats until one of us got back to relieve her. The crowd spilled out into the narrow streets and, while I stood under a tree, Susan went to get us something to drink. We had become separated from Brian and Beth.

"Having fun?" Susan asked me when she returned and handed me a paper cup of ice and coke.

"Yes. Yes, I am. Thanks for asking me along," I answered, "and thanks for waiting in line for the Cokes. Someday, I won't be as helpless."

"No, you won't, but sometimes you act as though you don't realize that."

"Sorry. Think of when you were sick your freshmen year. Didn't it seem as though time just crept along?"

"Yes, and people encouraged me. Beth and Kathy phoned me often. So, you do realize you're going to be fine?"

"I know I'm . . ." I stuttered, almost using one of my typical vulgarities. I began again. "I know I'm messed up, and many of the problems are permanent."

"And I know you will get along just fine," she replied and raised her cup and touched my cup in a toast.

"I wish there was some rum in these Cokes," I said, and Susan smiled. "Say, why didn't you add to the dinner conversation and tell us what you hope to be doing after graduation?" I asked.

"Why didn't you?"

"Come on, don't try to avoid my question. Besides, I'm not graduating in a year. What are your plans?"

"Journalism or something like it. I have an uncle who works for Xerox, and he claims technical businesses need good writers because the eggheads can't always express themselves. According to my uncle, it's possible to learn how to apply a technology by writing about it."

"The army uses publications called Field Manuals. You could get a job with the Department of Defense and make those usable."

Susan looked at me and said, "Whatever I do, I don't want to do it alone."

"I understand that, especially since I've been alone for the last two years."

Susan continued to grill me, "Now, I answered you. So it's your turn. You won't be graduating, but what do you want to be doing next year?"

"I can't say because I don't know." Using one crutch, I hopped over to the trash bin while holding my empty cup with my other hand. "Come on. Let's get back in there before the music starts."

"Wait a moment," Susan said as I took up my other crutch leaning against a tree. "Let's have ice cream together after the concert, just you and I."

"Fine, but let's go somewhere other than The Creamery. Half the audience goes there after the performance."

We agreed to go to the café on the veranda of the Athenaeum Hotel and, then, joined the streams of people packing themselves back into the pews.

We found that Brian and Beth switched places with Tom and Teresa. After sitting, I leaned forward and looked past Susan to Teresa. "Thanks for holding our spots. Are you enjoying the show?"

"Oh, you're welcome and yes, it's great! How's your foot doing?" Teresa asked.

"Good, it's good. It helps a lot to be able to stretch my leg out into the aisle." Susan and Teresa talked about music as the house lights dimmed.

The show started with a thumping beat from the bass drum; then trombones joined in, repeating the beat. After one refrain, the trumpets blasted in quickly, joined by the saxophones. The drums held the piece together as a virtuoso musician, for each instrument soloed the refrain. The audience gave each soloist rousing applause. This went on and on until, finally, the entire band became quieter and quieter; and I thought that the song was ending. But the entire band erupted in the swing beat, finishing the song with a blast.

The audience cheered and applauded, and the band leader came to the microphone. "What was the name of that song?" he shouted.

"Sing, Sing, Sing," many of the older audience shouted back.

Susan leaned to me and commented, "I'd say our parents had a good time in high school."

Her remark left me imagining my mother and father swing dancing to "Sing, Sing, Sing." I couldn't imagine my parents dating. They never talked of what they did as kids other than casual comments about school friends. Logically, they and even my grandparents must have hit the same bumps in growing up as I did. I wondered if either of my parents was jilted by someone—someone they sat at family dinners thinking about. My parents' life experiences didn't matter. I would bounce along through life just as my parents hadn't learned or benefited from my grandparents' lives.

During a pause in the music, I heard laughter and commotion from behind us—up in the entrance plaza—that ringed the seating. When the next song started, I heard cheering; and I looked back to see that people were swing dancing behind the top row of seating.

I nudged Susan and said, "They're dancing up, behind us. Want to go watch?"

She twisted and tried to see but looked puzzled; then we noticed a few people leaving their seats and going back up and out. She looked again and then back to me and nodded. Susan spoke to Teresa, and soon, others looked back to see the dancers. "Let's go,"

Susan said to me, and I shuffled with my crutches; and our group left to watch the swing dancers.

Dancers and their admirers filled the sidewalks around the main entrance to the amphitheater. To me, the dance moves seemed similar to rock and roll, with more jitter to them. The dancers pumped their knees high to the rhythm, sometimes waving with their free hand. At the end of a push apart, the partners imitated a snap, flinging their free arm out. The overhand twirls were graceful, sometimes ending with crossed arms and the girl pressed back against the guy. We enjoyed the exhibition, and I envied the guys. Susan and Beth were talking, and I heard something about four, four time. That meant nothing to me since I knew more about rocket science than music.

We remained outside the venue for the remainder of the performance, rather than push back to our seats. Gradually, the other two couples drifted away from us. Susan stood close to me as I, typically, leaned back against a tree for comfort. Down onstage, the trio sang a number of touching tunes, such as "I'm Getting Sentimental Over You." As that played, Susan turned to me and smiled. I gave a weak smile in return. I knew I was getting swept over the falls.

Later, another song matched our circumstances. "We'll Meet Again" contained the lyrics "We'll meet again. Don't know where, don't know when, but I know we'll meet again some sunny day." I smiled at Susan and said, "And that was here. And that was fourth of July."

Eventually, to the audience's disappointment, the program came to a close. Jimmy and Constance came to the microphone, and Jimmy spoke first. "Thank you, thank you! It's been wonderful to be with you, and sorry we don't have Champagne bubbles." The audience laughed, and he gave additional appreciative remarks. Constance announced the final song, "At Last."

The trio sang, "At last, my love has come along. My lonely days are over, and life is like a song."

Now, I regretted making comments about the lyrics of earlier songs. I watched the dancers as they embraced, moved, and turned to the music. Fortunately, Susan didn't make any comment either. How on God's earth could I lead a normal life?

The crowd erupted at the end of the song: standing, cheering, and clapping. The performers took a couple bows, and finally, Jimmy came to the mike and said, "Okay, we love you, too! A few more, a few more. Let's start with 'Night Train.'"

The song was melodic, a blues tune. Without a pause, the band ran directly into "Two O'clock Jump." Then came "Tuxedo Junction" and finally a rousing repeat of "Sing, Sing, Sing." The audience stood through the encore and let out a cheer for the obvious favorite song of the evening.

The ovations were enthusiastic, but now, the crowd wanted to get out of there as fast as possible. As people shuffled past Susan and me, we realized we hadn't kept track of the others. We debated just going to the hotel, but not wanting to be impolite, we searched the crowd for a moment until I had an idea. "I know, I'll raise my crutch and wave it around."

Momentarily, Brian and Beth came up to us. "What do you think? Wasn't that great?" Brian asked, smiling.

"It was!" I replied, "but why did Elvis get such a bad rap for wiggling around? That was vigorous shaking and squirming with a good deal of body contact."

"Yeah, true. And that was fifteen, twenty years before Elvis," Brian agreed.

Susan spoke up. "Say, Mike and I would like to take a walk, so if you would excuse us, you guys can go back or whatever you want. We'll be back at the dorm later."

Brian and Beth both gave suppressed smiles and told us that they, Tom, and Teresa had agreed to get ice cream at the crowded place I wanted to avoid. They gave us a cheery "Good night" and went on their way. I had the feeling I was walking out on a mine sweep; something bad may happen.

The flood of people had evaporated by the time Susan and I took a short walk down a sloping street beside the amphitheater to the Athenaeum Hotel. Clusters of people stood and sat in the lobby as we walked through. The clientele appeared to be all my parents' age but were more expensively dressed than my parents could afford. The men looked bored, which reminded me that there was no booze sold at Chautauqua. We walked through, past the main desk, turned, and passed the brass-trimmed doors of the darkened dining room, and out to the front veranda and the café.

"Hi, Sue!" a woman's voice called; and a young waitress wearing a large white apron, giving her the appearance of a European waiter, came up to us.

"Hi, Betty!" Susan responded, "are we too late for desert?"

"No, there's still half an hour to go, unfortunately for me. Did you go to the concert? How was it?"

"Fun! Really fun! People danced and everyone had a good time, even people our age."

"Oh, I hate working this shift on the weekends. Will this be okay?" Betty had shown us to a table at the railing and so giving us a view across the dark lawn to the lake.

"Oh, great," said Susan as she stepped around the table to the other side of me. I leaned my crutches against the railing, and we sat down.

"What may I get you?" Betty asked. I decided on maple walnut ice cream, and Susan chose strawberry.

Betty left, and after a moment, I asked Susan about her sister. "Say, you haven't mentioned—and I haven't asked—what's your sister up to?"

"Oh, a lot! You wouldn't have heard, but she was a handful for my parents after I left. According to my mother, our driveway was like a parking lot for guys' cars during her senior year. We've stayed away from each other during the summers. She has finished her first year at SUNY Binghamton and plans to study drama and be an actress. She is crazy enough to be a good one."

"What did you do summers?"

"We do have a lot to catch up on. Both summers, I worked for Xerox in Rochester and stayed at my grandparents' house in the city during the week. And what about you? You were in New Jersey the one time I wrote you, and then you went somewhere else before going overseas, but I don't remember where."

"Missouri, Fort Leonard Wood, in the Ozarks."

Fortunately, Betty served our ice cream; and I didn't have to elaborate on my time lost in the woods. The evening was humid with no wind. The evening was dark with it being just past a new moon. Two other couples were having coffee and ice cream on the patio. The younger of the couples seemed disinterested in each other, and I wondered if they had children asleep up in their room. The older couple was dressed formally as though there had been an opera or ballet performance. As we ate, we passed comments about the ice cream, the mosquitoes, and the humidity.

"I could eat a steady diet of that," I said as I finished and put my spoon down.

"It was great. It reminds me of when, during the summer, my parents would take us to Jenkins Dairy for ice cream. That was before the franchise stores moved in."

Betty returned and took our dishes. "I'm sorry, but I can't offer you more. It's past eleven, but you can sit here as long as you like," she said.

"Okay, I think we will linger a bit," Susan answered. I paid the tab, and Betty cleared the table. Immediately, my hands felt empty with no silverware to fiddle with. To pacify myself, I pulled a pen from my shirt pocket and began fingering it.

Susan reached down and brought her small purse up on the table. "I have something that you gave me that I'd like to return to you," she said as she opened the small purse.

Her remark snapped my lazy mind to attention, and I watched her hands. *I hadn't given her a ring so this couldn't be a big breakup scene,* I thought.

I saw a flash of red between Susan's fingers as her hands moved from her purse to in front of her. She moved her hands away and said, "Do you recognize this?"

I stopped breathing, and a chill struck me, making my hands twitch. I saw the crimson, velvet pouch with gold drawstrings that I had given her on our last date. "Yes," I replied in a flat voice.

"You said it might mean something someday," Susan said in a calm voice as she pulled open the pouch, spilled out the four pieces, and began assembling them into the word "love" but written vertically. "I do look at life differently now, and love—your love—means the future to me." She turned the small puzzle such that I could read it and slid it across the table to me.

I touched the puzzle and a strong déjà vu sensation swept over me, rendering me speechless. My mind was blank, and I struggled to say something. Anything. Finally, I spoke up. "I recognize it but never thought I'd see it again." I looked up at her and gave her a faint smile.

After long seconds of looking at each other, Susan reached out for the puzzle. "I know it's a shock," she said as she started to pull the puzzle back.

"No!" I said urgently, and I put my hand on hers, holding the puzzle in front of me. "I'm surprised." I broadened my smile and grasped her hand. "I never expected . . ." My voice trailed off.

"No, you wouldn't have. My letters would have given you a hint though." She gave me a wink.

"Yes, I'm sure. That was my screwup," I answered. I recovered enough to begin speaking intelligibly. "If I were the same person I was when I gave you the puzzle, I'd know what to say, what to do. But now . . ." I didn't say any more.

"Now, you're different. I'm different. Three years have changed us, especially you."

I didn't respond but continued to search for words, for understanding.

"Soldiers have been coming home with problems since the first soldier left home," Susan continued.

"We haven't been together long enough for you to understand," I replied. We continued to hold each other's hands.

"You're the first soldier I've welcomed home, and I'm not a psychiatrist, but I do understand human nature. I've studied people intensely through literature and deliberate observation. I know a lot about your situation. I bet you have trouble sleeping."

My eyebrows twitched, but I continued to look down at our hands covering the velvet pouch.

"And I've seen your discomfort in crowds. You look around as though you expect something to happen."

"Damn right!" I said, looking up at her.

"The reading list of one of my classes included *All Quiet on the Western Front*, a powerful book. Do you know it?"

"I've heard of it and know it's psychological, not heroics."

"And I bet you're not anxious to read it. Have you read anything since being back?"

"I've reread Steinbeck. But books can't describe—" I didn't finish my comment before she cut me off.

"No, but I've studied my own reaction to stress, being sick, and having to slug it out at school. School is no piece of cake."

"No, it isn't. I'm sure you haven't had an easy time."

"You aren't seriously interested in the future, going back to school or a profession. I see your fatalism over and over again. You don't think you can control your future because, for years, you couldn't. Am I right?"

"Not entirely," I finally objected to the amateur head shrinking. "Anyone that's been in combat knows you control your fate to a degree. It's possible to improve your odds of survival. Most of what you say is true though I don't apologize for who I've been made into."

"Yes, just as you say. Now, you do have control over your life. Circumstances have changed you but the real you, the Mike I knew, is there and can get back to normal." Susan looked at me intently, while I looked down at our hands. She continued, "I'm trying to point out that you have a normal condition, given what you've been through. I want you to admit that soldiers coming home do beat the problem. The problem has been written about since Homer."

"Oh, for Pete's sake, I'm not Odysseus!"

"And I'm not Penelope. The point is I can help you, and you can help me. I'm lonely. I want to share life, to love," Susan replied in a strained voice. She pulled her hand back, leaving me holding the bag. She continued, but calmly, saying "I realize it's been nearly three years since you gave me the puzzle, and your feelings for me may have changed. I do think you need help and support from someone."

I looked at her with a pained expression on my face. "My feelings haven't changed. I love you just as I did then. That's why I'm afraid of getting you wrapped up in my problems."

"Well, stop trying to do a far, far better thing than you've ever done and help me." She put her hand out, and I took it.

I felt an odd sense of relief as though a grave danger was past, and I was safe. I needed to walk, to move around. "Come on. Let's take a walk," I said after a moment, and I stood up. "Oh, damn it to hell. Where are my crutches?" I grabbed one, and Susan came around the table and handed me the other. We made our way down the front steps of the hotel, just as we had in the afternoon two days before.

A warm summer wind blew up from the lake, carrying the fresh smell of the water. We walked down across the grass to the street running parallel to the shore and, out of habit, turned to the left and walked toward the College Club and bell tower. The reflection of lights on the water showed the lake to be flat calm.

"I wish I could hold your hand," I said to distract from the odd creaking of my crutches.

"There will be plenty of chances for that. Tell me if you want to stop for a rest."

"I'm okay for now. Well, it's summertime, but the fish aren't jumping," I said looking out at the calm water. "And no one around here raises cotton."

"It is a nice night, but don't worry. I'm not going to cry."

To our left, across lawns and past trees, were other hotels with lights on. We could just hear the faint conversations of people out on the porches, escaping the heat of their rooms.

As we walked, my initial flash of romantic excitement faded, replaced by cold reality. We came to a pool of light under a street lamp, and I stopped and turned to Susan. "Tell me. Where does this leave us now? I need to know. I made a mistake before."

"We're in love. You said you love me, and I do love you. I want to spend the rest of my life with you. I'm a woman now, and I love as a woman."

She stretched out both arms to me, and I balanced on my crutches and reached out and took her hands. We kissed lightly and embraced, and she stayed close to me. "You are real, aren't you?" I asked her in a mock pleading voice, "you're not a mirage or a delightful dream, are you?"

"You don't need to flatter me even though I like it. You, especially, know how real and flawed I am."

We embraced again, and I awkwardly kissed her as I began to lose my balance. "I'll be better at that when we're sitting," I said.

"Or, as I remember, reclining." She playfully poked me in the ribs.

We walked out of the light and continued through the dark to the brightly lit College Club. "Let's go around, by the water," I suggested, and we left the street and walked between the building and the lake.

The happy music and laughter coming from the club seemed decadent compared to the dark street and near silent hotels we had just come past. A couple stood at the water's edge, arms around each other's waist, looking out across the lake.

"Would you like to go in?" I asked.

"No, but let's listen to the music awhile." We stood on the sidewalk, looking in the window at the dancers.

The next song played was "A Summer Place" sung by Andy Williams. Andy sang, "Your arms reach out to me, and my heart is free of all cares."

"Beautiful, just the way I feel," I said and I nudged Susan while holding onto my crutches. She smiled back at me, and we stood there for a couple songs; then I suggested we move on. "Say, I know a park bench at the end of the dock, just behind the bell tower. Want to go sit out on the water?"

Susan agreed, and we walked across a small patio at the end of the Club and ducked around a large bush. We were directly behind the Miller Bell Tower and walked out on the dock I had been on alone the night before.

"I didn't know this was here," Susan said with mild surprise.

"Isn't it neat? The bell tower, trees, and shrubs hide it."

We walked out to the end and sat down. A tiny sliver of the waxing moon came from behind a cloud, only to be quickly covered again. We squirmed to face each other, then embraced and kissed gently. I moved, kissing her cheek and then, brushing her hair aside, found her earlobe. I kissed it then gently bit her earlobe while giving a mock growl; then I said, "I'm hungry."

"Oh, you beast!" she replied and we both snickered.

I became serious, kissing Susan's shoulders and down her chest as far as I could move her blouse. Our legs fought to entangle with one another, but sitting on a bench a few feet from the water's surface made us cautious. Finally, I realized the limits of our position and relaxed.

"I would never have guessed," I said as I watched the tiny lights of cars as they drove along a road on the other side of the lake.

"Nor would I," Susan replied as she leaned her head on my shoulder.

"Well, I'd better get my act together and get some plans worked out," I said and then looked down at her. "You're sure you want me in this condition?"

"Yes, and we've been through that." She squeezed my hand. "What do you want of the future?"

"I want a degree. It's silly of me to try and convince myself that I don't. Everyone else in the gang will have a degree. I don't want to be left out."

"Sure, you can do it! And now, you'll have the GI Bill."

"I'll keep working after something technical even if my math isn't great. Maybe I'll take a few business finance classes in case that fits me better."

"I've got a wonderful adviser at Albany. She says employers consider a degree as evidence of your work ethic that you finish what you start and that you're dependable. I talked to her about careers, and she told me hardly anyone ends up employed exactly in the field they studied."

"Well, I am tired of worrying about the future. Good things are happening for me, and I'll just 'drive on' as the army told me." I paused for a moment and then turned and looked down at Susan. "Now, where should I drive on to? Would you mind if I tried to get into SUNY Albany for the spring semester?"

"Oh, well. Let me think," she replied, "that would mean we would see quite a lot of each other. Which, actually, would be great fun!" And she kissed me on the cheek.

I returned a quick kiss. "I'll start on the paperwork mess right away. Maybe my mother could take a couple days off, and I could drive over to the campus and fill out the application in person."

Susan perked up. "I'd be happy to drive you."

"Great! We'll leave tonight!"

Neither of us spoke for a moment but just listened to the sounds of the night. All the faint noises were natural; none were made by man or machine. A mosquito buzzed at my ear, and I waved it away. There were water sounds under the dock but were faint because the wind was flat calm. An owl flew past (probably after the many bugs). Finally, a modern sound intruded, as a jet (going from New York to Chicago maybe), flew very high overhead, sending down a faint hiss and crackle to us.

"We're going to make it," I said to break the silence. "I have a wonderful premonition that we will be happy. It won't be easy, but we will make it."

"Yes. Yes, we will. I'm sure of it, too. For the first time in ages, I'm optimistic, happy with the future." Silence intervened again and then Susan continued. "This bench is getting hard. Let's go on back to my room."

"Isn't Beth sharing with you this weekend?"

"No," Susan answered with a sly tone. "I got her a room of her own."

"Okay, let's see how fast I can make these crutches work," I said as we stood up.

It was midnight, and as we carefully walked off the dock, the bell tower startled us, ringing the longest chime of the day. Four sets of four notes rang out, followed by a dozen deep, hollow hour chimes.

"Gee, that's loud when you're right under it," Susan remarked after the twelfth hour stroke. We walked between the trees and through the dark shadows of the park, then up the brick street between silent houses.

I spoke up, saying "I've been thinking of Kathy. I'm glad she has found someone. Wayne would have wanted it that way."

"I'm glad to hear you say that. We all need a soul mate."